I0617746

STOLEN HIGHLAND DREAMS

THE HIGHLANDERS
BOOK 9

TERRY SPEAR

PUBLISHED BY:

Wilde Ink Publishing

Stolen Highland Dreams

Copyright © 2024 by Terry Spear

Cover Copyright by Terry Spear

All rights reserved. No part of this book may be reproduced or transmitted in any form or by any means, electronic or mechanical, including photocopying, recording, or by any information storage and retrieval system, without written permission from the author, except for the inclusion of brief quotations in a review.

Discover more about Terry Spear at:

http://www.terryspear.com/

Print ISBN: 978-1-63311-113-4

Ebook ISBN: 978-1-63311-112-7

SYNOPSIS

Finding a safe haven for her remaining family is wrought with peril.

Ella has been hiding in the Caledonian Forest with her brother and cousin since her would-be suitor massacred her family. A new laird now occupies her family's castle, but can she convince him to take them in before it's too late despite having lost her voice while her enemy search for her in the woods?

Dashiell has heard tales of the wondrous creature that protects the deer in his forest and is determined to capture the mysterious woman to uncover her true identity. However, the more he learns about her, the more he understands the danger she faces, and he is prepared to confront any threat to keep her safe and make her his.

If you like Lyndsay Sands Highland romances, you'll enjoy the Highland Series.

Be sure to grab your copy of the next installment of the Highlanders in Stolen Highland Dreams.

Stolen Highland Dreams is dedicated to my friend Moe Vann, a fellow female veteran who served in the Air Force and whose son is in the Navy. Thanks for your service! I love that you are a cyclist who does triathlons in your local area. You are a winner in my book!

PROLOGUE

"He shouldna lead. We must act now." "Aye, Lennox will give the signal." "Be armed. Be ready."

Her heart pounding, Lady Margery heard the whispered words of sedition in a room off the hallway, sounding gruff and masculine, before she headed down the curved stairs to reach the great hall to break her fast with her clansmen.

Or maybe they were just the usual complaints of clansmen unhappy with her da's rule. The same kinds of rumors had abounded before her da took over from his da three years ago. Wanting to know who was speaking to whom, she headed toward the room where she suspected the voices had come from.

With her heart beating hard, she paused and listened near the doorway but didn't hear anything else. She pulled her *sgian dubh* out from her boot, held her breath, and peeked into the room, but no one was there.

Still, she was worried that the men meant business, so she headed to her parents' bedchamber to warn them. She knocked on their door, and her da answered.

At first, he smiled at her, then frowned. "Margery, what's the matter?"

Her da could always sense when she was worried about something, maybe because of the deep frown creasing her brow.

"I overheard whispers in the hall about Uncle Lennox taking over the clan's rule."

Lennox was angry that their da had told the clan that Coinneach would rule when he died. Lennox had stormed out of the great hall, furious. She would have been sent to her bedchamber without a meal if *she'd* done that.

"For years, people have been saying that, even when your grandfather became the clan chief," her da reassured her. "I canna lead our people if I show fear because someone mentions overthrowing my rule."

"At least..."—tears filled Margery's eyes—"at least carry your sword to the table."

She was never weepy, so it annoyed her that it had come to this. But she couldn't emphasize enough how worried she was about her da's safety.

He hugged her and kissed her forehead. "I will make sure that some of my guards are armed."

"Do you know which ones are loyal to your brother?" It wouldn't do to arm the wrong ones!

"Aye. Dinna worry yourself about it." Then her da frowned. "We have more of a concern coming up."

His voice turned from cheerful and unworried to dark and concerned, making her even more anxious.

"MacAfee informed me that he and his men are visiting in two days."

"Nay." Would MacAfee never get the message that she didn't want to marry him and her da had no intention of wedding her to him either?

"We'll get through the meal with him just like we have all the rest," her da assured her. "Your mother and I will be down to the great hall momentarily. See to your brother. He is always late."

"Aye." She rushed off to her brother's bedchamber. When she reached the room, Finnegan was grumbling with a nanny about having his hair combed out.

At five years of age, Finnegan could be a handful.

"Go and meet us downstairs. I'll take care of Finnegan and bring him to your table in a few minutes," Margery told Millicent.

"Aye." Millicent curtsied and hurried out of the bedchamber, appearing relieved she didn't have to deal with Finnegan further.

Finnegan allowed Margery to comb his long blond hair out. "Why do you give Millicent such a hard time?"

"She is always in a rush and doesna take care to no' pull on my hair. It hurts when she does it." He looked up at Margery with his blue eyes wide. "Why are you here?"

"Da is tired of you coming to the morning meal late." Then she set the comb on the table beside the bed. "Come, we must hurry. I need to grab something from my bedchamber."

"Then we will be late, and you will be the reason, no' me, and they will still think it is my fault."

She smiled. "Then you shouldna be so late all the time."

She rushed him to her bedchamber, grabbed her sword and sheath, and attached them to her belt.

Finnegan's eyes were huge. He shook his head. "No one is supposed to be armed at the meals."

"Aye. Come, we must hurry."

"Da willna approve."

She tucked it so that the folds of her gown hid it. "Better?"

"Aye, but I still know it's there."

She ruffled his long blond, curly hair and dashed down the stairs ahead of him while he pounded them behind her.

At fifteen, Margery sat at the head table with her parents while her Uncle Lennox and cousin Michael, two years older than her, sat on the other side of her da. Finnegan sat with his nanny at one of the lower tables.

Everyone was eating. She didn't see anyone wearing swords. Not even her da. Which meant if someone tried to kill him or her mother, she would have to fight them off.

Uncle Lennox lifted his mug of ale and took a swig of it. Michael watched him as if waiting for his da to start the mutiny. Maybe Margery was being a bit paranoid. On the other hand, if she was right, maybe Lennox didn't plan to take over the clan this morning. Maybe tonight or tomorrow...or the next day.

Her uncle set his mug on the table and said to the gathered clansmen and women, "I'm sure you know how our da wanted me to lead our people, but Coinneach twisted his arm to obtain the position."

How could Lennox lie about such a thing? Everyone was silent, their gazes turning from Lennox to her da to see how he would respond.

Everyone had been there when her grandad had told the clan the news. No one had forced her granddad to give up command of the clan to her da.

She couldn't believe it. She looked at her cousin, Michael, to see how he viewed it. He nodded. Ohmigoddess, he was in on this, as she should have suspected.

Her own da frowned at Lennox, and she hoped to every god that existed that her da had heeded her words and that his guards were armed in case the insurrection took place today.

Her dad opened his mouth to speak, but his brother continued, "Enough of our people feel the same way. Today is the day to change the present circumstances. All those who back me say aye!"

Several men did. Her heart was beating like crazy. She glanced at her mother, whose face had turned ice white.

This was treason. Her uncle had to be mad. But when his men pulled unsheathed swords, Margery knew it was no longer just talk. His men were ready to fight their own kin to put Lennox in power.

Margery glanced at Finnegan. He was watching her, not their

uncle. Margery pulled out her sword, ready to kill anyone who tried to hurt her da or mother. Even her aunt and other uncle were sitting at the table and she was certain they sided with her da.

Her mother placed her hand on Margery's arm, indicating she didn't want her to fight any of the warriors, but she would to protect any of her kin who sided with her da.

Then Lennox rose from his seat, and she saw his sheathed sword. As soon as he pulled his sword out and turned his sword on her da, Margery yanked her *sgian dubh* out of her boot and bolted out of her seat. Her da was never armed at the table, and despite her warning, he wasn't armed today.

At the lower tables, the men clashed with a few of Margery's kin. Margery targeted her uncle when he tried to stab her da. Margery swung her sword at Lennox's sword arm as hard as she could, cutting him before he could hurt her da. He cursed at her, dropping his sword, and she cut him in the side with her *sgian dubh* after that before he could reach for his.

Two of her da's soldiers rushed forth and grabbed Lennox, forcing him back against a wall. He would die at their hands if her da commanded it.

But her da loved his brother, and despite what Lennox had done, he wouldn't have him put to death. "You are forever banished from our territory, brother," her da said. "All of you who engaged in the uprising are also banished. Keep their weapons. They will take naught from here but the clothes on their backs."

Margery had mixed feelings about it. What if Lennox encouraged more people to follow his cause? Most of their clan members loved her da, but she suspected Lennox would have given his cohorts more power if they sided with him in the takeover and they'd managed it.

Margery was shaking when her mother took hold of her arm. Margery's sword and *sgian dubh* dripped with her uncle's blood. Margery didn't even realize she was shaking from the fight until her mother touched her. She couldn't help but feel badly she'd had to cut her uncle, but she couldn't have allowed him to hurt her da.

Their healer, Mina, had left the table she was sitting at to see to Margery's uncle's wound, but Marjorie's da waved Mina away and she inclined her head in understanding.

Lennox, his son, Michael, and the rest of the men were roughly escorted out of the keep. Though Margery's cousin had not followed through to fight her kin, he'd held a sword in his hand, and a guard had quickly relieved him of it.

She couldn't believe it. He had always been her best friend. Maybe that was why he hadn't used his sword against her when she cut his da. Yet he hadn't hinted at what would happen on this day. How could he side with his da against hers when her da had done no wrong?

Her da took her weapons from her hands and laid them on the table. Then he hugged her tight. "You saved my life. For that, I will be forever grateful."

Her mother still looked pale, and Margery's five-year-old brother's eyes were still wide with shock.

Margery hoped her brother and mother didn't think she was a monster. At least her da had praised her and wasn't angry with her. How her friends would view her after this was another matter.

Worst of all, MacAfee would be here soon to cause more trouble.

Two days later, when things had settled down after Margery's uncle and his followers had mutinied and been banished from the lands, they heard that Laird MacAfee was arriving at Cairn Castle within the hour, and she knew what that meant. He was thirty while she was fifteen, yet he desperately wanted her for his wife. Her da had repeatedly said no, that she was too young.

He also didn't like the man, though MacAfee was powerful in his own right, commanding an army of sixty and having money and titles. But she hated the way he always leered at her as if he wanted her in his bed while she wanted to stay far away from him. She was glad her da said no to the marriage.

Then they sat down to dinner to celebrate the visit, though she knew her da only did it for appearance's sake, not because he wanted to celebrate the laird's visit.

MacAfee glanced in Margery's direction. "You know I want your daughter, and you canna deny I'm as good as a prospect as she'll ever have."

His words irked her. She wished someone else would want her that she wanted back!

Her da stood by his words and shook his head. "She is too young."

She knew her da meant, though he wouldn't say it—that she would never be his, no matter her age. She loved her da for it.

"Are you certain? Because I aim to take what I want." The threat in MacAfee's voice startled her.

Despite not liking him, he had always been jovial about it. As if he knew he would have her when the time was right. But this time, he sounded like her da wouldn't dissuade him no matter what.

MacAfee drained his mug of ale and held it up for a refill. "All right. Later then. I know you will see this through when the time is right."

That night, when everyone was preparing to retire, the battle began. Margery had been rocking her baby cousin, Amelda, to sleep when she heard screams and swords clashing. Her aunt rushed into the room to take Amelda into her arms.

"Go, find your brother! Get him to safety!" her aunt cried out.

Her heart beating like crazy, Margery ran out of the bedchamber and headed for her brother's room. Before she reached it, she saw her mother lying on the floor in the hallway, bleeding from the chest, her sword in her hand. "Get the baby and your brother," she breathed out. "Save them."

Margery ran to her mother and placed her hands over her mother's wound to try to stop the bleeding.

"Margery, go! They will kill you and all our kin. Go, now, while you can."

She heard cries of distress filling the castle; her mind was a blur as she couldn't think of what to do next. When her mom's eyes glazed over with the look of death, Margery was released from the momentary horror of indecision.

Tears filling her eyes, she ran off to her aunt's bedchamber and found her lying dead beside the bed. "Oh, goddess, no." The baby was sound asleep in her cradle, or the brigand who had killed her mother might have eliminated her also.

Margery carefully lifted Amelda from her cradle, swaddled her, and tucked her into a bag to make carrying her on her back easier. She ran out of the room, grabbed her mother's sword, and sheathed it. Hot tears slid down her cheeks as she looked at her mother one last time, but fighting on the stairs alerted her that she and the baby were in peril.

She dove into her brother's bedchamber and found him hiding under the bed, holding onto a wooden sword he practiced with.

"Come, Finnegan, we must run." If they could reach her parents' chamber in time, they could escape through a trapdoor to the secret tunnels.

Furious with her brother for not complying with her command when they could be slaughtered at any moment, she dragged Finnegan out from under the bed. Then, with his hand in hers, she gripped his small hand tightly, not wanting to lose him for anything, and raced out into the hall.

No one was there, thank the gods, and they ran for their parents' chamber. Before they could reach it, they saw a man, one of their own, fighting one of MacAfee's men.

She yanked Finnegan into their parents' bedchamber and shut the door, locking it. In there, they found their da dead. She tried to pull Finnegan away so he wouldn't see him, but he had already seen the carnage. She grabbed her da's sword and told Finnegan, "Go under the bed."

She didn't want to go first, fearing he would be too afraid to follow her. Slipping under it immediately, he seemed to prefer hiding under a bed. Then she joined him and pulled away the rug covering the trapdoor. She tugged on the door, but it wouldn't budge.

Men raced toward the bedchamber.

"Help me, Finnegan!"

He tugged with all his five-year-old might, aiding her, and they pulled it open between them.

"Go ahead of me," she said.

"It's dark."

"We will die if we dinna go. I must shut the trapdoor. You canna do it alone."

"It will be even darker then."

"You can feel your way down the steps with your toes. Go! Before we all die!"

Then he finally, reluctantly, very slowly, moved down into the passageway. Once he had moved low enough on the steps so she could join him, she closed the trapdoor, and darkness engulfed them.

"Once we reach the bottom, I'll go first and hold your hand, but I canna pass you on the narrow steps. Just hug the wall and use your feet to guide you."

He moved so slowly that she kept running into him. She was afraid that someone would soon discover their secret entrance to the tunnels and find them.

"Move more quickly," she whispered.

They finally reached the bottom of the tunnel, and with one

hand gripping her da's sword, she held Finnegan's hand with the other and moved as quickly as she could.

"How do you know the way?" he asked.

"Da showed me the way. We follow this straight until we come to a junction. Then we turn left. At another junction, we turn right, straight, and left again until we are outside and can enter the forest."

"Dinna let go of my hand. I willna remember all that you said."

"I willna."

When they finally reached the door to exit the tunnel, she and he tugged at the door until they opened it with a squeak. She cringed, hoping no one had heard it.

Thick brambles blocked the entrance, and she used her mother's sword to hack away at some of the vegetation. Her mother would have frowned on her using her sword for such a task. However, she had to remind herself that her mother wanted her to take any measure to get herself and the others to safety.

Thank the gods, Amelda was sound asleep the whole time. If she had begun to cry, all would have been lost.

Near the stream, their blacksmith fought another warrior, but Tannon was wounded, his side bleeding, and he struggled against the other man's attacks. She had thought leaving the castle would mean they were safe. But what a goose she was. This would be only the beginning of their fight to survive.

They had no shelter, clothes, or food, and with MacAfee killing everyone he could find—they were doomed.

"Stay here," she said, leaving Amelda cocooned in her pack with Finnegan.

The moon was full, and after the tunnel's darkness, it felt like light from torches filled the night sky.

She left her da's sword with Finnegan. It was so heavy that neither of them could swing it. She carried her mother's sword and ran to where the blacksmith fought the other warrior. Neither man, so busy trying to kill the other, saw her coming. She sliced MacAfee's man's leg where her da had told her it would cause the most damage.

The man turned on her with an angry roar. For an instant, she knew he would kill her, and her brother and baby cousin would be next.

But the blacksmith struck the brigand with such a blow that he felled him in one fell swoop. The dead brigand fell like a massive oak on top of her, and she feared she had died.

The next thing she knew, the blacksmith, badly wounded, was trying to lift the dead man off her. Her brother had come to assist him.

"Lady Margery," the blacksmith said, pulling her out from under the Highland warrior.

She meant to thank him. She meant to grab Amelda and her brother, forge the stream with the blacksmith, and bind his wounds, but away from here, where the danger still existed. But the words would not come. The tears were gone. She felt numb.

She put the pack carrying Amelda on her back, held the blacksmith's arm, and held her brother's hand, and they began to cross the stream.

In the darkness, a small light shone on an old woman, their healer, as she came to help them across the stream. *Mina.*

1

Five years had passed since the carnage had taken place at her castle, and Lady Margery, now known as Ella, was in the nearby village trading a pheasant for flour and oats, fearful that MacAfee or one of his people might see and recognize her and kill her. It was a constant worry for her, her brother, and her cousin.

After that day at the stream, when she and Mina helped her family and the blacksmith across it, she couldn't speak a word, no matter how hard she tried.

The dark-haired maid, Bhictoria, took the pheasant from her and gave her bags of flour and oats in trade. Like Ella, she was about twenty, but she was married. Ella would have liked to have been her friend, anyone's friend, but she couldn't risk the word getting out about who she was and where she was living.

"Have you heard the news?" Bhictoria asked.

Ella tried to concentrate on what she was saying and not glance around for danger like she was so used to doing, which could make Bhictoria suspicious. Ella shook her head.

"Laird Dashiell MacTavish has taken over Cairn Castle. He is hiring people from the village. I know you are no' from here, but mayhap he will hire you too if you have some skills he might need."

Ella's mouth dropped open. She'd seen a lot of movement in and out of the castle for the last month or so, always hiding while it was happening. She didn't realize someone else had taken her castle over.

"Aye. It was all so sudden. It has been a month, but you know how it is. When a laird and his people move in, they stay; generations later, the family still lives there."

Unless they were murdered as Ella's family had been.

"There's going to be a grand celebration between Laird MacAfee and MacTavish this eve, I hear. Some of us from the village will sneak in...or try to so we can enjoy the food and drink. You should come with us."

Ella attempted to smile, but the feeling wasn't there. She motioned to her with her hands over her eyes and mouthed the words—*see you.*

"We're willing to chance it. The worst they will do is send us away. So are you coming?"

Ella shook her head.

"All right. I'll see you when you have something else to trade and tell you how it goes."

Ella nodded, then headed off with her supplies. She walked two miles out of her way through meadows filled with heather and rocks, past crofts and pastures, sheep and cows looking her way. She always ensured no one followed her to see where she lived.

Once she arrived at the modest hut hidden in the forest, tucked away from prying eyes, she opened the door to find Mina and five-year-old Amelda patching up their worn garments.

The hut wasn't anything like their former life in the imposing Cairn Castle. When she dared to entertain the notion of trusting a new laird, doubt gnawed at her resolve.

Ella wrote in the dirt on the floor of their hut: *Where is Finnegan?*

"Gathering water," Mina said.

I have news, she wrote. She wrote about what Bhictoria had told her.

"'Tis good news," Mina said, her white hair bound up on her head as she took another stitch.

Ella shook her head. She wrote: *Nay, no' if MacTavish is friends with Laird MacAfee.*

"Dinna believe everything you hear or see, Ella," Mina said.

Finnegan hurried into the hut with a pail of fresh water. Then he saw the writing on the dirt floor. He set the pail down. "Who is Laird MacTavish?"

AS THEY HEADED BACK inside the keep, Dashiell MacTavish told his cousin, Fallon, "I still dinna understand why MacAfee wants to return here to celebrate with us after moving up north."

"I dinna either. Just like I dinna know why he bartered Cairn Castle for some of your lands up north. By the way, the food will be cooked and ready for his arrival."

"He wanted to hunt for game when he arrived. It would have been too late." MacAfee would know that so why had he sent a messenger to tell Dashiell that's what he wanted to do? "Is there something he is looking for in the forest other than game to eat?" Dashiell had heard rumors that something mysterious was in the Caledonian Forest.

Though no one would confirm that the rumors were true. But why give up his castle and lands here if MacAfee wanted to search for something like that? He could have just stayed here and done so at his leisure.

"Maybe he regrets having given up his hunting rights and wants to hunt once more in the forest," Fallon said, but he didn't look Dashiell in the eye.

"Is there some mystery in the forest?" If there was, Dashiell couldn't understand why he didn't see it. Though he wasn't superstitious, so that could be the reason.

"You know our grandmother would see things that were no' there."

Dashiell shook his head. He believed she had visions and knew they came to pass, but what did that have to do with the forest here?

"Riders!" Ruadh shouted from the wall walk.

"They are here," Fallon said. "Let's hope MacAfee doesna decide he wants Castle Cairn back."

"He isna getting it back."

Fallon smiled. "Aye, no' without a fight, and he wouldna win."

MacAfee rode into the inner bailey with his entourage of fifteen men.

"Disarm everyone but MacAfee," Dashiell told his cousin.

"Aye, right away." Fallon had several guards stop MacAfee's men and made them give up their weapons.

Even though Dashiell didn't believe MacAfee was a threat, he still had to take precautions for the safety of his own people. He didn't know MacAfee well at all.

"We are going on a hunt, aye?" MacAfee dismounted from his horse, his hair and eyes so dark a brown that they were nearly black.

"Nay, the meal is ready. Come, join us for a feast now." Dashiell had never been more eager to finish something than he was with this task. He glanced back at the forest and swore he saw a lass in a green gown, her hair a pretty red, but she quickly ducked behind a tree. He frowned. Had she come with MacAfee and was left behind?

"It is so good of you to celebrate with us," MacAfee said, stealing Dashiell's attention from the woman in the forest.

"We hope you enjoy the meal and drinks." Dashiell glanced back at the forest but saw nothing but the trees now.

ELLA HAD SNEAKED CLOSER to Cairn Castle, as dangerous as she knew her actions were. But she had to see if Laird MacAfee had truly returned. He had. And she'd seen Laird MacTavish for a moment. He welcomed MacAfee into his castle. *Her* castle. But not with open arms, a handshake, or a slap on the back. Maybe, he wasn't a true friend.

But then MacTavish saw her, and she melted back into the forest. She couldn't have him alert MacAfee he had seen a woman in the forest. She raced back through the forest, stopping to listen, not hearing anyone, and continuing until she reached the hut.

"He isna MacAfee's friend," Mina told her as she slipped into the hut.

Amelda ran and hugged her. "I worried about you."

Finnegan frowned. "We will need to learn when MacAfee leaves again. Hopefully, for good this time."

Ella nodded.

If MacAfee had moved out, why had he returned to celebrate with MacTavish? If Mina was wrong, Ella's seeking Laird MacTavish's help may be in vain. Whose word would he listen to? A friend of his, or someone hiding in his woods who was unknown to him, who had a wild tale about her family's death at the hands of *Auld Clootie* himself?

Mina scoffed. "You shouldna have gone to see MacAfee return to the castle."

Ella wrote on the dirt floor: *He didna see me.*

"Nay, or he would have come looking for you."

But she'd been driven to do it, to know for herself that MacAfee was welcomed into the castle. She wondered if the maid in the village had slipped in unnoticed to enjoy the revelry. She hoped Bhictoria and her friends had and hadn't been caught.

After Ella, her brother, cousin, and Mina ate pheasant and barley, they readied themselves for bed. She usually practiced sword-fighting with her brother at night but didn't want to chance it with MacAfee in the area again.

She lay down on her makeshift bed of straw between Amelda and Finnegan. She couldn't stop thinking of MacTavish and worrying that he was friends with MacAfee. What if MacAfee told Dashiell that if he found Ella in the woods to notify him, and he would take her off his hands? That she was dangerous to his people, or something like that.

She finally drifted off. *But then screams filled the night as Margery's family and friends were slaughtered. But then she heard celebration—between her enemy, the devil himself, Laird MacAfee, who had her kin murdered, and the new laird of the castle, Dashiell MacTavish. Her castle!*

A wolf howled and Ella was jolted awake, springing free from the depths of her nightmare. Her skin was slick with sweat and her heart was racing like a frantic drum. An eerie hoot from an owl echoed through the shadowy expanse of the Caledonian Forest, grounding her in the present moment.

Five years had passed since the horrific killings had taken place, yet she still couldn't stop having nightmares.

She blinked, taking in her surroundings. Her brother, cousin, and Mina were sound asleep on their fur-covered straw beds. A shiver traveled down her spine as she recalled MacTavish's association with MacAfee—a man who wished her dead.

Ella took a deep breath and tried to will herself to sleep. Unfortunately, her efforts to fall asleep were in vain. She had too much work and little time to complete it all. The sun would rise soon, and she needed to start her chores before dawn to avoid running into anyone in the forest.

Mina woke, sat up on her straw mattress, and studied Ella before getting out of bed. "They are no' friends. Trust me."

Finnegan stirred. "It is no' time to get up already, is it?"

Amelda was buried in furs, still sleeping soundly.

Ella frowned. What did Mina mean? She wrote in the dirt with her stick: *What?*

"You ken what I mean. You saw MacAfee arrive for the celebration at the castle. You know it was MacAfee celebrating with Dashiell's clan. You believe Dashiell now is also the enemy."

Mina had a way of...*knowing* things she shouldn't. The new chief of Cairn Castle *had* celebrated with her enemy there. All her instincts told her Laird Dashiell was friends with the devil, even if Mina didn't believe so.

Ella scratched in the dirt floor of their hut: *Aye, they were celebrating.*

"Aye, because MacAfee bartered the castle to Dashiell for some of his properties up north. MacAfee would never have given up searching for you otherwise. He and his people had to be... *persuaded* to leave."

Ella puzzled over Mina's words. She wrote: *How?*

"When people do evil deeds, sometimes the demons visit them." Mina smiled, but her expression was a bit devilish. "Dashiell didna know MacAfee before he approached him about exchanging the castle and lands for Dashiell's lands."

Ella paced, unconvinced.

Finnegan dressed. "I'm going to get the firewood."

He headed out of the hut.

"I know something about these things." Mina dressed.

Mina always knew something about things that no one else would know.

Mina released her breath in exasperation that she wasn't getting her point across to Ella. "There is more to all this than meets the eye."

Ella hastily wrote: *What?*

Mina sat down on her straw bed as if the weight of the news was too much to bear while standing. "Dashiell was to marry a bonnie lass, but the woman was interested in another."

Ella's eyes widened. She was shocked and felt sorry for the laird unless he was a tyrant, and that's why the woman had married someone else. Often, things weren't as they seemed at face value.

She scribbled in the dirt: *Against her da's will?*

"Aye."

Ella wrote: *Who did she throw the laird over for?*

"Your cousin Michael Gunn."

Ella's jaw dropped as she looked at Mina, unable to believe what she was hearing. Why had Mina failed to mention that her cousin was married? And worse yet, that he had taken Dashiell's bride before this? Ella couldn't help but feel ashamed that she was related to someone who would do such a thing.

Her distrust for her cousin grew even stronger, knowing that he had sided with his da in attempting to overthrow her own da from his position of power.

She chewed on her lower lip, then knelt and wrote: *Does Michael love her?*

Mina shrugged. "Women and men often marry without the thought of romantic love. Alliances are what are important."

Ella wrote: *Then this could have been my uncle's doing. Mayhap Michael isna happy with the arrangement. Maybe Dashiell wouldna have loved the woman, either.*

"'Tis all well and good, Ella. Dashiell wasna destined to marry the lass. She has no right to the castle. No' like you do."

Ella had told Mina enough times that she no longer did either.

Mina smiled brightly. "Help me prepare our porridge, and then you must practice sword fighting with your brother before sunup. You must always be prepared if the devil returns to the forest."

Ella frowned. She hadn't planned to practice fighting until MacAfee and his men left the area again.

"Oh, I should have mentioned. He and his men left way before dawn."

Ella wrote: *How do you know this?*

She thought Mina had been sleeping the whole night through. And why would MacAfee and his men visit and then leave in such a hurry? Unless he and Dashiell had a disagreement about something.

"I heard their horses traveling through the woods and investigated earlier while you slept."

Ella wrote: *You should have woken me.*

Ella didn't want Mina to get herself into harm's way.

"I was careful."

Ella began making porridge for breakfast. Amelda finally fully woke, and Mina helped her dress.

"Where's Finnegan?" Amelda asked as Mina plaited her hair.

"Gathering firewood."

"Oh, me too." Amelda ran off before Mina could finish her hair.

When they returned, Finnegan hurried to drop the kindling inside the hut. Amelda also brought in an armload of kindling.

After eating, Mina and Amelda cleaned up while Ella grabbed her and her brother's swords.

Amelda's eyes widened. "I want to go too."

Ella shook her head.

Finnegan took his sword from Ella and patted Amelda's head on the way out of the hut. "When you are older."

"I willna ever be older," Amelda grumbled and finished helping Mina clean the wooden bowls they had used for their porridge.

Ella and her brother moved silently through the dense forest, looking for a secluded spot to train and seek refuge if anyone encountered them. But then Warrior, the wolf pup they had been feeding when they found him alone in the forest, came to greet them. They both forgot their mission and petted him. He wagged his tail like crazy.

He was like them, an orphan, and they'd taken him in. Though growing big enough to catch rats, he needed to learn to hunt for himself. They still fed him fish when they caught enough. He licked their hands and faces, caught sight of a rabbit, and raced off.

"Come, we fight," she whispered to Finnegan.

They wouldn't have been able to do this if MacAfee and his clansmen had been in the area. Still, Ella couldn't shake off her uneasy feeling after seeing Dashiell celebrating with him.

Then, the thought of Mina crossed her mind, and she remembered what she had said about the demons MacAfee had to face. Mina had encountered wicked men like him before, and said their conscience never bothered them because they didn't have one.

Finnegan knocked Mina's sword from her hand, shocking her, her mouth gaping. He'd never been able to before.

He smiled, quickly covering his mouth before he laughed, his blue eyes sparkling with amusement.

She couldn't help that her mind was still on MacAfee and his horrible deeds. She didn't believe any passage of time would erase what she'd seen and experienced.

Being a good brother, he hurried to get her sword for her. She'd planned to fight with him longer to show him the next time he couldn't so easily disarm her when they heard movement some distance away.

He grabbed her sword, and she rushed to join him. The two of them hid in the tall bracken, waiting, listening, wishing they didn't have to hide while trying to practice their sword fighting to protect themselves.

"Over there!" a man called out. "The boar is there."

Hunters! They most likely were Dashiell's men. Maybe even

Dashiell was with them. She squeezed Finnegan's arm and motioned in the direction of their hut. *"Go,"* she mouthed.

"Aye," he whispered, and they kept low and hurried home.

"I heard something else!" a man shouted. "Someone fighting in the woods. Take care."

"Search for them," someone else said.

Ella's heart was beating triple time, and she rushed her brother back through the woods, keeping low to avoid being seen.

DASHIELL HAD OFTEN GONE to the woods to hunt and travel, but something seemed different this time. He couldn't explain what. Maybe he was more observant than usual, as his men seemed to be looking for something other than prey. When they hunted, they were ready for the hunt. But now, they seemed just as tense for some other reason.

Some of the men had separated from them, and boars could be dangerous for men and horses. Maybe that was the concern. Then Quinn, his advisor, joined them.

"We have had no trouble from brigands of late, have we?" Dashiell asked his cousin, Fallon.

"Nay," Fallon said.

"Yet, I sense an uneasiness from the men on the hunt."

Fallon shook his head. "Nay, just interested in hunting, as usual, Dashiell."

But he knew better than that. "Aye."

"I still dinna understand why MacAfee and his men suddenly wanted to leave the castle in the middle of the morning. I figured he would have stayed for a week at least," Quinn said.

"He looked terrified, sweating profusely, his eyes darting around the castle as if he was afraid of his own shadow," Dashiell agreed. "I was glad they left."

"Mayhap he sees ghosts," Fallon said.

"If so, his men have the same affliction." Whatever had happened, Dashiell was glad for it.

"We thought we heard something in the forest after MacAfee left, right before dawn. Something that sounded suspiciously like men sword fighting. We searched for anyone but couldn't see whoever might have been fighting. Now that it's getting lighter out, maybe we can find them," Quinn said.

"MacAfee's men?"

"Nay. They had left hours before that," Quinn said.

Suddenly, a small wolf pup emerged from the thick underbrush and caught their attention. The pup's soft gray fur covered his body, but his chest and face were white. His amber eyes were wide with curiosity, and his ears twitched as he watched them from the shadows.

Dashiell's brows furrowed in concern as he observed the curious creature. "*Madadh-allaidh*. A wolf."

"Dinna kill it. It's just a pup," Quinn said.

Dashiell glanced at his advisor.

"I believe someone is raising it." Quinn looked back at the wolf.

"A wolf pup? You ken wolf pups grow into wolves."

"Aye."

His people knew that. "Who is raising it?"

"It willna come near us, but he's thriving, and we believe someone is taking care of it."

"And he will thrive on the farmer's sheep if we're no' careful. Though they regulate our deer population, or they would eat all our new tree growth."

"Aye."

Dashiell had not planned on harming the wolf pup. In fact, he had thought about welcoming it into their group and ensuring it thrived under their protection. He was just surprised to see him alone without a pack to take care of him.

"Who would be taking care of it? No one in the village would, and no one would be living out here. The crofters certainly wouldna be caring for a wolf pup that could later come back to eat their sheep." Something wasn't being said.

His men sheepishly looked away from Dashiell when he turned to see if they knew about the wolf pup and who might be caring for him.

"All right, then we hunt." Dashiell had every intention of getting to the bottom of the mystery of the wolf pup when he could.

For now, they needed food for their clan after they'd had to feed MacAfee and his men.

The pup's glossy coat glimmered in the sunlight as it darted through the dense underbrush. It disappeared into the thick foliage of ferns and bushes, leaving behind rustling leaves and branches in its wake.

The houndsman freed the hunting dogs. The dogs, trained from birth to track and hunt, took off in a frenzy of barks and howls, their noses close to the ground as they followed a scent only they could detect.

They eagerly pursued their prey, baying loudly to signal their discovery. "It's a boar," Dashiell said. "Let's go."

Despite the direction indicated by the howling hounds, Dashiell was drawn to follow the young wolf pup and see where it would lead him and his men. Why did he feel the pull so strongly toward something that seemed to oppose his original plan?

2

———

Fearing she and her brother would get caught this time after MacTavish's men had searched for them practice fighting, Ella and Finnegan reached the hut, practically out of breath. Even still, they waited to ensure no one was about.

For what seemed like forever, they listened for the sound of the hunters, but when they were sure no one was nearby, they hurried to the hut and slipped inside.

"You have returned early," Mina said, surprised as she and Amelda sewed patches on Finnegan's spare plaid.

"I knocked Ella's sword from her hands," Finnegan said, speaking low.

Mina glanced at Ella.

Ella wrote: *We heard hunters in the forest, and they heard us.*

"You were no' seen?" Mina sounded worried.

"Nay," Finnegan said. Then he teased Ella. "Did you hear me? I knocked Ella's sword from her grasp."

Ella wrote in the dirt: *Certes. I was thinking of MacAfee, which is why you knocked the sword out of my hands. But you see what I have always told you: If you are distracted, you lose.*

He smiled. "Aye. You always say that." Then he turned serious. "I want to try and find work with Dashiell's clan."

Ella feared for his safety should he say something he should not and give them all away. Yet he would soon be a man, and he needed to continue to learn a trade and live a life of his own.

It began to storm, with rain pitter-pattering through the branches and then on top of the hut's thatched roof.

On days like this, they usually managed to do some chores in the rain while no one was out and about. Still, they waited for about an hour, hoping the hunters had caught their prey, and returned to the castle for a feast. When Ella thought it would be safe, she and Finnegan put on their hooded cloaks and moved quietly, gathering water from the stream.

Afterward, they returned to the hut with the water, and then Ella and Amelda went out to gather more nuts.

Amelda loved to help, and though Ella worried about her being quiet enough or moving quickly enough if they thought someone might have heard them, she knew her cousin needed to get out of the hut and enjoy the forest, too.

Finnegan even fished at the nearby loch and brought home enough trout for all of them for dinner. After they finished eating, it was time for bed.

For a week now, Ella had been dreaming about the new chief of Cairn Castle, Dashiell MacTavish of Glen Affric. She wished he was someone she could trust, especially since she had only been able to rely on her younger brother, her cousin, and the woman who had taught them how to survive for the past five years.

The handsome laird was dancing with her at a feast held in the great hall of her castle. She cherished the moment as he leaned down and kissed her, his mouth warm against hers. She felt the thrill of anticipation, of joining him in his bedchamber, of making love to him. Cheers went up throughout the great hall, and she felt embarrassed and happy to share the kiss with him in front of everyone.

She belonged with him at the castle—her castle, his people. It felt right. Her younger brother danced with a girl his age—around ten summers, and her five-year-old cousin stood on the sidelines, smiling and clapping. For too many years, Ella had seen her castle through the forest across the stream and dreaded returning to it, afraid of what she had seen done to her people, and yet, now she was at peace there once again.

Thunder crashed, and rain pattered on top of the shelter, waking her fully, and she realized it was but a dream. Ever since he'd taken over the castle, she had dreams of Dashiell and wondered why she would. She glanced at Mina, who was still sound asleep.

They had no idea what Dashiell MacTavish was like—though she had seen him through the trees while on a few hunts with his men as she had hidden in the bracken. Maybe that's why she had been dreaming of him.

He was a braw warrior, his chest covered in leather, his dark hair tied back, and his sculpted face, which had changed from concentration while on the hunt to a dimpled smile when he was amused at what one of his men said, had made her smile.

Finnegan wanted to see if the chief would hire him, and she worried about him. What if MacAfee learned where her brother had been living while he was working there? What if MacAfee and MacTavish truly *were* friends?

Ella got up and cooked the potatoes and mutton they had bartered for in the village with mushrooms and pheasant they had gathered in the forest, unlawfully, aye, but no one questioned where she got the food from, thank the gods.

"I want to work for MacTavish of Glen Affric," Finnegan told her again as they sat down to eat on simple wooden stools they had carved.

Ella shook her head but knew Finnegan had to make his way in the world. The hut they were hiding in seemed to grow smaller the bigger her brother grew. Ella was twenty-winters herself and knew she would never have a husband.

Not as old as she was and because she couldn't speak. Not after seeing her parents, her favorite aunt and uncle, and the rest of her clansmen and women murdered.

Ella considered Finnegan's eager expression, his blue eyes wide, a hint of a smile tugging at his lips. "You've got to let me try. I have some skills since I was an apprentice to the blacksmith in the nearby village. It was too bad that the blacksmith's boy is old enough now that his da let me go."

White-haired and having kindly gray eyes, Mina was as old as the woods and had lived there on and off forever, she told them when she gave them a safe haven. "Ella, Finnegan is right. He needs to find work at the castle. Also, you, Ella, and your cousin must return to Cairn Castle, your home and your heritage."

Ella didn't believe she and her family had any claim to the castle now.

"You would be safer if you could work there than living out here if MacTavish or his kin find you trespassing," Mina said.

"And you?" Finnegan asked.

"Me?" Mina scoffed. "Once the fighting began, I have lived here and will happily die here when my time comes." She pushed a loose strand of white hair behind her ear.

Ella wanted them to stay together—all of them. Mina had been with their family for so long and had helped them so much. Now that she was getting older, they aided her more, and Ella wouldn't abandon her.

Mina stubbornly felt the castle belonged to Ella and her kin. To an extent, Ella did too, but she didn't believe there was any way to rectify it.

They still worried that MacAfee would learn that Ella and some of her kin had survived the assault at Cairn Castle and that Ella might tell the king what had happened and have MacAfee punished. Ella wasn't sure the king would act against MacAfee anyway. If the king favored the laird, he might be able to get away with anything.

Where are you from? Ella wrote in the dirt, wanting Finnegan to tell her the story he planned to make up when he spoke to MacTavish's staff.

"From here," Finnegan quickly said. "Mina reminds us that it's better to tell what's closer to the truth rather than tell wild tales that would catch us up."

From the village, then? Ella wrote in the dirt.

Finnegan glanced at Mina, who said, "Thieves killed your parents. You're an orphan. You're from the area."

Your name? Ella wrote.

"Finnegan."

Nay. Your family name, Ella wrote.

"Fraser," Mina said. "It was your mother's family's name. No one will connect you with your da's clan then. Never mention the Gunn name."

What would he work at? Ella wrote, asking Mina. Ella didn't want to be separated from her brother. She felt she had to take care of him, though he was a hard worker. Just like she had to take care of their cousin, who was like their little sister. Ella didn't want to lose any of them.

Not after all they'd been through, and since they had no other family—except for Uncle Lennox and his son, Michael. She figured Lennox would kill her if he could himself after she cut him with her sword and *sgian dubh.* But her da banished them from the clan for trying to rule over their people shortly before MacAfee laid siege to their castle.

"Finnegan can work at the armory as a blacksmith, with the horses in the stables, or any other chores. Finnegan, you must find a way to bring the rest of your family into the fold," Mina said. "Ella can sew, take care of the children, hunt, fish, serve as a healer, and when she can speak again, she could teach reading and writing."

Ella was so exasperated with herself that she couldn't speak still. They'd had to be careful when MacAfee still owned Cairn Castle and hunted in these woods. Now that MacTavish owned it, he had the same rules. No one was allowed to hunt or gather food or wood in the forest without his permission. No one was allowed to live there.

Their blacksmith, the only other survivor from her clan, had been badly wounded but had recovered with Mina and Ella's aid. He'd helped them expand Mina's tiny lean-to into a small hut so well hidden in a patch of briars that no one had ever discovered that a group of people lived there.

He had left the area soon after that, knowing it was too small for him to stay. The chance of all of them getting caught would have been too great.

They had to be careful not to speak when others traveled through the forest, though that wasn't a problem for Ella. They only lit a fire when they knew no one would be in the woods. When they went to the village for supplies, they had let on that they now worked for MacTavish, and no one questioned them.

He had hired a few villagers to fill some positions, the villagers had said.

"You have to let me try," Finnegan appealed to his sister.

It would probably be easier for him to learn another trade at ten than wait until he was older. He was so eager and just as industrious as she was.

You can never reveal who you are if MacAfee returns to the castle.

"Nay, of course no'. He would want me dead. All of us dead," Finnegan said. "I will go on the morrow then."

Ella prayed he would be well-received, but she would be glad to see him return to them safe and sound if he wasn't.

"What about me?" Amelda asked. "Can I go too?"

"You can help Ella do whatever chores she is doing if she ends up at the castle," Mina said. "Maybe Finnegan can find a way to bring you both over there."

You too, Ella wrote. She wasn't about to leave Mina behind in the woods. Without her guidance and love, Ella couldn't have managed to care for her brother and cousin in the forest when they'd been so young.

She'd had no training on surviving in the wilderness on her own. She'd learned to dance, sew, and manage the staff. None of that had helped with living off the land and avoiding detection like they'd had to do. Her da had allowed her to train with a sword and *sgian dubh* at least, which had already proved invaluable.

"Aye," Mina said.

"I dinna ken why you canna just use your magic to return us to the castle," Finnegan said and took another bite of his pheasant.

"The magic is within you in the words you speak, how you treat others, your helpfulness, and your kindness," Mina said.

Ella smiled. They knew Mina could do things others could not, but they were careful never to speak of it to anyone. They didn't want anyone to accuse her of being a witch.

"What did you dream of last night?" Finnegan asked Amelda.

"Of butterflies. Lots and lots of butterflies." Amelda waved her hands around as if they were butterflies taking flight.

At least she hadn't seen the horrors Ella had witnessed except for her beautiful dream of MacTavish. Her brother hadn't seen as much as she had during their flight from the castle either, she hadn't thought.

Finnegan was trying to make a point. He swore that Mina made them dream of happy things so that he wouldn't continue to have nightmares about the fighting he'd seen. Amelda had been too young, but she still had pleasant dreams.

Except for Ella. She had nightmares. For the life of her, she couldn't understand why she would have dreams of MacTavish now—his dark beard, piercing blue eyes, distinguished, tall, strong jawline, impressive.

She had told Mina about it, not how he looked, but that she had seen him. Of course, Mina wanted her to talk to him and ask for employment, but she could not.

Once, to her shock and pleasure, Ella had seen him remove his shirt at the loch where she bathed. He'd washed his bare chest. He was muscled, just beautiful. She'd seen men half naked before practicing fighting in the inner bailey when her da was in charge. But no' bathing in such a sensuous way.

She so wanted to touch and wash him, and...och, she had been so in awe, it was a good thing no one had seen *her*! And she did not tell Mina about that either.

"What about you?" Finnegan asked.

Ella shook her head. Not only did she not want to share anything about her dreams, she didn't want to write them down on the floor when she was hungry and wanted to eat the rest of her food.

"I dreamed of being a great warrior." Finnegan drank some of his mead.

Ella looked up from her bowl at Finnegan. Sure, she had been teaching him to swordfight, but only so he could protect himself if needed. She quickly glanced at Mina. She oft wondered if Mina was sharing premonitions with them through their dreams, which made Ella think of dancing with and kissing Dashiell. Nah. She just wished that to be true.

Mina smiled a little.

"Well, and about catching the biggest fish ever. I also made friends with the deer like you do, Ella." Finnegan ate some of his bread. "I know you dinna believe I remember what had happened to us, but I do. I wasna a baby like Amelda. I was the age Amelda is now. I dinna remember everything. Just flashes."

She was sorry he'd remembered any of it.

"You were moving us too quickly into the tunnels before they discovered us for me to see as much as you must have seen. I will never forget hearing the screams and the sound of swords striking swords and shields. And the man calling out to his men to take care that they didna hurt Lady Margaret."

Ella took a deep breath and nodded. Sometimes, she wished she had all her memories back, but other times, she didn't. She had wondered if he had remembered seeing their da dead, but she never spoke of it to him in case he had blocked it from his memories.

"Why can I speak then?" Finnegan asked.

Sometimes, Ella thought, Finnegan asked too many questions.

"People deal with trauma in different ways," Mina said.

"Ella doesna even remember what she saw," Finnegan said.

But Ella did! She just didn't want to discuss it with him and make him relive more of it. Or for Amelda to learn about it.

"She saw enough to affect her profoundly," Mina said. "Simultaneously, she was terrified that she would lose the two of you."

She thought it might have been when the massive warrior had fallen dead on top of her, and Tannon and her brother had struggled to move him. She remembered being terrified that she was going to suffocate to death and wasn't able to speak any further after that.

"Will she ever get her voice back?" Finnegan asked.

"She must."

Ella had tried! Goddess knows she had. But it was like having a night terror: She wanted to cry out in fright at seeing the horror before her and couldn't utter a sound. Only now, it was always during her waking hours.

After they ate and cleaned up, they did their chores outside the hut. They gathered nuts, wood, and water, cleaned their clothes in the nearby stream, and then spent hours sewing. They ate, and then it was time to work on sword fighting.

"Can I go too?" Amelda asked.

"Nay. You need to be abed," Mina said.

Then Ella belted her sword, and so did Finnegan. She grabbed a lantern, kissed and hugged Amelda goodnight, and wrote in the dirt: *Sleep well.*

"Aye," Amelda said, looking drifty-eyed already.

Ella knew taking Amelda with them wasn't a good idea. If they ran into trouble, it would be harder for them to escape to the safety of the hut.

She and Finnegan walked silently, as they always did on their nightly sword practice, in case anyone was in the woods. They'd never had any trouble, but they had to be resolute in keeping themselves safe.

She had thought of practicing in the meadow near the loch but was afraid someone would see them, and they wouldn't be able to escape successfully. The trees and bracken would conceal their lantern light in the woods, and they could easily evade an enemy.

When they found the area where they had room to practice, she set the lantern down on a rock, and then they unsheathed their swords. Their swords clanked as they fought each other. Finnegan was so strong; she was proud of how skilled he had become and how powerful his swings.

His footwork had been improving, but hers had too. Now that he was stronger but not as tall as her, he made her work at it.

After they practiced until they were tired, she heard horses off in the distance. Immediately, she thought of MacAfee, and she wanted to kill him in the worst way. She had to remind herself that MacAfee was no longer there; instead, they were probably MacTavish's people.

It didn't mean Dashiell would be with them even if they were MacTavish's clansmen. However, she would love to get a glimpse of him again. Dreaming of him was preferred to having nightmares.

"MacAfee?" Finnegan asked as she put out their lantern light.

She hurried them deeper into the bracken, far away from where they'd been practicing their swordsmanship in case the riders had heard them and were trying to locate who was out fighting in the forest.

She shook her head, but he couldn't see her response in the dark.

The riders should have gone in more of a straight line toward where they had been practicing, but instead, they were drawing closer to where she and Finnegan dropped down in the bracken to wait it out before they returned to the hut, carrying lanterns to light their way.

"Quinn, I heard them back that way," a man said.

"I know, Fallon, which is why we're going this way," Quinn said. "I believe they went this way. Watch carefully and look for a body."

She realized then that the men believed that she and her brother had truly been battling it out between them, not practicing sword fighting, which would make more sense. She'd heard their names before.

Quinn was the advisor to MacTavish, and Fallon was his cousin, the clan's tanist, second in command of the clan. She felt guarded relief that it was them and not MacAfee's men. However, she couldn't help wanting to kill MacAfee. More than anything, she wanted to right the wrongs, as much as she could, for what he had done.

"Are you sure what we heard was two people fighting with swords or something more..."

"Mystical?" Quinn asked. "Like the Nymph of the Forest?"

"Aye, the fey has friends?"

"Sword fighting? Come on, Fallon. We say naught about this to Dashiell," Quinn said. "He will think we are losing our minds.

Nymph of the Forest?

The horses rode away, and once they thought it was safe

enough, Ella and Finnegan headed back through the forest to the hut and got ready for bed. Mina and Amelda were already asleep.

Ella prayed she was doing the right thing by letting Finnegan go to Cairn Castle for work in the morn. She hoped no one would learn who he was and tell MacAfee that he had not killed all her kin as he had thought and put Finnegan's life—and theirs—at risk.

3

Mystery, intrigue, and rumors of strange happenings in the Caledonian Forest drew Dashiell MacTavish into the shadowed woods early that spring day, although he disguised his mission as a hunt.

A hunting expedition for the elusive two-legged creature he had overheard his clansmen discussing in hushed voices in the darkened passages of Cairn Castle this morn.

He wasn't superstitious and didn't believe in witches or ghosts or that a hare crossing his path would cause bad luck, as many of his clansmen believed. Even so, he wished to discover what his clansmen thought they had seen in the ancient forest. Surely, something that could easily be explained away.

He knew *he* could explain it away. He had seen nothing unusual on previous hunts he'd been on with his men.

The whisper of a chilly southerly breeze tickled the leaves of the massive oaks, the gentle tune of their fluttery voice overcome by the sounds of horses' hooves. The clansmen's mounts tromped on the spongy woodland floor, and his hounds milled about as they moved deeper into the forest.

Dashiell and his entourage stopped as the filtered sun danced across the branches stretched out to them. His advisor, Quinn, spotted a red deer drinking from a stream two hundred yards away and leaned over in his saddle to point out the prey to him.

Dashiell reached for his bow and nocked the arrow, but he glimpsed a silhouette behind the deer when he pulled the string taut. Lowering his bow, he stared at the shadow, then without taking his eyes off the figure, he whispered, "What is that behind the deer? Can you tell, Quinn?"

His friend from childhood shoved a wisp of blond hair out of his blue eyes, their clansmen staring at the sight as well, and then he turned to Dashiell. "I believe it is the Nymph of the Forest."

He sounded so serious that Dashiell stared at him in disbelief. He hadn't expected his advisor to have been taken in by the rumors.

"The what?" Dashiell had believed the elusive creature to be a man, not a woman, if this was the one the others had whispered about. He had assumed that the man was a hermit unlawfully living in his woods if the tales were true.

If he allowed one man to live there, there was no telling how many others would invade his woods and hunt and forage in them until there was nothing left for the members of his clan to eat.

"Some of our men and I have seen her a couple of times on recent hunts. Others have as well. Many have observed her since we moved into the keep this past winter before you joined us. They say she is a protector of the deer of the Caledonian Forest."

Protector of the deer?

"We shall see, shall we no'?" Dashiell raised his arrow to his bow.

These were *his* hunting grounds, and no slip of a maid would prevent him from bringing home meat to feed his people. He had to ensure his clansmen would not be taken in by these superstitious beliefs and prove them wrong.

When he pulled the string rigid, the deer twitched its ear, her warm brown eyes observing him.

Before he could release his arrow, the slim figure of a woman moved into view. Dashiell *froze*.

The lass's dark green gown and a matching veil covering her hair made her appear like a specter, blending in with the woods like a chameleon camouflaged in its surroundings. Yet he saw the glint of a sword hanging from a belt at her waist.

A chill swept up his spine as he realized how at risk she could be should he, or one of his men who were hunting, hit her instead of the deer. He wanted to say as much as possible, to warn her away, yet he could not utter a word for his life.

Intently, he studied her, trying to learn more about her—her age, figure, and hair color hidden beneath the veil. When she lifted her hand as if to stop him in his mission, it was as though he was carved into stone, unable to move.

If he'd been of sound mind, he would have crossed the stream, captured the lass, and proven to his people that the woman was only that. Not some fey creature with mystical powers.

Except the woman enraptured him, made his blood race, and forced him to acknowledge that there was more to his interest in her than he wished to admit. His men were just as enthralled, and even his hounds stood silently watching her, their tails straight behind them, their ears perked, their brown eyes watching the deer...and observing the lady.

Then the wolf pup—he was sure it was the same one he'd seen before—pushed through the ferns and nuzzled her leg. Had his men seen the woman with the wolf pup before? Was that why Quinn thought someone had been caring for him? More than just someone, but the fey woman? But he hadn't wanted to reveal the truth?

At the motion of her hand, the deer turned and fled. As if she had released her hold on Dashiell, he let loose the arrow, sending it winging across the stream, where it found its mark in a lichen-covered trunk of a yew nearby with a thwack!

Dashiell turned his head quickly to observe more of the lady, but she and the wolf pup had vanished as suddenly as the deer. Staring at the deep green and lighter green leaves fluttering in the breeze, narrow shafts of sunlight filtering through the dense forest where the lady, wolf, and deer had disappeared, he frowned.

After pausing for a moment, he smiled as he considered the novelty of the situation.

He put his bow and arrow up, not to be thwarted by the woman. "'Tis a hunt. Let us retrieve all three, shall we?"

His men eagerly agreed, and spurring his horse on, Dashiell led the hunting party across the shallow stream, sending rivulets splashing. He headed deeper into the filtered shade of the timber-lands, determined to find the woman, capture her, and question her about who she was and what she was doing there.

After riding a short distance and not finding the woman as he'd expected and somewhat disappointed and surprised at her fleet-ness of foot, Dashiell turned back and motioned for his men to release the wolfhounds.

The scenting hounds were used for tracking prey and had taken down a few English knights from their mounts during battles between his men and theirs in years past. They would bring her to heel.

Greatly anticipating the woman's capture, he waited until the hounds' howls rent the air.

"Come! They have found our quarry!" His blood racing with the thrill of the hunt, Dashiell turned toward the dogs' barking.

They rode to the location of the ruckus, and his gaze caught sight of the lady's leafy green gown billowing out behind her and her silky red hair trailing past her back, following the flow of her skirts, her green veil gone.

"Over there!" he shouted and pointed with his bow, then rode toward the lady. He saw no sign of her as he drew close to where he had spotted her.

Turning to his men, he said as he maneuvered through the woods, "You saw her come this way, too, did you no'?"

The men all shook their heads, whereupon Dashiell took a deep breath, knowing he was not wrong, and continued to make his way toward the sound of his hounds. When they arrived on the scene, they found the dogs had cornered a boar, its ivory tusks protruding threateningly as it charged the dogs and men about it.

Dashiell stared at the animal, then shook his head, disappointed that he had not found his real prey—the woman. "That is neither the deer nor the...what did you call her?"

"The Nymph of the Forest." Quinn looked just as disappointed.

"Why has no one ever told me of this?" Annoyed that his people would keep the intriguing creature secret from him, he was determined to catch her and discover all there was about her. He imagined she was some waif of a woman who lived in the village nearby and frequented his woods, harvesting mushrooms and berries— which was forbidden.

Quinn said, "We have never had a good view of her. Nobody has ever been closer than we were to her today. In the shadows of the trees, we wondered if our imaginations were creating the illusion of a woman in your forest. A woman could never live out here on her own for very long. We didna believe you would wish to be bothered with unfounded rumors and such."

Glancing back at the beast as it charged at the hounds again, Dashiell said, "Kill the boar. We will have him for the evening meal. The rest of you come with me. I wish to find the woman."

He was still annoyed that his clansmen would not bother him with such a matter. The woman was intriguing, to say the least.

He followed the horses' tracks back to where they had seen the deer at the stream. Studying the ground from his horse, he finally dismounted and examined the riverbank more closely.

His men were sure to wonder why he wouldn't hunt for food

when it was one of his favorite activities. But today, the woman consumed his thoughts.

Quinn and the others joined him, and Dashiell pointed to footprints in the mud.

"Look here." He placed his shoe next to the imprint. "'Tis the woman's small footprint. She isna a figment of our imagination." Kneeling at the stream's edge, he reached for a clump of violets dropped nearby. He twisted them back and forth in his hand. "Wild violets grow abundantly in the meadow. She must have come from there. What did you see of her?"

"She is wearing green gowns that blend in with the forest. I dinna ken how she could get so close to the deer without spooking them, but when I saw her before, she stood near the deer as she did today. Then she spied the hunters and shooed the deer to safety."

Dashiell considered the notion. "Perhaps 'tis the same deer. Mayhap, she raised an orphan."

"The others were bucks."

Dashiell loved a good mystery as well as the hunt. "What about the wolf pup?"

Quinn cleared his throat. "Aye, we saw here with the pup as well."

"I knew you were no' telling everything you knew about the pup."

"I couldna without revealing she had been with the wolf. Many of our clansmen have seen her, but they were afraid to report it for fear that you would believe they had been partaking too much of the ale or had gone mad. One of our men heard some of us discussing the lass in the great hall a week ago, and that is when they came forward and told me about her."

"Why did no one tell me about her before?"

"You dinna believe in witches or such. I dinna believe you would wish to hear such news."

"Nonsense. I wish to know all that goes on throughout my land."

Dashiell and his men searched for clues as to where the woman had disappeared until the light turned a brilliant orange tinged with pink. Then, as it darkened to a deep blue, the light faded from the sky. Though he wished to continue beyond any reason he could account for, he finally ceased their search.

"We may as well return to the castle. We will find naught more concerning the woman tonight in the dark of the woods, I dare say." He raised his brows at Quinn. "Do you think me too serious, then, Quinn?"

His advisor smiled. "Nay. I just didna think you would be interested in the story."

"Aye." Dashiell would not wish anyone to think he believed in such tales as rational as his people knew him to be.

When they arrived in the outer bailey of Cairn Castle, the supper bell rang. "We are just in time. I hope they knew we had just returned and hadna planned to eat without us." He only jested. He knew very well his clansmen would not.

A stable boy quickly took Dashiell's horse's reins and led the horse to the stable while Dashiell and his advisor walked ahead of his men into the great hall filled with clansmen and women already gathered about the bare trestle tables.

Dashiell stalked toward the head table elevated at the backside of the great hall, overlooking the arrangement of the trestle tables, and turned to his advisor. "Is the lady from the village, do you think?"

"I have made some inquiries. They say she is the Nymph of the Forest, as we do, though the blacksmith said he had heard her name was Ella. The butchers and liverymen say she has magical powers, and the thieves who used to roam free in the forest avoid it now."

"Well, that is good." However, Dashiell thought it was utter nonsense. "Why were you making inquiries about the lass, Quinn?"

"I was curious about her."

Dashiell considered Quinn's normally stern face, a hint of amusement in his expression. His advisor bowed to him, took his leave, and joined his wife at the head table. Was his advisor *more* than curious about the mysterious woman?

He had been solely dedicated to his pretty wife, and Dashiell had never seen Quinn's gaze or interest stray to another lass. The way he had kept the lass secret from Dashiell bothered him. Quinn seemed more than intrigued with her.

When Dashiell took his seat at the center of the table, he attempted to listen to the hushed murmurings concerning Ella all around him since the new sighting had incited tongues to wag. The talk might have been partly since he had now spied the wisp of a woman, confirming they were not the only ones to have seen her.

He dipped his spoon into his bowl of fish stew when Lady Yvaine, widow of his late uncle, leaned over to him. "I understand you have finally seen this mysterious nymph yourself."

"Barely enough to believe she is naught more than shadows."

Yvaine pinched her gray brows together and made a small, amused face. "Ah, but I have heard you made further discoveries concerning the woman—the size of her shoe and that she has been to the meadow in the valley as well."

"Perhaps."

"I hear she sprints as fast as the deer and that even the hounds canna locate her as she confuses their scent. You do know Quinn has tried to catch her twice before?"

Dashiell raised his brows and stared at his advisor, who was laughing with his wife. "Nay, he dinna tell me this." He had suspected there was more to the story than his advisor had been letting on. He shook his head and took another scoop of the stew.

"Aye, since he has seen her, he thinks of naught else and has made many excursions into the forest, trying to track her down. His wife has been rather perturbed over his recent overwhelming interest in the lady."

Dashiell observed Wynda leaning over her husband as she handed him a slice of boar. Quinn grasped the meat between his teeth, and Dashiell shook his head. Quinn and his wife seemed content enough, which was more than he could say about his own ill-fated relationships with women.

"I am certain Quinn is curious, as am I and all the other clansmen on the hunt today." Dashiell downed his ale, then poked his boar with his knife and lifted it. "We will find this woman soon. Twelve clansmen inspect my forests every third year, but I will have them do it in a few days."

"That's a good idea." His aunt drank some of her mead.

"They will be searching for more than the erection of a mill or fishpond or any enlarged clearing or land that has been enclosed without my authority or any abuse to cut wood this time. I will also send out my foresters, who act as my gamekeepers. Everyone who enters the Caledonian Forest will be on the lookout for the lady. We will find her."

He realized after speaking he sounded way too interested in the woman himself, which he hadn't meant to do. The word would spread through the clan. Well, it couldn't be helped now. He *was* intrigued with the woman.

"They say she turns into a great horned owl at night. That is why she is in no danger from the wild beasts who roam the forest."

Dashiell smiled at the notion. He had never thought his aunt to be so superstitious. "Is that so? We will see." He chewed on his boar meat, but seeing Yvaine watching him, he paused. "You have something further to say to me, as I know that inquisitive look in your eyes."

"You know what your grandmother would have said about her."

"She was of the fey."

"Aye. What did you think of the lass?"

"I didna get enough of a look at her, I am afraid. How long have you known about her?"

"Since Quinn first saw her."

"Why did you no' bring this to my attention before?" As extraordinary as the lass was, someone should have told him!

"I have never seen the lass. Someone who had seen her should have made you aware of her presence in the woods."

As the lady supped her soup, Dashiell frowned at her. "You usually tell me everything that is going on, whether I wish to hear of it or no'. If you were no' a lass, I would have made you one of my advisors some time ago."

Yvaine smiled at him. "Why, what a nice compliment. Had I been a man, I would have been honored to serve as one of your advisors."

"I am still waiting for my answer, my lady." He swirled the ale in his tankard. After drinking the remainder, he poured himself another tankard full.

"I am afraid I have forgotten the question."

Dashiell studied her, knowing his aunt did not speak the truth. Despite her age, she was as quick-witted as any of his advisors. "Why did you no' tell me of the lady of the forest before?"

"Truthfully, I wasna sure how you would take it."

"What do you mean?" He didn't need her to speak in riddles.

"You are a most solemn individual."

He glanced at Quinn. "I have heard that already today. Does everyone think this of me?"

"I wouldna ken."

He observed Yvaine pull apart her boar. In her mysterious way, she was trying to tell him something, but he had no idea what. "Tell me, how am I too serious?"

"I didna say you were *too* somber."

"You ken my meaning. What makes you think I am serious?"

Yvaine sipped more of her honeyed mead. "When we celebrate some great good that has transpired, you have the greatest feasts. No one would rather be anywhere but with you at these times. But you never join in any of the games. You watch and enjoy seeing your people having fun but never participate. No' even when MacAfee and his men were here most recently."

"There is no need." He sliced off a piece of brown bread. "Everyone has worked hard during the year, and the celebrations are a time when the ladies can let down their hair...so to speak." He smiled when Yvaine raised her eyebrows at the notion.

Immediately, he thought of Ella and her glorious red hair, catching a shimmer of sunlight rippling across its waves. He let out his breath, wishing he could have scooped the woman onto his saddle and run his hands through her unbound hair. He wondered then where her veil had gone and if he could find it clinging to a branch in the forest.

Seeing his aunt waiting for him to say more, he added, "And the men can relax. I enjoy seeing everyone enjoying themselves. But you speak of these special occasions...when we are no' celebrating?"

"You dinna seem enthusiastic about much of anything. You are rather somber for your youthful age."

"With our continued troubles with the neighboring clans, a clan chief canna be frivolous."

"Frivolity can be a good thing. I have heard the whimsical can aid digestion."

Dashiell nodded. "If you were my advisor, my lady, what would you advise me to do?"

He glanced at his people, laughing, talking, enjoying the boar and ale.

"Participate in the games, for one, I would say, if I were your advisor."

"When there are no games to play?"

She shrugged.

"I must decide to marry soon, and I have no interest in any woman in that regard. I must make this choice, and love is not a consideration. Instead, I willna doubt have to marry one of our neighboring chiefs' daughters. Two are spoiled beyond repair, and I willna have them abusing my people."

"All sound reasons, my laird."

"Another lass trembles before me as if I am the most fearful man she has ever gazed upon. I've heard one is interested in meeting me, but I dinna know what she would be like. How can I be in good spirits with such a gloomy prospect?"

Yvaine smiled, lifted one gray brow and a piece of bread to her lips, and said, "Mayhap, you will marry the Nymph of the Forest."

He grunted. The woman belonged in the village, cavorting in the meadow or the woods, not helping him run his staff and castle. "Now you see why they dinna make women, advisors, my lady."

4

"You saw him on the hunt? The chief of Cairn Castle?"
Mina asked as Ella combed Mina's long, soft white hair.
She frowned at her, appearing exasperated with her.

Ella knew Mina wished she had tried to communicate with the laird.

Ella nodded. No man was as impressive. His tall composure as he was seated on his big roan made her feel even smaller. His muscular figure was imposing and commanding. She heard the other hunters with him tell him about her. He was searching for her for the first time while on the hunt.

He was the one who gave the orders, the one everyone listened to, the one she couldn't take her eyes off.

It was the second time he laid eyes on her. Though he might not realize she was the same woman he had seen in the forest when he was welcoming MacAfee at her castle. She had been more out in the open with him than with his other men. She'd only allowed brief glimpses of herself with them once she'd ensured they were not affiliated with MacAfee.

When his men told him about her, she wanted desperately to speak with him, to tell him her whole story, but she couldn't. Not without a voice. What if he locked her up in his dungeon for being in his woods, and she couldn't return to Mina and her family?

She was surprised Dashiell hadn't shot the deer when she held up her hand to stop him. What a foolish gesture she had made! He could have hit her *and* the deer! For some reason, he had just frozen with indecision. She'd gotten away, but she was just lucky.

She knew where to run and where to hide, and her green gowns helped to conceal her in the woods. Worse, her veil had snagged on a branch, and she'd had to return in the dark to find it once the men had stopped searching for her. She was glad they had not found it.

She stroked Mina's hair some more. She was grateful that Mina had taken her and her kin in and protected them over the years. It was Ella's turn to care for the kindly, old woman.

Though in the village, when Ella had gone for supplies, she'd heard the whispered words that Mina was a witch, and no one dared cross her. No one knew Ella lived with her, or they might have called her a witch too. Mina was not a witch. Gifted, aye, but not a witch.

Mina sighed. "After all these years, I had hoped you would find your voice. You must, you ken. The chief willna help you if you canna speak with him. He and the others of his ilk will think you daft."

That was why Ella hadn't allowed the laird to find her. She had thought the same.

"You canna live with me always. I am old. Older than some of the trees in this forest. Your place is within the walls of the keep, safe from harm, Ella, no' out here in the woods with me. No' now that MacAfee no longer rules there. It should be safe at Castle Cairn now, but you must learn to speak again. Amelda and your brother also need to be there."

Mina took a deep breath, turned, and took Ella's hands in hers, her gray eyes soft, yet her jaw was set. "I have called you Ella, one who is a beautiful fairy, one who enjoys life. You are no longer a young girl but a woman full grown. 'Tis time you have a guardian who can protect you, and you can use your true name, take your rightful place, and make a home among your people."

Her people. Dashiell's people were not her own. She'd watched the men hunting, the women gathering flowers in the meadow, and the lads fishing in the stream, and she knew they were not her clansmen.

Oh, how she had hoped she would recognize someone she had known. Anyone from her past. Like the blacksmith who had aided them.

But her people were gone. All gone. She'd hoped beyond hope that some of them had made it out alive, that she'd seen some of them escape. The more she thought about it, the more the darkness closed in on her, shutting out the memories.

She wasn't sure she wanted to live in the castle. They lived a simple life out here of fishing, catching birds, and gathering mushrooms, herbs, and berries, which she sometimes bartered at the market so they could buy other supplies they needed. They took care of each other. Yet, she knew it was forbidden to be here.

"You canna protect the deer of the woods always, lass. If you are no' careful, you could be injured. The laird has every right to hunt in his woods. So do his men. They claim these woods for their own. When they, in truth, are *your* woods to claim. No' that anyone will listen to you—a woman without a voice."

Ella nodded.

"With a name that could mean trouble for you should you share it with anyone—unless you have MacTavish's protection. I've been thinking it over. I fear you dinna have long before some of MacTavish's men or the laird himself discover us. Instead of being caught out here, you must...you must seek the laird out and beg for his protection."

Ella thought her brother should get work first and find his way in the world. For now, this was her home. She knew Mina would never agree to leave the forest. Ella envisioned living in the castle where the darkness awaited her.

She could sense it deep within her bones every time she approached the place. She had a strong aversion to going there, yet an inexplicable pull towards it. She knew that if she weren't cautious, she would meet the same fate as her people before her.

Mina scoffed. "You will havena choice before long, Ella. I pray you will find the courage to..." She shook her head. "I was wrong to take you in. I should have found a family to care for you in the village. Even if you didna live in the castle, you would have had a family."

Ella shook her head vigorously. Mina was their family. Even if she denied it, Ella believed Mina had needed them as much as they had needed her.

Mina sighed. "I ken, lass. You might no' have been safe there, either. MacAfee and his men searched the village on and off for years. Come, let us prepare the stew. Mark my words, you must ask for the laird's protection before long. I am no' long for this world. I've prepared you for my passing, taught you all I know, but in the end, you canna live here forever like I have."

Ella looked at Mina and stubbornly raised her chin. She thought she could live here in the hut so buried in vines and moss that it was invisible to the rest of the world. But Amelda needed to be with others.

Mina had been like a grandmother to them, though she had told her for years that Ella was not to call her that. She was not their grandmother. That Ella was destined for more.

But Ella would never abandon her. When the time came, and Mina was gone, Ella would try to get work at Cairn Castle if they would allow her to bring Amelda.

∾

Unable to quit thinking of the woman in the woods, Dashiell readied himself for bed, yanked off his boots, and spoke with Christopher, an orphaned Saxon of sixteen summers that Dashiell had saved in a tavern brawl and who had pledged his loyalty ever since, serving him as his personal guard.

"You have hunted with me before in the Caledonian Forest." Dashiell sat on the edge of his feather-filled mattress. "Have you ever seen Ella, the Nymph of the Forest?"

Christopher smiled and shook his dark curly hair, his amber eyes dancing with amusement. "Nay. However, I had heard of a woman from the Caledonian Forest for many years since I was young. I was born at Wharram Percy on the Yorkshire Wolds, you know."

"This woman couldna be very old."

"Nay, my laird."

"What have you heard then?"

"The lady I have heard of lives deep in the woods where no man ever goes, no hunter, no forester, no thief. They say she has magical powers, and if any invade her territory or threaten her in any way, they vanish, never to be seen or heard of again."

Dashiell laughed. "Nonsense." He removed his sheathed sword and his belt and frowned. "Besides, the forest within our clan's boundaries is ours. It isna hers."

"'Tis only a tale." Christopher hung up Dashiell's belt and sword.

"Of course." After changing into a clean léine, Dashiell climbed into bed. He yanked his fur covers to his chest, folded his arms behind his head, and stared at the ceiling.

"Do you wish for me to get you anything?"

"Aye, the lady in green."

Christopher smiled. "I believe she is an owl tonight."

"So I have heard. Sleep, Christopher. I need naught else tonight."

When Christopher climbed onto his own trestle bed beside the west wall, Dashiell wondered about the woman, who she was, why she was in the forest, and how she had befriended the deer until his eyes grew heavy with sleep, and he finally shut them and drifted off.

A mist filled the forest—cool and serene, the sunlight filtering through the dense leaves. Dashiell approached the stream on horseback, staring at the familiar surroundings, thinking of her—the red-haired nymph when he spied a deer drinking from the brook. He nudged his horse closer.

In the muted greens of the forest, he saw Ella holding a spray of violets in her hand as she seemed to appear next to the deer suddenly. The animal stopped drinking from the brook, lifted its head, and stared at him. Not at Ella, as Dashiell would have expected. The deer regarded her as though she was just another deer, joining him, unafraid.

Seeing the deer's attention diverted, Ella looked in the same direction and observed Dashiell. He was dressed in his shirt and plaid; otherwise, he was as cloaked in the woods as she was. The sun's rays grew bolder, burning away the mist, and now he could see the woman more clearly as her hair flowed freely, cascading over her shoulders and reaching her belt.

His loins tightening, his need to capture her compelling him to move closer, he urged his mount forward as she watched. As if she did not fear him, she knelt beside the water's edge and placed the flowers in the stream. Her fair skin shone in the filtered light of the trees as she stood.

Her gaze followed the flowers as they floated, dipping and rising on the swells in the tumbling water for some time. She looked back to see Dashiell still observing her. In that instant, he saw a terrible sadness in her green eyes, tears shimmering, ready to spill.

Before he could react and cross the stream and learn who she was, she turned, moving like a wisp of green silk caught by the breeze, flowing, blending, and vanishing into the woods.

"No!" Dashiell shouted.

"What's the matter?" Christopher jumped from his trundle bed as three clansmen rushed into the chamber, swords drawn.

Dashiell stared at them for a moment, still foggy-headed, trying to remember what had disturbed him. Then, he frowned. "It was only a dream."

"Of Ella?" Christopher asked.

Dashiell lay back down without saying a word. Aye, that was what he had dreamed of—*her*, Ella tantalizing him, teasing him, forcing him to desire her when he had no idea who she truly was.

"They say that once you catch sight of the lady, your dreams are no longer your own."

Looking over at the young man and his clansmen, who were waiting to hear what he had to say about Christopher's claim, Dashiell assured them, "She willna rule *my* dreams."

His men looked at him with skepticism as if *they* knew better.

ELLA WOKE FITFULLY in the hut that night, thinking of everything Mina had told her. She'd had the weirdest dream about the chief of Cairn Castle again.

Only this time, she had been crouched at the stream, tears in her eyes, as she set a handful of wild meadowland violets on the water as a tribute to her mother, da, and the rest of her clan every spring while the flowers were in bloom.

Dashiell was watching her, trying to get closer to her, like a wolf stalking its prey, slowly, ever so slowly, observing her every movement, any indication that she would take flight.

While he'd been staying still, she hadn't minded him spying on her. If he'd kept his distance, she would have continued to stay by the stream, her heart heavy with sadness.

Tears had streamed down her cheeks, and she had desperately tried to free herself from the depths of sadness. Then she finally awoke, realizing it had all been but a dream.

Ella glanced at her brother, Mina, and her heart dropped when she saw Amelda was no longer on her straw mattress tucked under her furs.

Her heart beating out of control, Ella hurried out of bed and dressed. Then, she shook her brother awake and pointed at Amelda's empty mattress.

Her brother wiped the sleep from his eyes, jerked his blankets aside, and stood. "I didna hear her leave."

Mina was sound asleep, and Ella didn't want to wake her. She grabbed her sword and *sgian dubh* and hurried out of the hut. Armed with his sword, her brother quickly followed her.

Amelda squealed off in the distant woods, and they ran to her aid. Ella's heart was practically pounding out of her chest. After protecting Amelda for the last five years, Ella couldn't believe she could lose her young cousin now.

They raced through the tall bracken when she and her brother normally moved swiftly but quietly. She was afraid they would be too late. They scared a roe deer that leaped out of their path. At any other time, they would use lots more caution as they moved through the brush, not wanting to be seen or heard.

"What are you doing alone in the forest?" one of five bearded men asked as he held Amelda's wrist.

She struggled to free herself. She looked as terrified as Ella felt as she and her brother hid in the bracken nearby.

Ella was glad her brother wasn't as headstrong as she could be, or he might have bolted into the men's path and tried to take them on.

"Have you lost your mother? Your da, wee lassie?" the same man asked.

His kind manner put Ella slightly at ease. Though he could pretend to care about Amelda to learn who she belonged to and why she was alone.

"If you dinna let me go, Ella will make you pay for it," Amelda said, her chin up and defiant, but her eyes were filled with tears.

Nay, she didn't just say that. They were never to say their names in the woods unless forced to, and then they would give another name.

Ella motioned to her brother to stay. He shook his head. She grabbed a nearby twig and wrote in the dirt: *Stay. If I need your help, I'll motion to you.*

She didn't know if the men were some of MacAfee's, and she didn't want them to know her brother was also out here if she could help it.

Finnegan nodded, though he was frowning. She knew he didn't like her plan.

Ella cautiously made her way to the clearing. She didn't want to startle the men who might think brigands were setting upon them if they were not themselves villains.

When she moved out of the trees, the men turned to see her. She pointed her sword at them as if they would be afraid of her display of aggression.

Ella!" Amelda cried out, jerked her wrist free, and ran to throw her arms around Ella in a grateful hug.

Ella backed into the bracken with Ella, and then she, her cousin, and her brother raced off.

"That's her!" the one man exclaimed.

"Aye, I know. We must catch her."

Ella motioned for her brother to take Amelda away from her, and they ran off to the west, where they would hide in their special places, thatched covers over shallow dugouts they had made in strategic places throughout the forest. They were off the trails where humans, deer, and wild boar traveled.

They didn't want anyone accidentally finding their hiding places and searching for others. She could envision them putting sentinels out to watch for them should they try to use them again.

Ella popped up to let the men glimpse her so they would follow her and not her brother and cousin so they could get away.

"The lasses went this way!" one of the men said, his voice a mixture of disbelief that they'd seen her and enthusiasm at the prospect of catching her.

She swiftly changed her path several times, keeping low after that so that she couldn't be followed. After five years of practicing and playing hide and seek with her brother and cousin, they were very good at it. She didn't know why her cousin had been so far from the hut before Ella had woken.

The men had been close behind her, traipsing through the woods, noisily making their presence known, while she had been quiet, quick, and concealed like the deer.

She'd heard them speaking low for a while, but now they were so far away that she took the chance to head back to the hut. She hoped her brother and Amelda had returned safely.

When she finally arrived near the hut, she waited, not moving, to ensure no one was around. Then she saw her brother and cousin dash into the hut.

She gave a relieved sigh. Then she heard something rustling through the brush near her, snuffling and snorting, its pig eyes catching sight of her. She raced to the hut and ran inside.

"Were they after you?" her brother asked, panting, breathless.

She shook her head, put her fingers on her face, and indicated tusks.

He said, "Boar!"

Ella put her finger on her lips. They were to always speak quietly during daylight hours. Looking at Amelda, Ella raised her hands and brows in question. Why did she go outside and run so far from the hut?

"A kitten was mewing nearby. I had to find it," Amelda said. "She ran away, and the men found me."

"You are no' supposed to leave the hut without one of us being with you," Finnegan said.

Her brother was often Ella's voice of reason, so she didn't always have to write everything down. Though she was teaching them how to read and write simultaneously, she would prefer it if she could talk, too.

Finnegan shook his head. "You know we canna have a cat or dog here. They would meow or bark and give us away. You dinna remember, but Ella had to work extra hard to keep us safe when you were a baby, crying for food or because you were wet and needed to be changed."

"Aye." Amelda looked down at the dirt floor.

Ella knew Amelda had been scared to death when the men had caught her, and she'd done wrong, but she could understand how she felt about having a pet to love. She wrote in the dirt: *No harm done. We're all safe.*

Amelda looked at Finnegan, and he read the words to her. Amelda pursed her mouth. "You have a puppy."

Ella sighed. She wrote: *The pup is a wolf and mostly on his own.*

"Aye," Finnegan whispered. "He doesna come around here much."

Are you going to the castle this morn? Ella wrote in the dirt.

Finnegan said, "Nay. No' after what happened with Amelda."

Mina opened her eyes and frowned. "Why have you not begun to do your chores?"

5

After checking on a new foal one of the mares had birthed, Dashiell had just left the stable when Fallon, Quinn, and five more of his men galloped into the inner bailey, looking flushed and excited.

Instantly, Dashiell feared that an enemy clan was within striking distance, but he suspected if that were the case, they would have been shouting the warning all the way to the castle.

"Ruadh and some of our men saw her," Fallon said. "Ella!"

"What?"

"And a wee lassie," Quinn said. "She had to be about five. And Ella is of marriageable age. Ella brandished a sword at them. It wasna a weapon carried by the local citizenry."

"And the little one? Was she armed as well?" Dashiell couldn't help but jest about it.

His cousin was known to make up wild stories for light-hearted fun, though Quinn was more circumspect than Dashiell once they reached manhood.

"Mayhap," Quinn said. "She could have had a wee *sgian dubh* in her boot."

"Was the little one her child?" Dashiell had never thought the lass would be a mother and may even have a husband since no one had seen a man or a child with her before.

"Or a younger sibling," Quinn said. "I'm sure they're related as much as the man said they looked similar, though the little one's hair was more blond than red. Ella was as protective of her as a wolf would be of its cub."

"So where are they?" Dashiell knew they must have lost them in the forest since they had not brought them here. He was sorely annoyed with himself for not having seen her himself this morning, but he'd had to check on the new foal.

Fallon said, "Ruadh had hold of the little one's wrist while questioning her when Ella charged out of the bracken, sword raised, and he lost his grip on the young one."

Dashiell raised his brows at Ruadh.

"Sorry, my laird."

"They were so startled, she caught them unaware," Quinn said. "We were disappointed not to have been in the vicinity."

"'Twas a good thing you hadna encountered one of our enemies." Dashiell was even more intrigued. How would a young woman in the forest know how to use a sword, let alone own one? He hadn't considered that before, though he recalled how she was wearing one both times he had seen her. "What did Ella say?"

"No' a word," Quinn said.

Dashiell was annoyed that the lassies had gotten away, but he wanted to laugh at his men for losing the lass and her charge to a sword-wielding young woman who hadn't even spoken a word to them!

Before the sun rose, Ella collected firewood to heat the porridge while Mina, her brother, and Amelda slept. She tried not to disturb them since she figured they needed extra sleep if they hadn't awoken.

They always cooked their food before sunrise and after sunset to lessen the chance of anyone in the woods seeing the smoke from their stone hearth. The woods were so forested that the smoke was gone before it reached the peak of the tall trees.

When she returned with the firewood, she was surprised to see Mina sleeping soundly on her bedding. She went to check on her, but she was breathing just fine.

Finnegan hurried out of bed, mouthing, "Sorry for not getting the firewood." He left the hut to gather more timber. Once he broke his fast, he planned to head to the castle, sternly telling Amelda that she wasn't to chase after cats or dogs in the forest.

Ella began to cook the porridge, and Amelda woke and quickly dressed. She started to help bring out their wooden bowls. Mina finally stirred. She sat up but didn't move to get up yet, which wasn't like her.

"Are you all right?" Finnegan asked as he brought in a load of firewood and put it in the box where they stored it.

So he had noticed the change in Mina also.

"Aye. I'm just getting old, tired, and achy. You are going to Cairn Castle this morn, aye?" Mina joined them at the table as Ella served up the porridge.

"Aye. As soon as I eat and do whatever Ella needs me to do."

"Naught else. You need to get yerself over there early to get work. Take your clothes with you, in case you dinna return," Mina said.

"Aye. I have my bag packed."

Then they ate silently, Amelda still half asleep like she always was early in the morning. Once they had eaten, Amelda cleaned their bowls, and Ella hugged Finnegan.

Ella wrote: *Good luck to you, brother.*

Amelda hugged him too. Mina just smiled. "You will do it, lad. You have it in you to be a great warrior."

Finnegan's eyes widened, and his gaze shifted from Mina to Ella. Oh, heavens. She hoped he would never be a warrior after all the fighting and killing she'd seen.

"I will return if they willna take me on," Finnegan said. "If I get work, I may no' be able to meet you here."

"Nay, no' here. If anyone should follow you, it could be dangerous for us all," Mina said.

"I will try to befriend everyone I can and see if I can find work for you and Amelda," Finnegan said to Ella.

Ella nodded but didn't believe they would consider employing them sight unseen. Amelda might seem too young for anyone to hire.

He smiled, waved at them, and hurried off. He seemed eager to do something other than live in the woods in the small hut. Ella understood his need to grow up and become a man.

EARLY THAT MORNING, Dashiell dressed and headed for the stables. As he strode through the inner bailey, his cousin Fallon, seeing him alone, approached him. "I see that you are getting ready to go somewhere."

"Aye, aye, I am in a hurry."

"You must no' go out alone."

Dashiell stared at the open gate. "I hadna planned to. Have Quinn and the rest of those who usually join us on the hunt ready themselves at once."

"Aye." Fallon ran his hand through his dark blond hair, a fine stubble covering his chin, and then his cousin rushed off.

Dashiell strode to the stable and waved to a groom. "Saddle my horse."

"Aye, my laird."

Dashiell left the stable and stared at the stone castle, then smiled as Quinn hurried outside, slipping his *sgian dubh* into his boot. He had expected him to join him if he was as intrigued with the woman as Dashiell was. "Are you ready for another hunt, Quinn?"

"For the forest nymph?"

"Of course. What else? This willna get you into too much trouble with the missus, will it?"

His blue eyes sparkling, Quinn smiled. "I see Lady Yvaine has spoken to you about the matter. I am just curious who this lady is, that is all."

"That is what I told my aunt." Dashiell's horse was led out of the stable, and ten more of his men joined him. "We are hunting for Ella today."

"No' deer?" one of the men said.

"Of course, if we find a deer, we will have venison on the table this morn. Otherwise, I will be happy to retrieve the forest nymph."

Christopher rushed out of the keep, his eyes wide. "You were no' going to leave me behind, were you?"

"I wouldna wish Ella to take over your dreams."

Christopher shook his head.

Dashiell would not dream about the woman again. "Now, where has the lady been sighted before?"

"Always by the stream. And always with a deer," one of the men said. "Sometimes with the wolf pup."

"She has the hair the color of sunset red-gold, silkily caressing her shoulders and back." Dashiell mounted his horse, still thinking about the way her gown flowed over her hips and her breasts—she was definitely a full-grown woman, not a wisp of a lass as he first had thought.

As they headed out of the castle grounds, Quinn asked, "How do you ken that? I couldna tell with the distance we were from the lady and the way the veil covered her hair. Forest shadows danced across her features, making her appear not quite real."

Dashiell stared at his advisor for a moment. "I could have sworn her hair was...oh, I saw her even more vividly in a dream. She had lost her veil."

"A dream?"

"Aye, have you had a dream about the lady? Christopher says that anyone who gazes upon Ella dreams about her afterward."

His advisor looked away. "Aye."

"Really? Prithee, tell me what you dreamed of." The hunting party entered the forest fringe, and an owl hooting made Dashiell smile, thinking back to his men's words. "Mayhap, she is still an owl."

"Aye. As I have said, the lady always accompanies a deer near the stream that runs through the Caledonian Forest, even in my dreams. I didna see the color of her hair as I was mesmerized by her gown."

"Her léine?" Dashiell smiled. "I will have to pay more attention to her dress the next time. What about her gown interested you so, pray tell?" Although he could imagine what had captured his advisor's eye.

"As I said before, it was green, like the color of the leaves of the trees. When I approached her, I could see delicate designs embroidered on the bodice..."

"Now I see what caught your eye." Although Dashiell hadn't seen the designs on the bodice, he was more entranced by the swell of her breasts.

Quinn laughed. "Just because I am married, I am no' dead."

Unable to conceal his amusement, Dashiell nodded. "Continue with your story."

Everyone was listening, appearing eager to hear what the others had to say about the woman.

"Well, just once, I reached the stream without her leaving. She watched me as if she was as curious about me as I was about her. The deer stood with her as if it was unafraid of me. When I stepped into the water, the lady dropped her flowers into the stream and disappeared. And the deer also. Right before my eyes."

"You have dreamed of her on more than one occasion then?"

"I have dreamed of her every night since I first encountered the woman. 'Tis the oddest thing as I dinna normally dream about anything...at least before sighting the lass."

"I see." Dashiell rubbed his chin, stubble covering it. "Well, the lady will not rule *my* sleep. Is this why you wish to capture Ella?"

Quinn shook his head. "She has the most appealing lips I have ever seen. Besides her gown, I see her mouth, slightly parted, pink as the buttercup, willing, waiting for my embrace. Then, she disappears before I ever taste the sweet nectar from her lips."

Dashiell laughed. "I will have to check out her mouth as well." He had seen her eyes filled with tears, which had drawn his attention more, and he couldn't help being disturbed by it, even if it had been just a dream.

Glancing at the other men in their party, Dashiell asked, "Has anybody else dreamed of the lady?"

Several of the others nodded.

One of the men spied a deer, but Dashiell shook his head. "We will wait until we are at the stream. What about you, Fallon? What did you dream of?"

"Like you, I saw the lady's locks. I didna notice anything about her dress."

Dashiell laughed. He didn't believe a word of it, nor did he think any of the men did either, as they chuckled in response.

"So, what else did you notice about the lady?"

"She had the most beautiful almond-shaped eyes. She stared back at me, beckoning me to come to her, but when I neared the water, she disappeared," Fallon said.

Green eyes, shimmering with tears.

Dashiell frowned, bothered again by recalling her distress.

Quinn motioned to Dashiell as they came to the clearing in the woods along the bank of the stream and spied a deer drinking from the gurgling water.

"She is not here," his advisor whispered. Quinn glanced at Fallon, who nodded. "We heard a battle in the forest two nights ago."

Dashiell looked at him. "A battle?"

"Between the fey and someone else," Fallon said. "You see how she wears a sword. We heard fighting and found no one."

Dashiell shook his head. He had never thought his men would be spooked over nothing in the dark woods at night.

The men all remained mounted on their horses, hidden in the thick foliage and shadows of the trees as they continued to watch the deer.

After observing the stream for an eternity, Dashiell finally said, "I dinna believe she will come here." He reached for his bow and an arrow, nocked it, and prepared to shoot when the woman suddenly appeared.

"Look, there," Quinn whispered as he pointed at the lady.

Dashiell lowered his bow and waited. "What is she doing?" he asked as he watched her scrutinize them. "Can she see us?"

"She seems to be able to, but I thought the thickness of the trees massed before us hid us from her sight."

"I wish to get a closer look. Will she run, do you think?"

"Aye. I am sure she will take flight if we move toward her."

The lady finally took her eyes off the forest, knelt at the stream's edge on the stony bank, and placed flowers into the water. She watched the flowers float in swirling crescents down the stream, and Dashiell whispered, "That's what I saw her do in my dream."

Considering her entire appearance, he smiled. She was beautiful—her hair, face, eyes, and body. The fabric hung snugly to her curves in the cool breeze, making him long to get a closer look. He saw the sheathed sword belted at her waist.

Dashiell wanted to see her up close with every fiber of his being. "I must get nearer."

"What do you wish for us to do?" Quinn asked.

"Stay here. Perhaps if only one of us approaches her, the movement will not alarm her."

He handed his bow and arrow to Christopher, but before he could nudge his horse into the clearing, the lady began to hum a haunting tune that drifted down the stream and carried away by the breeze.

He sat taller in his saddle and frowned. "I recognize that tune, but without the words, I canna recall what it is." He looked at his companions, but no one seemed to know. "All right, I will attempt to get closer to the woman."

Prompting his horse to move out of the forest, Dashiell took a few steps toward the stream's bank while focusing on the lady's movements. She seemed to take no notice of him, and he turned back to smile at his companions. Quinn waved him on, his expression anxious.

Dashiell continued to the edge of the water downstream from the lady and stared at her when she touched the deer and rubbed its cheek. The deer licked her hand, and she smiled. Then she turned to observe Dashiell walking his horse alongside the stream, attempting to get closer to her. She shook her head at him, and his heart sank.

He knew then that she would bolt. He saw it in her eyes as if she were a deer, fearful he would hunt her down.

She darted into the forest while the deer dashed off in the opposite direction. When the lady ran, Dashiell kicked his horse and took off after her, sending water skyward as he splashed across the stream while his friends soon joined him in the pursuit.

After searching for over an hour, he stopped his horse, and a frown creased his brow. "I dinna see how the lady can disappear like she does."

"What did she look like up close?" Quinn asked.

"I have never seen a more beautiful woman in all my life. She is just like you have described to me in your dreams, only she is real. Oh, to touch her face, her hair, her lips...I believe I am in love."

Quinn shook his head. "The other clan chiefs willna be happy about this."

"They need no' know about this."

"Five chiefs wish you to wed their daughters. What will you do now? You have shown no interest in the ladies."

"I will have to find the right lady, then, will I no'? If I do, I willna be chasing after a dream in the woods all day."

Quinn sighed deeply. "I am happily married, yet here I am, searching for the lady myself."

"Aye, but today, you are searching for the lady for *me*."

A chorus of laughter from his clansmen broke out as they headed back to the castle.

"Will we no' try to take a deer back with us before we return?" Fallon asked.

"Nay, with the boar we brought home, we will have plenty of meat for the next few days. We will let the lady's deer be for the time being."

As for the lady herself, Dashiell intended to capture her quickly to satisfy his growing curiosity.

6

———

Dashiell overhead everyone talking about the mystery woman in the forest when he entered the great hall to break their fast. He guessed everyone knew about her now. Some were talking about plans to capture her.

When he sat down at the head table, Lady Yvaine watched him as he drank his ale. "Have you had dreams of Ella? Wynda says her husband often dreams of the lady. The first time, he made the mistake of telling her about it when he awoke in the middle of the night. Since then, she says he wakes every night, sitting up all at once, and she knows he has had the dream again."

"You are the most curious woman I know."

"Aye, well, 'tis no' me who is hunting for the lady for several hours in the morn before we break our fast."

He nodded. "My uncle had always said you had the quickest wit of any woman he knew."

"He was a good man."

"He was at that. So what else do you know of Ella, my lady?"

"She is a temptress."

"A temptress?" Dashiell said, amused. "What do you mean?"

"If you saw me standing on the bank of the stream, would you pursue me?"

He laughed. "You are old enough to be my mother."

Yvaine smiled. "Just the same, you would not take any interest in me. However, you and the other men canna get enough of seeing the lady. She is a temptress. Watch out for her or she will rule both your dreams at night and your thoughts during the day."

Dashiell took a drink of his mead and looked across the great hall to see the men who had been on the hunt with him speaking to the rest of the clan while they ate. "I can just imagine what they are saying about the experience today."

"They are saying"—Yvaine scooped up a spoonful of stewed fruit—"that their beloved laird has fallen in love with a temptress."

"She doesna rule my life, Lady Yvaine. You are wrong about that."

"I have heard that you have suspended dealing with the troubles our clansmen would have brought before you to resolve midday."

"I am entitled to do such a thing if I so determine that the circumstances warrant."

"Ah, but what do you plan to do then?"

He didn't speak, not wanting to admit to his aunt that he could not quit thinking about the lady in the woods.

Yvaine finished her bread and then waited as the servant took her bowl away. As the minstrel strolled over to the table, his aunt said, "I surmise you will have a sudden urge to go on a hunt again this afternoon. Dinna take anyone new with you or the plague will soon spread."

"Nonsense." Dashiell listened to the minstrel sing his song. "That song!"

"What?"

"The lass hummed a tune. I canna remember the song she was humming because she sang not the words. Perhaps the minstrel will know. Now I canna recall the tune she hummed." He motioned for the minstrel to stop his song. "Do any of you who hunted with me today remember the tune the lady hummed in the woods?"

The men all shook their heads.

"Continue with your song, minstrel." Dashiell frowned at the table.

"I have heard Cameron is having his daughter escorted here for you to consider as a bride choice."

"What?"

Yvaine laughed. "The forest nymph has stolen your thoughts away."

He sighed and finished his mead. "You are right, Lady Yvaine. I will return to the hunt this afternoon."

ELLA CLEANED up after they finished breaking their fast and was ready to do her chores. She picked up her writing stick and wrote on the dirt floor. *What would you have me do today?*

She always asked if Mina wanted her to do something other than what Ella had already planned. She prayed Finnegan was doing all right at the castle. He hadn't returned so that had to be a good sign, she hoped.

"Find more mushrooms and herbs. Our stores are getting low. We need fresh water also. We could do with a wee bit more firewood and kindling."

She wrote: *Be back soon.* Well, with all the chores Ella had to do, she would be back as soon as she could. Ella worried more and more about Mina. She was taking longer naps now, tired after doing very little, and seemed to be fading away. Ella wanted to do everything for Mina so she could rest more.

Amelda went with Ella to help collect mushrooms, herbs, and berries and then she would return to the hut. Ella never wanted her cousin to be away from the hut as long as she was, afraid if someone spied them, Amelda wouldn't be able to hide as well as Ella could. Aye, she was smaller, but she wasn't as fast as Ella. Or as quiet.

They headed down the path where they often found mushrooms, but they soon heard men moving about, talking low, one of them saying, "We must find the lass. Dead or alive."

"Aye."

Dashiell's men wouldn't say that, and a shiver ran up Ella's spine as she recognized the man's voice. Years ago, he had shouted, "*Tha mi ag iarraidh orra marbh!*" He had wanted them all dead. But who? Yet his comment brought a flood of memories back.

Men yelling, women screaming, her mother dying, and commanding her to save her brother and her cousin.

All she knew was the man was *olc. Evil.* Maybe he wasn't looking for her, but she feared he was because he was one of MacAfee's men. She didn't think they would be here by MacTavish's invitation. What other lass would be in these woods?

She and Amelda hid in the thick bracken and listened to them as they talked to one another. She couldn't believe they would speak while on a hunt. She might not be their usual prey, but she was just as wary of them as the deer in the forest would be. And certes when they were talking about killing the lass, she knew they were up to no good.

She slowly unsheathed her sword, praying that MacTavish's men would be in the forest, see these men, and send them on their way. Amelda touched her arm. Ella put her finger to her lips to make sure she didn't speak.

She had tears in her eyes and Ella hugged her and kissed her forehead. They had survived for five years; she wouldn't let McAfee kill her without her at least paying him back. She wanted to send Amelda back to the hut, but she was afraid she would be seen.

"MacAfee, should we no' call out the name the villagers gave her? Ella?"

Her skin chilled. That confirmed they were looking for her, not some other lass. And that MacAfee was with them. She also had a *sgian dubh* in her boot, but she couldn't fight all of them. Maybe not even one of them. She knew they would want to kill Amelda also since she was Ella's kin.

"And alert her that we are after her? God's wounds, how daft can you be?" MacAfee said.

The devil himself.

"If we call her by name, she will think us friend, no' foe, since we are no' living at the castle," the man insisted.

"If any of you listen to this man and do as he suggests, you will be dead at my hand!" MacAfee said.

She heard at least six male voices speaking to one another and knew she couldn't take on any of them.

To her relief, their horses' hooves clomped on the forest floor, and the men's voices faded away as they moved farther away from her and her cousin. She wondered if Dashiell had allowed these men to come into the forest to hunt for her. She suspected not. She wished she could get word to him without putting herself and Amelda at risk.

She hoped they would not find their hut and harm Mina in any way. Ella had to do her chores again and return to the hut immediately.

Once the sound of MacAfee and his men faded away, Ella sheathed her sword, grabbed Amelda's hand, and ran through the woods, listening for any sign of anyone nearby. Not hearing anyone in this direction, they kept going until they got close enough to the hut and stayed nearby, hidden in the bracken.

Again, she listened, not wanting to dash into the hut when someone might witness it and know it was there. They stayed still for what seemed an interminable amount of time. She and Amelda ran for the hut when she was certain no one was about.

Making their way into the small abode, they must have looked a sight, their hair having come loose and tangled with twigs as they escaped.

"What's wrong?" Mina asked, coming to them, taking hold of their arms and pulling them into a hug.

In times like these, Ella knew Mina still had the inner and outer strength to keep her going.

Ella grabbed her writing stick and wrote on the dirt floor. *MacAfee!*

"Here? In our forest?" Mina asked, her words hushed.

Ella nodded vigorously. She wrote—*Wants me dead. Or alive*—she added. Though she suspected he wanted her dead.

Tears filled Mina's eyes, and she hugged Ella against her chest. "I'm so sorry, lass. I was afraid this day might come. How did he know that you had even survived?"

Ella hugged Mina, then pulled away from her and wrote—*Villagers.*

"Wagging tongues. If I hadna had to teach you to barter with people, to learn more about the people in the village, I would never have sent you there." Mina let out her breath and hugged Amelda.

Ella shook her head.

"It couldna be helped. You couldna be sheltered here all your life. You needed to talk with—well, be around other people. Besides, I hoped that where I couldna help you to speak or remember what had happened to you, mayhap someone in the village might have helped."

Chores?

"Only when they are gone for certain."

Word to Dashiell?

"Aye. I wish we could send word to him, but you canna speak and you risk MacAfee or his men catching you if you try to reach

MacTavish. He will no doubt be angered when he learns MacAfee is looking for a lass to kill in his forest." Mina motioned to the sewing basket. "Sit and sew. You have no' finished your new gown."

Ella had outgrown several léines over the years, and most had been patched together from the ones that were too small—all but two. One was the beautiful gown she'd been wearing when Mina had discovered her at the stream. Mina had washed and dried it and neatly folded it away.

Amelda would grow into it one day. And the other was the green gown she wore when encountering Dashiell and his men. Mina had given her coin to purchase the fabric, and Ella was still working on the embroidery for a new gown. At least in her mind, it wasn't so that she could look like a fine lady, but to learn how to sew finer garments if she were to work on Dashiell's staff sometime in the future, sewing gowns for ladies.

But she didn't want to sit and sew. She wanted to warn Dashiell about the men in his forest. She wanted him to kill the devil. And she wanted to do her chores. She hated to be confined when there was danger about. But she also worried about Finnegan. What if he wasn't hired and tried to return home but ran into these men?

"I ken that look, Ella. Sit. And. Sew." Mina patted her shoulder.

Ella sat down with the basket of sewing supplies and began to work on the gown, trying to concentrate on embroidering the neckline while listening for danger outside their hut. Amelda was also trying to learn how to sew and was working on a simple scarf.

Ella wished she'd seen MacAfee's face. She knew his voice, and she would recognize his face. Would she regain some more of her memories if she saw him? She wished Mina would tell her more about him.

"He is a bad man, Ella. He canna be allowed to find you. That is why you must find your voice and speak again. You must discover all your memories, and you must appeal to Dashiell to take you in. Until you do, you'll be in the worst kind of danger all over again, now that MacAfee believes you live in the forest and is bold enough to come here without MacTavish's consent."

Ella feared more for her cousin, Mina, and her brother should he return to the hut.

Mina helped Amelda work on some of *her* embroidery stitches. "No more looking for anything in the woods. No more trips to the village. Not until those men leave."

Mina took hold of Ella's hand, tears in her eyes. "The nightmares you have are about real things that have happened in your life. The battle was in your castle. Cairn Castle. They were real. You must remember what had happened. I...I think if you return to the castle, you'll find your voice."

Ella set her work aside and wrote on the floor. *What about Finnegan?*

"He's a canny lad. You have taught him well. He will be careful should he return to the forest."

What if Dashiell felt threatened by Ella because she might hold some claim to the castle? Then again, she doubted anyone would ever believe her.

7

A lad of about sixteen unexpectedly rode into the inner bailey on horseback while Dashiell and some of his men practiced sword fighting. Everyone stopped fighting as Dashiell turned to see who the newcomer was. The boy had a black eye and bloodied knuckles.

Dashiell sheathed his sword and approached the messenger, Fallon quickly joining him in case of trouble.

The lad dismounted. "I'm kin of the MacNeills, Geoffrey, and I've brought word that James, his brother Angus, and their cousin Niall are coming to see you. They bought bulls in Stirling market."

Dashiell smiled. He needed good news.

"Um, they're intrigued by what is happening in the forest."

Dashiell frowned.

"I was meant to come earlier but ran into trouble on the way here."

"Oh? What trouble?" Dashiell would punish whoever harmed anyone in his territory. "Is that why you have a black eye and bloodied knuckles?"

"Aye. Two men asked me if I was a member of the MacTavish

clan. I said no. I was with the MacNeill clan. They wanted to know if I knew about Ella of the Caledonian Forest. I said no, though my brethren and I have heard of her. They didna believe me and beat me up. But I beat them up as well."

"Two men against one lad?"

"I ken. They should have sent more against me."

Dashiell chuckled. He sounded like a MacNeill all right. "Come, we'll get you some ale."

But then James MacNeill, one of his brothers, Angus, and their cousin Niall headed for the gates with three Highland bulls in tow on their way back to the Highlands. He hadn't seen them for about three years. He was glad to welcome his friends back.

James, Angus, and Niall gave Dashiell hugs. The ten men with them smiled and greeted him. James frowned at Geoffrey. "What happened to you?"

"I was set upon by two men."

James glanced at Dashiell. "I'm sending out a force to look for them."

"They look worse than me," Geoffrey insisted.

Dashiell said to Fallon, "I want you to take a dozen men and search for anyone who might have beat up the lad."

"Aye." Fallon took off across the bailey, calling out names of men to join him as he quickly gathered a force.

"I see you have good-looking bulls that you're gifting me," Dashiell said to James.

They laughed. "You should have gone to market with us. We're starting our breeding stock and hope to have a good head of cattle with these," James said.

"As long as no one steals them." Dashiell knew they'd had problems with that in the past.

"We resolved that issue a while back and have no' had any difficulty since then," James said.

"I'm glad to hear it. Come, join us for the nooning meal. You'll stay for a few days, aye?"

"Aye, we were hoping you would offer. As long as the bulls can stay in the outer bailey," James said.

Dashiell laughed. "Aye. Will they be in your outer bailey when you return home?"

"Nay, too much of a mess to clean up. We've heard there are strange goings ons in the Caledonian Forest, and we dinna want to lose them to...uh, strange and mysterious forces," James said.

How had his friends, who lived so far away, known about that when Dashiell hadn't?

"Strange and mysterious forces?" Dashiell wanted to know just what they had heard.

"The Nymph of the Forest?" James asked. "We should be asking you what you know of her."

They looked at Geoffrey and frowned. "What exactly happened to you? Did you encounter thieves?" James asked.

"I ran into two men who wanted to know if I knew of the lady of the forest," Geoffrey said. "Truly, I look better than they do."

"Who were they?" James asked.

"I dinna ken. They didna say their names."

"Fallon and the others will hopefully catch them," Dashiell said, wondering who would have done such a thing to Geoffrey without provocation. They would pay for it.

Dashiell brought them into the great hall, and the MacNeills sat with him at the head table. Dashiell's aunt moved over to sit with his advisor and his wife, happy to do so. He loved her for always being so accommodating when he had important guests visiting.

"We've seen her on the hunts across the stream when we're in the woods," Dashiell said.

"A fey woman," Angus said as the servers began bringing venison to the table.

"I dinna believe in things of a mystical nature." Though the woman was sure making Dashiell wonder about her.

The MacNeills laughed.

"Then you wouldna mind if we joined you on the hunt to see this woman," James said.

"All who see her—" Dashiell began to say that they would dream of her, but he thought it would sound like he believed in it.

His friends were hanging on his every word and when he paused, James said, "Aye?"

Dashiell shook his head.

"You ken we'll learn the truth," James said. "Everyone in a castle talks."

"'Tis said that if you see her, you will dream about her from then on." Dashiell drank some of his ale.

His friends smiled and drank their ale and ate their venison. They didn't believe it.

"You have seen her?" Niall asked.

Dashiell knew what was coming next. "Aye."

"Do you dream of her?" Niall asked.

Dashiell didn't want to tell them he did, but he knew his friends would know the truth before long with the way his people gossiped. "Aye."

All three of the MacNeills sat back.

James considered Dashiell for a long time. "The others who go with you on the hunt also?"

"Aye."

James smiled. "I'm glad we stopped in on you to see this fascinating woman. We have heard tell she is uncommonly beautiful and for the most part blends into the forest."

"Like a fey woman," Niall said.

"She may no' appear for you. She doesna always show herself," Dashiell said.

"Then we may have to stay longer to ensure that we finally do see her," James said.

As strong-willed as James was, Dashiell knew there was no deterring him from his mission unless he had trouble back home and had to leave.

"As you wish. You're welcome to stay as long as you like, except your men have to clean up after your bulls."

The brothers and their cousin laughed.

"We were surprised that you had bartered for the castle here. Why did MacAfee agree to give it away?" James asked.

"I was surprised as well, but I was delighted to be given the opportunity to barter for it. I got the bargain in the deal. We'd been drinking at a pub when he and his men arrived and I knew he wanted some of my land, which I wouldna sell to him. He looked haggard like he hadn't been sleeping for days."

James frowned.

"All his men did, and I wondered if he'd been in a battle with another clan, but I didna pry. He joined me at my table and said he had a proposition. I didna believe he truly wanted to barter his castle and lands, but he said he was serious, and I agreed."

James shook his head.

"I still assumed he would sleep on it and change his mind, that mayhap too much ale had addled his mind, but his men seemed just as eager to move out of the castle."

"I've never met the chief. But I did meet one of his men shortly after you took over the castle. I asked him why his chief bartered away his castle. He said it was time to move on. We keep our castles to pass down to our kin for centuries unless another clan takes us over."

"Aye, that's just what I thought," Dashiell said.

"I canna imagine MacAfee wanting to give up his castle for your land, as valuable as it was," James said. "It still isna as valuable as the castle and the land and forest surrounding it."

"Aye. So he didna specify any other reason?" Dashiell asked.

"Nay."

"Mayhap the Nymph of the Forest was scaring off his deer and had spooked his people," Niall said. "Or—"

"They had nightmares about the nymph." James didn't sound serious in the least. "Since your people dream of her after seeing her, maybe no' everyone dreams good things."

Smiling, Dashiell shook his head. He remembered all the good times they had had over the years when they'd been able to get together. Even James's brother Malcolm, Dougald, and their good friend, Gunnolf, who had been raised alongside them, were his best friends.

"Aye." Niall nodded as if he truly believed it.

Dashiell wasn't sure if he was jesting or not.

"That's why he and his men looked so haggard," Niall said.

Angus laughed and slapped Niall on the back. "You would make a great storyteller."

Dashiell and James agreed.

WITH THE TIME that had passed, Mina finally agreed that Ella needed to forage for food. "Be vigilant. Return here immediately if you see any sign of MacAfee or his men."

Ella nodded, eager to leave the hut and do her chores.

They hadn't heard from her brother for the three days he'd been gone, and she had worried about him. Amelda wanted to go with her to do their chores, probably tired of being confined to the hut like Ella was, but she shook her head and wrote in the dirt: *Not this time. If I find the men have left the forest, you can. But we canna risk it right now.*

She'd been so worried about Amelda when they had heard

MacAfee and his men so close to where they'd been hiding that she didn't want to put her in danger again.

Ella left the hut to do her chores as they desperately needed food and water, and Mina could not do the work. Ella was cautious, ensuring she heard no one in the forest searching for her.

Even though she gathered wild garlic, elderflower, honeysuckle, wild cherries, blueberries, sloes, wild mint, wood sorrel, Scots pine needles, and rowan berries, she kept thinking she had to tell Dashiell that MacAfee had been hunting on his lands—for her.

Still, she was concerned that Dashiell might think she would try to claim the castle was hers next. Or he might not even believe her.

At least she had stored up enough acorns and chestnuts from last winter to eat, especially since Mina seemed to be eating less and less, so Ella didn't need to fish for a few days. And Finnegan wasn't eating here any longer. At least they had mutton and cabbage to make a pottage for the evening meal. They needed firewood also.

She spent all morning gathering the food, spying a pine marten scurrying off, and then returned to the hut to leave the bags with Mina and Amelda.

"No sign of anyone, I take it?" Mina took the bags from her. She peered into them and smiled.

Ella shook her head. She wrote in the dirt: *Firewood*. She was always glad when she had gathered enough food to make Mina smile.

"Aye. And water."

"Can I go with you, Ella?" Amelda implored.

Ella nodded because she hadn't seen anyone in the woods and knew her cousin needed to leave the hut for fresh air. They headed out to gather firewood this time.

She usually had to go farther into the woods, but they found more firewood closer to the hut since she hadn't gathered wood and kindling in a while. They couldn't leave it stacked up outside the hut either, or it could be discovered, and someone could watch to see who came for it.

Amelda quickly gathered an armload of twigs, and Ella pointed in the direction of the hut, telling Amelda to return with it now. Amelda hurried off with it, and once she entered the hut, Ella gathered more firewood.

She heard nothing but the birds in the trees twittering away with each other. She saw a red deer but no sign of any men. A hawk flew overhead, catching her attention. She carried more twigs and a couple of branches into the hut and grabbed two buckets.

Mina and Amelda began sorting through all the food Ella had gathered. Ella wondered if Mina was ever tired of talking to Ella when she couldn't converse with her.

"Be careful," Mina said.

This was the most dangerous of missions. Ella would be exposed when she went to the stream if MacAfee or his men were about. If she saw Dashiell or his men, she could write a message in the dirt on the shore where they had gone before. If only they would remain on their side. She was afraid if Dashiell or the others saw her, they would cross the stream.

When she got there, she waited in the cover of the bracken and woods, watching and listening for any sign of anyone. She was certain no one was around and quickly gathered her water in the buckets and decided she needed to return them to the hut first.

If she didn't, and they saw her, they would chase her, and she would have to leave the water behind. After she took the water to the hut, she would return to the bank and write the message.

She was afraid Mina would not want her to leave again once she dropped off the water-filled buckets, but when she arrived, Mina had left the hut. Amelda was preparing a meal. "Mina had to...you ken."

Ella nodded and set the buckets of water inside. She wrote: *Be back soon.*

Then she hurried off to the stream again to write her message in the soil, hoping someone in Dashiell's party could read. When Ella reached the stream, she saw Dashiell and his men and decided to take the chance to leave the message. She also noticed new men were riding with him.

They were seated on their horses next to him in a place of honor and friendship, all three men dark-haired and dark-eyed. Brothers? She didn't believe they were MacAfee's men. She prayed they weren't.

They were all staring at her.

"I am Dashiell MacLeod of Cairn Castle, lass. Who are you, and where do you come from?" Dashiell sighed. "We are having a fine feast in the keep this eve. I wish for you to join us."

Frowning, Ella shook her head, then stepped out of the shadows of the trees and walked with a cautious step toward the bank with a stick in hand, hoping he didn't try to rush her.

Just stay on your side, she silently told him. Yet, Mina's words came to her, niggling at her. *"Go with him. He and his people can protect you."*

But Ella couldn't leave Mina behind. And she wasn't sure that Dashiell would want to take her cousin in either.

WHEN DASHIELL SAW ELLA, he was certain he could not draw close to her before she took flight like a frightened bird. His MacNeill friends were quiet, curious, and rivetted like he was. A breeze caught her gown and tugged at it, the same with the veil on her hair, showing off some long red curls.

Dashiell nudged his horse to walk halfway to the stream, then paused. His heart nearly stopped when he saw her advance toward the stream. She was so close yet so far away.

She watched him as he waited, observing her, wanting to prove she had nothing to fear from him. She stood at the water's edge, parted her lips as if to say something, then crouched down and drew in the dirt. It took the greatest fortitude to hold back and not dash across the water, seize her, and take her back to Cairn Castle to learn who she was.

She lifted her stick as if she was done, then glanced at him to see that he had edged closer to the stream on his horse. She shook her head at him, causing her hair to toss from side to side with the motion, then turned and ran into the forest.

"Nay! Dinna go!" he shouted, his voice a mixture of pleading and command, his blood pulsing in his veins. He galloped his horse across the water.

His men and friends soon caught up with him to aid him in searching the surrounding area for signs of where the lady had disappeared. When he finally paused, he saw his advisor smiling at him. "What?"

"You invited her to eat with us? What would everyone have thought?" Quinn asked.

"I am sure she would have been the topic of conversation." Dashiell was furious beyond measure that the woman would continue to elude him.

"She is of the fey," Niall said as if he knew the truth.

"She is most unusual," Angus said.

"Worthy of investigating further," James said.

"From her reaction to your invitation, I would venture to say the lass doesna like the idea of visiting the castle," Quinn said.

"Perhaps she worked for MacAfee's staff before your people took over, and she was let go," James said.

"She seems skittish toward any who try to get close to her," his advisor said.

"Mayhap she has heard I am too serious." Dashiell looked about for more clues of the woman's whereabouts. "When did you say people started noticing the lass in the woods? How long ago was this?"

"For the old lady, they say she is as old as some of the trees in the forest...seventy, eighty-years old at least. As for the girl, she has been seen here for several months. Accounts varied. A blacksmith said he had seen her as long as five years ago, but nearly everyone else has said she has only been around this past year."

"How odd. Well, do any of you see clues as to where she disappeared?"

"I see deer trails all over," Fallon said. "She must use them to travel wherever she goes when she leaves the stream."

"All right then, we will split our forces and check where the deer trails lead. Perhaps we will get lucky. Meet back at the stream before dark. If any find the lass...hold her at the stream so I may speak with her."

Dashiell, his advisor, his MacNeill friends, and three of his men took one of the trails while the others split off into different groups and headed down some other paths. Dashiell's trail finally came into the meadow, where the path led down to the loch. He stared at the grasses that flowed with the breeze.

"Do you think she could hide in the grasses since they are so tall this time of year, Quinn?"

"Possibly."

His heart thundering, Dashiell stared at a figure standing by the loch. "Is that her, do you think?"

"Nay," his advisor said. "She isna wearing the same green gown, is smaller in stature, and her hair appears too dark to be the same lass."

Niall shook his head. "She isna the same woman."

"Come, let us see her anyway."

When Dashiell and his men approached the girl, she curtsied to him. "Do you know of Ella of the Forest, miss?"

"Of course."

"Have you seen her then?"

"Aye, here in the meadow, twice."

"Have you spoken to her?"

The girl shook her head. "She didna see me, and I was afraid of her. I only watched her as she went to the loch and bathed, then returned to the forest. The other time, she gathered flowers and returned to the forest."

"Why were you afraid of her? Did she do anything threatening?"

"Oh, nay. Do you no' think it odd that she lives alone in the forest the way she does? The villagers say she is a wild woman raised by a pack of wolves. Some say she is one of the fey kind. A woodland fey. They call her Ella."

Niall cleared his throat. "I told you."

"They do, do they?" Dashiell ignored Niall. "Thank you, miss." He turned his horse back toward the forest. "Imagine that...a woman raised by wolves who protects the deer in my forest, then turns into an owl at night, and she's one of the fey. This I have got to see."

The MacNeills agreed.

James said, "This will be a tale worth telling."

"If she is of the fey, no' just a lass living in the forest you should be careful," Angus cautioned.

Fallon suddenly joined them. "I didna believe the lass was doing anything but drawing in the dirt with her stick, but she wrote something."

They all headed back that way. "What, pray tell, did she write?" Dashiell asked.

"She wrote—MacAfee."

Dashiell studied Fallon. "How could the lass even know how to write?" Then he frowned. "Is that all she wrote?"

"Aye. If she had meant to write anything else, you might have scared her away before she could," Fallon said.

"I thought the same," James said.

Dashiell was sorely vexed with himself over that. "MacAfee? What is the significance of her writing it here?" Here, Dashiell thought he would catch her and learn all about her, but now he had a new mystery.

How did she know MacAfee? How did she know how to read and write if she was a wild woman? Was she telling him that MacAfee still owned the forest? That Dashiell didn't belong there?

8

B efore anyone could follow her, Ella hurried into the hut and saw Mina napping. Amelda was working on her sewing. Ella quietly closed the door behind her and locked it with the latch, glad she'd at least been able to hastily write MacAfee's name on the shore.

But she'd had no time to write anything more than that when Dashiell tried to approach her, and she ran off. At least she had done all her chores. But she was annoyed with him for trying to sneak over to her side while she had been writing and couldn't say all that she needed to. Would he even figure out what she was trying to say? Most likely not.

She feared Mina would scold her for not allowing him to approach her. If she knew Dashiell had offered to have Ella eat with them and she said no, Mina was sure to be upset with her. But what if he hadn't allowed Ella to return for Amelda and Mina?

What if Mina had no longer been able to care for Amelda, and her cousin would have had to fend for herself? At five years of age, Amelda couldn't manage. What if Dashiell had released her, followed Ella to the hut, and destroyed it because no one was supposed to live in his forest?

But what if he took them all in?

Mina woke and stared at her for a moment. "I thought you had returned with the water, but then you were gone again."

Ella wrote on the ground—*I left a message for Dashiell at the stream.*

Mina raised a brow, left the bed, and began to make their meal —pottage made of mutton and cabbage. "You told him about MacAfee."

Ella helped her make the meal and nodded.

"About him coming for you?" Mina asked.

Ella wrote on the floor—*Just MacAfee's name.*

Her expression turned into a scowl, her shoulders more slumped than usual, Mina appeared to be exasperated with her.

Dashiell tried to cross the stream.

"You should have gone with him!"

What about you? What about Amelda? Would you go with us?

Mina continued to make the meal. "I am old. I dinna belong there."

You belong with me. With us.

Mina studied her.

Together?

"They willna want an old woman like me."

Ella smiled. She wrote: *We will go together.*

She would not leave Mina behind. She had been like a grand-mother to them, teaching them, scolding them, loving them.

"If they willna take me in? You will be with them. As I have said, I am no' long for this world."

Ella never wanted to leave her behind. If Dashiell took them all in, maybe this would work. But she wouldn't go without Mina.

We go together. Since that was decided, Ella poured the pottage into bowls for them, and they sat down to eat.

Mina looked at Ella so seriously and said, "You will bring him here."

For too long, they had tried to keep their hut hidden. She couldn't believe what she was hearing. Mina had always said she didn't have foresight, but Ella suspected she did.

"Aye. 'Tis destined to happen that way. I have seen this in a dream today. I have no' seen what happens after that, but he will come here because you will bring him here."

"When?" Ella mouthed the word.

"That I dinna know."

THE MACNEILLS again sat with Dashiell at the head table that evening at supper. They were eating pigeons cooked with oyster shells. When he saw his aunt observing him on the other side of Niall, he said, "Aye, Lady Yvaine, what words of wisdom have you for me this evening?"

"I was wondering, now that you have heard wolves raised the lady...what do you intend to do with her, should you catch her?"

"We havena even come close to apprehending her."

"Do you really believe she would eat supper with us?"

"Would you have objected?"

"She would have had to put her hair up. I am no' so sure she would have been willing to abide by our etiquette."

"I dinna believe the young lady was terribly interested in eating with us."

"The clan chiefs vying for you to wed one of the daughters will no' be pleased. I only jested when I said perhaps you should wed the lady."

He looked up from his meal and turned to Lady Yvaine. "Whomsoever would think such a thing, my lady?" He looked back down at his plate and shook his head. "I have the clan to think of and alliances to make. I would no' think of marrying a woman who lives in the forest when it is illegal to do so."

"I know you are quite taken with her, but do you no' think it best to leave the lady be?"

"I am glad you are no' my advisor. This is the most interested that I have been in anything in my life. I thought you said yourself I wasna very enthusiastic about anything."

"Quinn should be advising you to stay away from the lass, instead of encouraging you the way he does. The men all desire to go with you on the hunts now." His aunt drank some of her mead.

"Well, at least I have taken your advice on that matter. No one will join me on the hunts except those who have always hunted with me."

"Who are you considering as a bride choice?" James asked, "if you dinna mind sharing?"

"No one. I know I must, but I have had no interest in the women who could provide an alliance with another clan." Dashiell was honest with his friends. The brothers and their cousin had taken extraordinary measures to win over the lasses they had fallen in love with. He didn't expect anything like that to happen in his case, but he hoped he could find love like they had.

"He willna have none other than the nymph herself," Niall predicted.

"Wait until you dream of her," Dashiell warned.

"When the shepherdess Anna threatened me with a pitchfork, I knew I had met my match and have never looked anywhere else. She is the only lass for me," Niall said.

"The same with Eilis and me," James said. "No other lass would do."

"Aye." Dashiell believed they would dream as he and the others on the hunt always did.

After finishing his fowl, he listened to the minstrel sing a new ballad as the trenchers were removed to give to the poor in the village. As new thick slabs of coarse bread were set before his clansmen, he saw Quinn kiss his wife's cheek.

"You do know the word will soon reach the other clan chiefs of this matter? Like I said, they willna be happy that you have taken such an interest in this unknown woman," his aunt said.

"Ah, my lady. You reproach me for being too somber, and now that I truly take an interest in life..."

"It isna life that you take such an interest in, but the temptress." She scoffed.

"Aye, well, I canna stop thinking about her; you are right. What harm is there in that?"

"If you dinna find a lady to marry, there will never be an heir. What if Fallon were to marry? And have a bairn? He could be the next chief. You must consider your people and your holdings."

"I am. One part at a time. Right now, I am concentrating on the Caledonian Forest."

And one Nymph of the Forest that Dashiell could not get his mind off no matter how much he tried.

THE NEXT MORNING, when Dashiell dressed for the hunt, the lass filling his thoughts as usual, a young towheaded lad, Paden, came to him with a message. "A lady is here to see you."

"Who? If she is not the lady of the forest, I dinna wish to entertain her."

"She is Lady Lynette of the Cameron Clan, and she says that her da has sent her here to visit with you per your request."

Dashiell had forgotten all about it and glanced at Quinn as he arrived at his bedchamber. "I understand the hunt is to be called off because of the arrival of a lady to meet you. The MacNeills will be sorely disappointed as they are eager to see the woman again in the woods."

"No." Dashiell pulled his shirt over his head. "I willna be dissuaded from the task at hand."

"And the lady?"

Dashiell belted his great kilt. "She may visit with your wife and the other ladies in the gardens or wherever else my aunt and the other women gather when sewing and the like."

"Aye. I will inform the lady you will see her later then."

"At dinner."

"Aye." Quinn and the boy quickly left.

After finishing dressing for the hunt, Dashiell headed down the stairs and met up with the MacNeills, who were just as ready to join him.

"Did you dream of her?" Dashiell asked.

"Nay," James said. "I dreamed of Eilis, as it should be—swimming with her in the loch, riding with her, and more that I dinna wish to discuss."

Dashiell smiled. If he could be married to a lass he loved as much as the two of them loved each other, he would be thrilled.

"I was dreaming of Anna trying to skewer me with her pitchfork. I shouldna have mentioned that last eve," Niall said.

Everyone laughed.

"And you, Angus?" James asked.

Angus shrugged. "I dreamed of trying to rescue Edana's brothers from the dungeon and then of bidding in Stirling for the bulls. Dinna tell her I had dreamed of both."

They laughed.

Still, Dashiell was surprised they hadn't dreamed of the lass.

When they approached the massive doors to the inner bailey, the lady seeking a marriage proposal approached him and curtsied. "I am Lady Lynette, from Gloucester. My father has sent me to see you."

She was pale, fine-boned, her black hair peeking through a veil of white. Her gown was pale yellow, which made her appear all the more wan. She was not appealing in the least, her smile insincere, her blue eyes as pallid as the rest of her.

"Aye, I am well aware of the circumstances of your arrival, but I am on my way to hunt."

"I would like to accompany you if I may."

"Women dinna go on hunts with me, my lady." Not because Dashiell objected to the women of his clan hunting but because none had ever been interested in going with them. In Lynette's case, he didn't believe she was up to the task as pale as she looked.

"Is it because you have business other than hunting in the forest these days?"

Dashiell glanced at Quinn, who shrugged.

"I dinna know what you mean," Dashiell said to Lynette, then hurried toward the north doors. One of his men pulled one of the doors open to let them pass. Lynette chased after him, Quinn following on her heels, and the MacNeills in hot pursuit.

"I can ride as well as any man if you fear I will fall behind. Or is it that you fear I will discover your secret?"

Dashiell stopped in his footsteps, making the lady nearly collide with him. "What secret is that, Lady Lynette?" Already, he didn't care for her sharp tongue.

"This so-called woodland nymph, Ella, is some commoner you have taken as your mistress."

He stared at the woman, her pale mouth pinched, and her pale blue eyes held no warmth. At first, he couldn't believe, if the woman was looking to marry him, how she could be so antagonistic, but then he had an idea. He told Quinn, "Perhaps we should take the lady with us."

"You canna be serious." Quinn's brows rose with the pitch of his voice. He appeared thoroughly surprised.

"You have no say in it," she said to Quinn as if she was already the lady of the keep.

"Mayhap the lass will react differently to seeing a woman," he explained to Quinn, ignoring her comment. "All right," he said to the lady, "you may come, but you will do as you are told."

"Of course." While she was helped onto her horse, Dashiell, his men, and the MacNeills took off for the forest and she had to kick her horse to a gallop to catch up to them.

They finally reached the stream, and everyone remained quiet when they saw a deer step into the clearing.

Lynette said, "There is a deer. Are you not going to shoot it?"

"Shh," Dashiell harshly said, instantly regretting he had allowed the woman to join them.

After sitting in the woods for an eternity, Quinn said, "I believe she isna coming."

"Aye, but we expressed that notion yesterday, and then there she was."

"The fey have no schedule to keep," Niall said.

"Fey." Lynette scoffed. They waited and then she said, "I dinna believe you men would sit watching a deer like this and no' kill it. Have done with it, then let us return to the castle and have our dinner."

"Perhaps Lady Lynette has scared the woman away," Quinn said.

Dashiell frowned, his gut clenching with irritation. "She has to come."

"Are you no' going to kill the deer?" Lynette asked. "If I could shoot an arrow, I would kill it myself."

The woman was fiercely grating on him. He would never agree to marry such a woman.

"If she willna appear, we might as well return to the castle," Dashiell reluctantly told the MacNeills and his men. It was a mistake to bring the woman with them.

To everyone's surprise, Lynette nudged her horse out into the open and walked toward the stream as the deer stood watching her. "I have never seen a deer so tame," she said, looking back at Dashiell.

"Look." Dashiell pointed to a spot in the woods behind the deer.

He could not quash the elation he felt at seeing Ella again. Bewitching is what she was. "She was there all the time." He walked his horse up to the stream to join Lynette. Ella stared at the sight of the lady. "I believe you intrigue her for some reason."

"I dinna see what the attraction is for the woman. She is naught more than a wild animal letting her hair down like that for all to see. And be careful! She is armed!"

Dashiell saw she was holding a stick like she had yesterday. Did she mean to write in the mud again? To give him another message? "She has the most beautiful tresses, do you no' think?" he asked the MacNeills.

"Nay," Lynette said, "and furthermore..."

Ella stepped into the sunlight.

Dashiell smiled. "I believe she isna afraid of you. See if you can cross the stream to her."

"Cross the stream? Whatever for?" Lynette stared at him, her black brows furrowed.

"I wish to see if she will come to you. Ask her name."

"What do I get for it?"

"I will be truly grateful."

"Very well, perhaps you can show me your gratitude in a dance held in my honor." Lynette kicked her horse and guided it across the stream. "And a marriage proposal soon after."

Dashiell could manage a dance. A marriage proposal? Never. He smiled when Ella stood still for the lady on her horse. When Lynette reached her, Ella touched Lynette's dress and smiled at her.

"Tell me who you really are!" Lynette said harshly, frowning down at the woman.

Ella looked at Dashiell, then took hold of Lynette's horse's reins and pulled her into the woods. As soon as they disappeared from Dashiell's and the others' sight, he and his men crossed the stream, but not finding them, he stopped the search.

"How will I explain this to her da?" Dashiell asked, mystified and angered all at the same time.

James shook his head. "I didna believe she was of the fey, despite what my cousin has said. Mayhap, he was right."

Dashiell said, "We have to find Lynette." So why did he want to find the nymph instead?

A woman's scream in the forest caused Dashiell to spur his horse into the forest, where he found Lynette sitting on the ground, hidden in the bracken, holding her head as if it pained her.

Her horse was nearby, nibbling on grass, only pausing to look at them.

He leaped from his horse and rushed to her side. "What has happened, my lady?"

James was beside him instantly, Niall also, as Angus was still searching for Ella.

"That creature hit me! That is what happened. She must have been jealous of me and tried to kill me."

"Kill you?" Dashiell looked at his men, then motioned for them to search for Ella. The first thought he had was if Ella had wanted to kill the lady, she could have, armed with a sword as she was. "What did she say to you?"

"She said that this was her forest and that she didna mind seeing you here, but she didna wish to see your lady friend too."

Dashiell frowned, not understanding why Ella appeared intrigued with the lady and then would hurt her. He helped Lynette to stand.

"Oh," Lynette said and grasped his arm.

"Are you all right?"

"Nay. I feel a little dizzy." Leaning against him, Lynette gave him a weak smile.

"I am sorry that this has happened to you. The lady seemed so gentle..."

"Gentle?" Lynette said, raising her voice. "She has the devil in her."

"Aye, well, I will escort you back to the castle now." Dashiell caught a glimpse of James shaking his head. But whether it was because he thought ill of Ella or because he believed Lynette was making a fuss about nothing, Dashiell wasn't sure.

"I dinna believe I can sit on my horse alone."

"You wish to ride with me then?"

Dashiell suspected she was faking the incident. She didn't appear injured anywhere and he'd known enough lasses over the years who were talented in the art of fainting.

She held her head as if it pained her. "If you dinna mind."

"Nay, if it helps to make up for this business with the woman." Dashiell motioned for one of his men to take the lass on his horse.

Lynette's expression fell, then she scrunched her forehead as if she was irritated by the idea of riding with someone other than him, possibly even considering it beneath her.

He couldn't believe Ella would attempt to injure Lynette. "Where have you been all this time? We searched for you in the woods and couldna find you." That completely puzzled and distressed him.

"She led me to a loch nearby surrounded by a field of flowers."

He realized his men had remained in the forest looking for the women. He lifted her to his clansman's horse, and Dashiell's men rejoined them after they had no success finding Ella.

Disappointed, the party headed back to Cairn Castle.

"There was no sign of her?" Dashiell asked Quinn once they were alone at the keep.

"Nay. Though it seems odd that Ella would have attacked Lady Lynette."

"Do you believe the lady lied about being attacked?" Dashiell had never met Lynette before. He didn't know what she was capable of.

"Aye. I try to keep an open mind when it comes to women."

Dashiell nodded. "I have my doubts as well. Plan for a dance for tonight, though it seems that if Ella had injured her so badly, she wouldna be feeling well enough to dance. Ensure my healer sees to her and learns just where she was injured and the extent of it."

"Aye, my laird."

"There will be no more hunting in my forest for the week."

"But, my laird..."

"None, Quinn."

"What of your other guests? The MacNeills?"

Dashiell shook his head. "We'll find other ways to entertain ourselves."

ELLA WAS SO CONFUSED. She realized she didn't know how to interact well with people. Not when she couldn't talk to them. At the village, Bhictoria was the exception. For the first time ever, Dashiell had taken a woman on the hunt in the forest, though she didn't hunt.

She was dark-haired, blue-eyed, and beautiful. Ella had wanted to show her the beauty of the loch and the wildflowers. She thought that's why Dashiell had brought her there—so she and the lady could be friends. When the woman pretended injury and blamed Ella for it, she couldn't understand why she had done so.

Ella was beside herself with upset when she fled to the hut and explained what had happened to Mina. Now Dashiell would never offer to take her, Amelda, and Mina into the castle for safekeeping.

Mina read Ella's writing on the dirt floor and sighed. "It seems Dashiell is courting the woman, but she is envious of the way he has been searching for you and wants to make sure he sees you as someone evil, not good."

Ella couldn't believe it.

"You have the words. You need to coax them out and explain to them that you didna hurt the woman. Though she is undoubtedly a lady, I very much doubt he will believe your word against hers."

Yet so was Ella. Not that anyone would believe it.

"You should have gone to live with them before this. This only makes things worse. Instead, I should say that it will make things more difficult for you. But you've lived through so much already. You will get through this." Then Mina frowned. "Did you truly speak to the woman?"

Ella shook her head vigorously, though she wished she'd been able to, and told her right off.

"Then if Dashiell should learn you canna speak, he will ken the lady lied."

9

"Nay! I dinna need you to look me over," Lynette screamed at the healer.

Dashiell overheard Lynette refusing to let Mai examine her injuries and said to Quinn, "Lynette isna injured."

Dashiell was irritated with the woman for trying to get Ella in trouble when she had done nothing wrong. He wanted to take Ella into his castle more than ever and learn all he could about her.

"I would think no', or it was so minor that Lynette would have appeared to have been making the whole thing up," Quinn said.

Dashiell nodded.

"What about the celebration?"

Dashiell had given it a lot of thought. "We eat; those who wish to dance will dance. I willna deny our people a chance to enjoy themselves. Instead of honoring Lynette, 'tis in honor of James and his kin's visit."

"Aye, I'm glad of it. I'll make the announcement. Will you dance with Lynette?" Quinn asked.

"I will, but only one dance."

"Aye." Then Quinn announced that the dance honored the MacNeills' visit, and Lynette gasped.

It served her right to tell tales.

Smiling, James, his brother, and cousin raised their tankards of ale to Dashiell in thanks.

Lynette's face was crimson. Dashiell's people had already shared the news that she had lied to him about Ella injuring her. No one liked liars.

Fallon offered to dance with Lynette, and then the dancing began.

"How much did you have to bribe your cousin so that he would dance with the woman?" James asked, knowing how Dashiell and his people felt about Lynette now.

Dashiell chuckled. "He has free time for a week."

James laughed.

"Believe me, no one wants to have anything to do with the woman now that they feel she has lied about Ella. What would she do if we were to marry, gods forbid, and she treated my staff the same way? Causing distress and strife? I could see that happening."

"Aye. You canna trust someone like that. No telling what she might even say about you at some point," James said.

"Exactly." Even so, Dashiell and his people and the MacNeills had a wonderful time enjoying the celebration, and like he told Quinn, he left the high table to dance with Lynette one time only.

When Dashiell retired to his bed after the dance in the wee hours of the morning, he closed his eyes, wanting to employ Ella at his castle, anything to get her to join him here. But then he remembered Quinn's words about the younger lass that Ella had protected. Where was she?

He finally fell asleep and found himself dancing with Lynette.

Still, when her black hair loosened about her shoulders, turning lighter as he held her hand in the circle dance, he saw the face of the forest nymph, her beautiful green eyes holding him hostage, and her slight smile endearing.

He couldn't believe she was there and touched her cheek fondly. Shaking her head as her hair tossed with the motion, she backed away from him, then turned and ran into the darkness of the forest.

"Nay!" Dashiell shouted. He woke, sat up in bed, and stared at Christopher.

"Should I send for your healer?"

"Nay. But a tankard of ale would be welcome."

After several minutes, Christopher left the room and returned to find Dashiell pacing across his bedchamber.

"What took you so long?" Dashiell asked as he took the tankard Christopher offered to him.

"A maid was getting Lady Lynette some ale as well. I inquired about the problem; apparently, the lady has also suffered from a nightmare concerning the lady of the forest."

Immediately, Dashiell thought of Niall's comments concerning why MacAfee might have bartered his castle away. "Did the maid say what Lady Lynette's dream was about?"

"Nay. She was in a hurry to return to the bedchamber. She said she was crying hysterically."

"Over a dream?"

"Aye."

Dashiell couldn't understand why Lynette could have a nightmare unless it were her own doing because of her deceitfulness about what Ella had done to her. With him, Ella was all sweetness and light.

Later, in the grip of sleep, he again saw Ella as she knelt beside the stream and placed flowers in the water, humming her tune. *She saw Dashiell and stood, but when Lynette came up behind him, came around in front of him, and leaned her head against his chest, Ella backed away and slipped into the darkness of the forest.*

He sat up in bed. "I canna sleep any further."

"Aye," Christopher said, rolling out of his trundle bed.

After Dashiell and Christopher dressed, they walked into the hall. Quinn crossed the floor to greet him. Dashiell asked, "What are you doing up at this hour?"

Quinn shook his head. "I was about to ask the same of you."

"I canna sleep." Dashiell sighed.

"Me either."

"Apparently, Lady Lynette had a nightmare," Dashiell said.

"About Ella?"

"What else?"

"Aye, well, my dreams of the lady are no nightmares; I can never quite reach her," Quinn said.

Dashiell let out an exasperated breath. "Aye, mine are the same. I believe Lynette's nightmare was of her own making."

"Aye. I couldna agree more." His advisor motioned with his head toward the curving stairs. "It appears Lady Lynette could no longer sleep either."

The lady curtsied to Dashiell when he turned to face her. "I didna think I would find so many awake at this hour in the morning."

"I was told you had a nightmare."

"Aye, well, I dinna wish to discuss it."

"Perhaps if you tell me what happened, you willna be so frightened by the dream any longer."

"I wasna frightened." Lynette looked away from Dashiell's stern gaze. "Many women and children were in the castle. Soldiers slaughtered everyone. Everyone but that woman."

"Ella? What would she be doing in a castle?"

"It was a dream. That is all. She is evil. She just stood there watching as everyone was massacred, saying naught, just watching."

"That is all?"

"Is that no' enough? The screams were terrifying. Every time I close my eyes, I see the horror reenacted, and the screams continue. I canna sleep any further this morn."

"Quinn and I have business to attend to, my lady. We will see you later." Then Dashiell saw the MacNeills coming to join them.

"Did you have dreams that woke you from your sleep?" Dashiell asked them.

"Nay. We heard all the talking and were surprised you were leaving the castle," James said. "We will go with you. What are friends for?"

"Aye, thanks be to thee." Dashiell grabbed Quinn's arm and led him outside into the inner bailey.

"Where are we going to now?"

"On a hunt."

The MacNeills smiled, looking glad to be searching for the fey woman again.

"At this hour? I thought you said there would be no more hunting..."

"We are hunting for owls."

"Aye," Quinn said.

After waking Fallon and having their horses saddled, they headed deep into the forest. They made their way to the stream where the noise of frogs and crickets filled the night, and the howling of a wolf set off the rest of his pack.

"There," Quinn said as he spied four deer heading for the stream.

One of the deer watched for signs of trouble while the others drank their fill, but when Dashiell readied his arrow to his bow, Ella stepped in front of one of the deer. The arrow flew its course, and she warned the deer away and then fled.

"Gods' wounds!" Dashiell said. "Ella has a death wish if she tries to protect the deer in my forest when we are hunting."

"She is only here by the stream. If you hunt elsewhere..."

In truth, he didn't care about hunting the deer as much as he wanted to find the lass, and he wanted to know the truth concerning Lynette. He stared across the stream and could have sworn he heard something. "Did you hear something strange?"

"Aye, the rustling of shrubs. Something is over there still," James said.

"Perhaps I have nicked one of the deer after all. We will cross the stream and see."

"It willna be good if you have injured the fey woman," Niall warned.

Dashiell prayed he hadn't hurt the woman.

After fording the stream, the men dismounted from their horses, and Fallon lighted a torch. While searching the ground, he found signs of blood. "You hit one. Fresh drops of blood are scattered here all over the stones."

The men stuck close together as they walked their horses, searching in the darkness with only the torchlight showing the trail of blood. "The deer seems not to have weakened much," Fallon said.

"If it is a deer." Angus sounded worried.

Dashiell was too.

They reached the end of the trail, and Dashiell paced back and forth. "A wounded deer canna vanish like this. Or the woman. We will wait here until first light. Then we will find this wounded animal if the wolves dinna make a meal of him first." Certainly, if the lass had been injured, he had to stay here at all costs to locate her and have his healer take care of her.

Fallon and Quinn made a campfire while Dashiell backtracked the trail of blood. After re-examining the trail for half an hour, he returned to the campsite. "I have found no sign of my arrow. It didna graze the beast. It must be embedded in him."

He sat down with everyone at the campfire, watched the eerie glow in silence, and then frowned to see a mist rising from the forest floor.

Fallon cleared his throat. "None of us can believe that Ella harmed Lady Lynette."

"I have to agree with Fallon," James said, "though I have no sound basis for it. Still, she seemed genuinely interested in befriending Lynette, no' doing her harm."

"Aye, I dinna trust Lynette at all." A sudden movement in the leaves accumulated on the forest floor nearby made Dashiell and the others stand. Dashiell picked up his bow and arrow and readied it. Fallon and Quinn unsheathed their swords. "Get the torch," Dashiell whispered to his cousin. "The sound came from over there, did it no'?"

"Aye." Fallon led the way, holding the torch.

James, his brother, and his cousin likewise took out their swords and circled where they'd heard the sound.

All of them searched the forest floor. Seeing Dashiell's arrow poking out of a pile of leaves, Dashiell waved to his companions to encircle the wounded animal. Using their swords, Fallon and Angus pushed the leaves aside.

"It canna be." Dashiell stared at Ella, who lay still half-buried by the leaves.

Dashiell reached for the arrow still lodged in her arm, but the lady shook her head and held her hand out to keep him away. He didn't blame her for being afraid of him when he never wanted her to feel that way.

"Hold her down. I must free the arrow and stop the bleeding, or she willna live," Dashiell said.

Quinn grabbed the lady's good arm, and Fallon held the torch for Dashiell to see while James held her injured arm against the ground. After cutting the arrowhead off, Dashiell and Angus pulled the rest of the arrow free, then Dashiell held his hand to the lady's wound.

"Does anyone have something to bind the wound?" Dashiell asked.

"Here." Niall offered him a slip of cloth.

"We must get her to Cairn Castle. I will have my healer see to her at once." Dashiell saw that she had passed out. "She hasna died, has she?"

His heartbeat quickened, and he felt sickened all at once.

"Nay. When you pulled the arrow free, she passed out from the pain," Fallon said.

"She uttered no' a sound." Dashiell was thoroughly mystified. No hardened warrior could feel that kind of pain and remain silent.

"Nay," James said.

"I tell you, she is of the fey," Niall whispered.

Dashiell remounted his horse, and then Fallon handed the lady to him. After they extinguished their campfire, they returned to the castle. Everyone was beginning to do their early morning chores when they arrived, but the word soon spread of Ella's capture. Several men met Dashiell in the inner bailey to see the injured woman.

A young lad Dashiell had never seen before seemed the most distraught. He had pushed through the growing crowd of men to see the lass, and all Dashiell could think of was that the lad would have dreams of her now.

"Who are you?" Dashiell asked, feeling he should recognize the boy because he seemed familiar.

"Finnegan," the lad said.

"He's working with the blacksmith," one of his men said.

Two of his men rushed to Dashiell's side and took the lady to one of the guest chambers while the healer was sent for. When Dashiell entered the bedchamber minutes later, his healer shook his head. "She has lost a lot of blood. She may no' live."

Dashiell stared at Ella, hating that he had done this to her when he only wanted to know everything he could about her. "See that you do everything for her that you can."

"Aye."

James and his kin were waiting downstairs, looking as concerned as he felt.

Dashiell told them, "She may no' live."

"If she truly is of the fey, she will heal herself," Niall said. "What would you have us do?"

"There is naught that you can do. We'll break our fast in a little while."

James patted him on the back. "Let us know if we can help in any way."

"Thanks to all of you. I know you wish for the best." Dashiell had never felt this disheartened ever.

Several of the members of Dashiell's clan approached Dashiell. "They say you shot her to capture her finally."

"I aimed at a deer. She got in the way." Dashiell quickly brushed past them.

"Will she live?" Yvaine asked as she walked behind him.

"You will have to ask Mai that question. I am certain no one knows the answer for sure."

Lynette caught up to him when he walked up the stairs. "I hear you have captured the devil."

"She may no' live." Dashiell saw that the woman had no empathy for Ella after he had accidentally hurt her.

"She doesna deserve to after what she did to me."

Dashiell couldn't believe Lynette would say that to him. Dashiell might have killed the lass. The way Lynette showed no compassion at all for the woman who could very well be dying was telling.

"Ready my bath," he said to Christopher when he walked into his bedchamber. He needed to clean off the blood from the lass's wound before he ate with his people, though he had no appetite. He had to be there for his clan.

"Aye."

Dashiell cleaned himself off in his wooden tub, and Christopher said, "I understand the lady is truly beautiful."

Ella was, only now, she was pale as Lynette, and he prayed to every god and goddess known to man to save her.

"The lady I heard tell of was supposed to be so ugly even a charging wild boar would turn and run away at the sight of her."

"This is no' the same lady." Ella was beautiful.

"She is said to have magical powers, the lady I have heard tell of. She has driven sane men mad, though no one knows how."

"And women?"

"I have never heard of her harming a woman."

"Who is this woman supposed to be? Has she a name?"

"No' that I ever heard of. My mother always referred to her as the lady of the forest."

"And she is evil?"

"Oh, nay."

"But you said..."

"Oh, I am sorry. She was always kind to anyone who deserved her kindness. It was those that tried to hurt her that she retaliated against."

"I see."

"She protected the deer in the forest. They were her favorite animal."

"Like my forest nymph."

"Aye. I wondered, once I had heard of her, whether she could be the daughter of the one I knew of."

"She is too beautiful if what you say is true about the other."

A knock on the door made Dashiell wave his hand at Christopher to get it. From there, Christopher said, "Fallon wishes to see you about Ella."

"Send him in."

When Fallon entered the chamber, he said, "Your healer says

the lady is awake if you wish to see her. She had to have Ella tied to the bed as she tried to run away."

"In her condition?" Dashiell jumped up from the tub. "I will be right there."

He slipped into his shirt and belted his plaid, yanked his boots on, and Quinn met up with him as he strode through the hall. "I hear she has come to. May I see her also?"

"Nay, no' just yet." Dashiell entered the room, expecting to question the lass, but her eyes were closed. "I thought she was awake," he said to the maid attending her.

At hearing his words, Ella opened her eyes.

Walking over to the bed, he said, "Your eyes are green, just as I remember in my dreams. Who are you?"

When she didn't answer, Dashiell looked at the maid and she shook her head. "She will say naught. Your healer believes she canna speak."

"She is mute, then?" Dashiell couldn't be more surprised. He frowned and looked back at the lady. "Can you no' speak to me?" To the maid, he said, "She isna deaf, too, is she?"

"We dinna believe so. She seems to listen to all that is being said."

He considered Ella's wrists tied to the bed frame. "Is this necessary?" Did his people believe that she had hurt Lynette after all?

"Your healer said if she tries to run away any further, she willna live."

"Run away?" Dashiell said to Ella, "I willna release you until you tell me who you are. You have naught to fear of me or from us. We dinna believe you harmed Lady Lynette."

Ella's eyes widened, and she shook her head, indicating she hadn't hurt Lynette. He was glad to see it.

"Has she eaten?" he asked the maid.

"Nay. She had just now regained consciousness."

"See if you can get her to eat something."

When the maid left the room, Ella closed her eyes.

He pulled a chair beside the bed, sat down, reached over, and touched her hair. She opened her eyes. "I am no' going anywhere. Tell me your name." The lady's lips parted as if she was going to speak, but the words would not come. Dashiell shook his head. "I must know who you are."

Even now, under his roof, she was his captive, and he still knew no more about her than he did before.

10

More than anything, Dashiell wished Ella could speak to him and tell him everything he needed to know—who she was, where she'd been living, where the young girl was that she'd rescued from his men, and why she'd written MacAfee's name in the dirt.

Mai returned to take care of the lady so he could attend the meal.

At the morning meal, Lady Yvaine leaned over Niall to speak to Dashiell. "Many are dying to see Ella. They say she canna speak."

"Perhaps she only knows the language of the owls and wolves of the forest." He paused to poke his spoon into the pork stew and added, "Let us no' forget the deer."

"Will you no' permit any of your ladies to see her?

"Nay, they may dream of her."

"We have never dreamed of her," James said. "While you were with her, I spoke to several men who hunt with you, curious. They all had different dreams, but all about her."

"'Tis good we dinna dream of her," Niall said. "Our lasses wouldna be happy about it."

"They would know she had bewitched us." Angus ate some of his brown bread. "And that we wouldna be at fault."

His aunt lifted her goblet, "It does no' seem fair that only some of your men have seen her. Lady Whittington wishes to see what has interested her husband so. I wish to learn how the lady has entranced you so. Why will you no' permit me to meet with her?"

"When she has recovered, Lady Yvaine. She seems afraid of anyone who comes into the room."

"Paige, who attends her, says Ella doesna seem afraid of women. And a young lad saw her, and she seemed cheered."

Dashiell frowned. "What young lad?"

"I dinna ken. We believe that Lynette lied about Ella harming her. If the lass canna speak, she could no' have said the things to Lynette that she claims."

"I believe the lady should be given a chance to recover first before she has too many visitors, and I agree with you about Lynette, even before I learned Ella canna speak, but I want to know who the lad was."

"You were with her alone in the chamber."

"She was tied up. She could no' harm me." Dashiell glanced at his aunt, frowning at him. "What?" He knew what his aunt was getting at, but he also knew she only worried about what his people would say, not that he would take advantage of the injured lass.

"The poor girl was defenseless."

The MacNeills chuckled.

"Oh, you worry about my intentions toward Ella. They are honorable, my lady."

"She shouldna be alone with any man. Remember, she is a temptress."

"Aye, that she is." Why was he thinking about how much he craved tempting her into staying with him?

When a rack of venison was served, a servant dutifully cut the meat for Dashiell, but as it rested on his trencher, he frowned at the sight. He poked at his venison. Suddenly, he felt the weight of his aunt's gaze upon him. She watched him intently, her keen eyes taking in his every movement. He met her gaze and saw concern etched on her face.

"Is something the matter, Dashiell?" she asked, her voice low. Lady Yvaine looked down at Dashiell's uneaten meat. "Is it no' any good?"

"What?"

"Your venison."

"When I look at it, I see Ella standing before the deer. I canna believe I injured her so."

WHEN THE MEAL WAS FINISHED, Dashiell told the MacNeills he would see them later. He returned to the guest chamber and smiled to see Ella awake. He asked the maid, "Did she eat well?"

"Aye," Paige said, waiting beside the bed.

"Who was the lad who visited her?"

"I dinna ken. I had never seen him before."

"I must know your full name, Ella," Dashiell said.

"Mayhap, she can write her name."

"Aye. She wrote a name on the shore at the stream. Get some parchment and ink. We will see if the lady can speak to us that way."

Looking back at Ella, Dashiell studied her hair, which cascaded over her shoulders in soft red-gold curls, gleaming in the sunlight that filtered through the window. He noticed her observing Paige as she left the room.

He sat in the chair beside the bed and touched Ella's hair. He stroked her hair tenderly, feeling the silky strands between his fingers. "You have the most beautiful tresses I have ever seen."

She just watched him, her eyes gazing at him. Dashiell felt a sense of peace wash over him as they sat silently. Despite the chaos and uncertainty of the world outside, he knew that everything was right in this room with Ella. And he vowed never to let anything come between them again.

When she didn't flinch, he pulled some of her hair away from her cheek and touched her cheek gently. "I must know who you are. Have you always lived in the forest?" Ella looked at his plaid again. "What is there about my plaid that fascinates you so?"

Ella's eyes grew big when the maid returned with the parchment and writing instrument. She shook her head as Dashiell untied her good hand.

"She seems frightened. Perhaps she canna write," Paige said.

Dashiell took the parchment and pen and wrote his name. "She can write. At least she wrote a name in the sand. Mayhap, she has never seen parchment and ink before. I am Dashiell. That is my name." Then he showed it to Ella, but she shook her head again and shrank away from the parchment. "What is the matter with her?"

"I dinna know."

Ella stared at the parchment, then as Dashiell offered it to her, her eyes grew round, and her face paled. He pulled the parchment back, but the lass fainted dead away.

This time, unlike when Lynette had pretended to feel faint, he did not doubt that Ella had truly been terrified.

Paige patted her hand as Dashiell stood up from the chair. "Get my healer at once."

"Aye."

"Young lady," Dashiell called to Ella. "Can you hear me?" He touched her cheek, and her eyelashes fluttered. Then she opened her eyes and looked around for the parchment. "I have put the parchment away. There is naught to fear in that. Whatever is the matter?"

He took her hand and kissed it as she observed him. Then he

smiled to see she still didna withdraw from his touch. "That is better. At least you are no' afraid of me anymore. I am so sorry for hurting you. I aimed for the deer."

She nodded.

"Had I known you would step in front of the deer, I wouldna have released the arrow. Then again, I probably would never have been this close to you. How can I get you to communicate with me?" He waited for a response that would never come, then shook his head. "I never expected this."

The lady put her lips together as she tried to say a word and touched Dashiell's shirt.

He smiled. "You are trying to talk to me, are you no'? That is good. Perhaps in time, you can." Mai and Paige rushed into the room, and Dashiell said, "I believe Ella is all right now, Mai. The sight of a piece of parchment frightened her terribly. I thought she could write to me and tell me more about herself."

"If you dinna need me, one of your ladies is having difficulty in childbirth," Mai said.

"Olivia?"

"Aye."

"Go see to her then. Let me know the outcome as soon as you can."

"Aye."

The healer bowed to Dashiell, but Ella held out her hand to her.

"What is it, lass?" Mai reached for her hand, and Ella grasped it firmly. "I must go and help Lady Olivia."

Ella shook her head and pulled at Mai's hand, not letting her go.

The healer said to Dashiell, "I must go."

"Lass, Mai must see a lady having trouble having her first-born child. Do you understand?"

Ella nodded and tugged harder at the healer.

"Do you want to go with me?" Mai asked.

Nodding, Ella continued to hold onto the healer's hand with a tight grip.

"I dinna think it is a good idea," Dashiell said as Ella looked at him.

"Mayhap if she knows magic...," Paige said.

Dashiell and Mai glanced at Paige and frowned, which caused her to suddenly look at the rushes on the floor.

"All right," Dashiell said. "But you are in no condition to run around the castle yourself. I will help you to the ladies' chamber. If you upset Lady Olivia in any way or make the situation more difficult than it already is, I will return you here at once."

Ella nodded, then Dashiell helped her to stand, but she became unsteady on her feet, so he lifted her in his arms and carried her to the ladies' chamber. When they arrived, the other ladies stared at Ella in Dashiell's arms.

"What is she doing here?" one of the maids asked as Dashiell carried Ella into the chamber and set her in a chair next to the bed.

"She wants to help Olivia," Dashiell said.

Olivia stared at Ella, who reached for Olivia's hand, took hold of it gently, and began to hum a tune.

"You must leave now," Mai said to Dashiell.

"Aye, if you need me, I will be outside the chamber." He worried about Olivia and her bairn, but also about Ella should she faint again from the loss of blood this time.

OLIVIA RELAXED, and Ella touched her forehead like Mina had taught her to lessen a person's pain. She placed her hand firmly there and spoke silently. Olivia nodded and took a deep breath. The woman's dark hair flowed over the bedding, her forehead sweaty, and her dark brown eyes widening.

"What is she doing?" the maid asked.

"Whatever she is doing, it is working. The baby is nearly here," Mai said.

After a few more minutes, Paige exclaimed, "There, oh, the baby is a boy! Oh, Olivia, you have had a son."

Olivia smiled as she waited to see her son, and then Ella patted her hand and stood to leave. "Wait, young lady," Olivia said.

Ella hesitated as she clung to the bedpost with her good arm, her head spinning. She knew she needed to lie down before she collapsed.

"Thanks be to thee."

Ella smiled and nodded, but as she made her way to the door, her hand trembled slightly as she reached out to open it. Her fingers felt clammy against the cool metal handle, and she struggled to keep her balance.

Her steps were unsteady, and her vision blurred. Before she could unlatch the door, her knees gave out, and she knelt, struggling to regain her composure before one of the maids rushed over to help her. She hated feeling so weak and out of control.

"My laird!" Paige called out from the ladies' chamber, and Dashiell feared the worst. That Ella was causing trouble for Olivia as she gave birth or was in peril herself.

He rushed into the room and found Ella unconscious in Paige's arms on the floor. His heart pounding furiously, he lifted Ella off the floor. He glanced at Mai to learn what she felt about Ella's condition.

"Ella has lost a lot of blood. She needs to lie abed for at least the next week."

"And Olivia and her baby?" Dashiell asked, thinking the lass hadn't been able to help her.

"Mother and son are doing fine, with Ella's help, I might add. She needs to be one of our healers. I will see to the lass in a moment after I have finished what needs to be done here," Mai said. "Dinna let her escape you again."

11

D ashiell couldn't believe he had injured Ella so. He prayed to all the gods that she would come through this okay.
Paige covered her with blankets.

"Let me know when she is awake again." He was glad to know Ella had helped Olivia in childbirth. Was she a healer? If so, they could use her on his staff in a heartbeat. Though he really would keep her here for any reason. She just had to be well again.

"Aye."

Paige sat beside the bed and began to sew on a tapestry. Dashiell left the room, nearly running into Lady Yvaine, who waited beyond the door. "I am sorry, I didna mean to startle you so."

"What have you to say about Ella now, my lady?"

"Naught at all."

"Come now, you always have an opinion on any topic. What are my clansmen and women saying about the lass?"

Dashiell and his aunt walked toward the stairs, and she said, "They think 'tis remarkable that Ella wished to help another lady in need, especially after what happened to Lady Lynette. Though, of course, none of us believe her tale. Ella did help Olivia, I am told. Lady Olivia wishes her to be her maid, now."

"She does, does she? We dinna even know who Ella is. Were you told that the lass collapsed in the ladies' chambers?"

"Aye, and that she fainted at the sight of a piece of parchment in the guest chamber as well. I thought that particularly odd."

"What do you make of that?"

"A piece of parchment is nothing to be afraid of unless she has some memory of parchment that she fears."

"Perhaps a fire was started with a piece of parchment." Dashiell had wracked his brain, trying to come up with a reason for Ella's frightened reaction.

"Or something terrible happened when she was writing on parchment."

"Mayhap someone gave her a piece of parchment that had a particularly bad bit of news for her," Dashiell said.

"Aye. There are many possibilities." His aunt looked up at him, adding, "What if she can read and write more than just MacAfee's name?" She shook her head. "It would mean a great deal and make the situation all the more curious."

"I believe she can. Unfortunately, it means we canna get her to communicate with pen and parchment with us."

"Did you know that Olivia says Ella spoke to her?"

"She did? What did Ella say?" Dashiell asked.

"Olivia didna remember her words. The oddest thing is that none of the other ladies, nor Mai, even heard Ella speak to Olivia," his aunt said.

"What did the lass do exactly?"

"From what anyone could gather, she calmed Olivia to the point that she could have her baby without further difficulty."

"I wish I knew who she was," Dashiell said.

"She is Ella, the Nymph of the Forest, naught more."

"Somehow, I dinna believe that is so. Nor do I think you believe that either."

Lady Yvaine smiled. "Nay, I think she is quite an extraordinary creature. She might even make someone a good wife someday."

"If you are referring to me…"

"No' you."

"No one would marry such a lady without knowing who she truly is." However, he was quickly reassessing the notion.

"I understand she is very beautiful. Once a man sees her, he desires her both night and day."

"Who?"

"You for one. You canna get through a day without thinking of the lady."

AFTER PRACTICING sword fighting with the MacNeills and his own men, Dashiell—though he had fought valiantly, his mind had been on Ella to such an extent that he lost most of his battles, which had concerned everyone who had fought him—returned to the guest chamber to see Ella later that afternoon but found her still deep in sleep.

He sat beside her bed for some time, then retired from the bedchamber. "I will have court this afternoon," he said to Quinn in the entryway of the keep.

"As you wish. How is the lady?"

"She is sleeping soundly. The healer says it is what she needs most now."

His advisor nodded and then left to gather the necessary staff to begin the court proceedings. Dashiell sat and waited to hear the first case while the MacNeills watched the proceedings. James had told him that he wanted to learn how Dashiell handled his people's conflicts to see if he could learn anything from him.

Dashiell knew James to be a fair and non-judgmental clan chief who decided matters in the best way possible.

The clerk cleared his throat as the accused man knelt before Dashiell. "This man was caught poaching wild boar. He said the boar killed several of his sheep."

"You must let us know about such a dilemma if this happens again," Dashiell said. "I would have had hunters take care of the matter."

"I beg your forgiveness."

"Aye, well, I will let you off this time without a fine, but the next time...what did you do with the boar after you killed it?"

"I shared it with the villagers at a feast."

Dashiell nodded. "You may be dismissed. Next case."

The sheepherder left the room while two men and a woman bowed to Dashiell. "In this case, this man sold his wife to this farmer for the price of two pigs. Now, he wants to have his wife returned and wishes to pay for the pigs he had received in payment for his wife. The farmer doesna want to give up the woman."

Dashiell raised his brows. "Why would you sell your wife... never mind. Pay the farmer for the pigs, and the farmer will release your wife back to you. I dinna wish to hear of this again in the future. Next?"

The farmer, the man, and his wife hurried out of the room. A young woman and her husband came before Dashiell.

After genuflecting to show their respect to the clan chief, the clerk said, "In the next case, this man's wife willna consent to conjugal relations with him. She says it is because he has been seeing other women, most of a disreputable nature. She wishes to have nothing further to do with him. He says she constantly ridicules him, making his life nothing more than a living hell at home."

"Cease your wanderings, sir. If you will promise this..."

"Aye, I will."

"And you, young woman, must quit your derision of your husband and make his home pleasant enough that he willna wish to be anywhere else when his workday is through." Dashiell said, "The next case?"

A clansman approached Dashiell, bowed, and waited for the clerk to read his petition. "Torrington states that his wife is too close a relation to him and wishes to have his marriage to her annulled," the clerk said.

"He does, does he? You have been married five years and have three children with your wife, Torrington. What made you decide that your wife is too close a relation to you suddenly?"

"I didna know of some of her relations on her mother's side until recently."

"I see. It isna that you tire of your wife's affections and desire the intimacies of some other, is it?"

James, his kin, and Quinn smiled at Torrington.

Dashiell said, "You will stay with your wife and have many more fine sons. Next."

The clerk read the next complaint as Torrington stormed out of the room. "This butcher states the boy stole a berry pie from his windowsill that his wife set there to cool before they sat down to supper."

"Has the boy done such a thing before?"

"Nay."

"Why would you do such a thing?" Dashiell asked the lad of about seven.

"My mother was ill. We hadna anything to eat for several days."

"Is this true?" Dashiell asked his clerk.

"We checked his story out. It is true."

"Then the boy willna be punished. Is your mother well enough now?"

"Aye."

"And your father?"

"He died last year."

"If you should need help in the future, we have a food surplus we give to those less fortunate than ourselves. I dinna wish to hear of any who steal to avoid starving to death. Are you the eldest of your brothers and sisters?"

"Aye."

Dashiell shook his head. "If you were starving, would you no' appreciate it if some kind man offered you a pie to help you out?"

The man glared at the boy and reluctantly nodded.

"Next case."

"This man was caught stealing from a laird's purse while he shopped at the market. The thief normally would have been in the woods and stolen from any who use the trails through the Caledonian Forest, but since the strange happenings there of late, he has targeted the villagers."

"Since you desire to steal from the hard-earned wages of those who work for their living and dinna seem to have any intention to work for your own keep, you will be confined for three months. Mayhap a stay in our dungeon will encourage you to find honest work in the future."

Dashiell glanced at the clerk, who shook his head. "There are no other cases."

"Good. Then," Dashiell said to Quinn and the MacNeills, "I will check on our guest before supper."

"I applaud you for your handling of these cases," James said. "Though I've never had anything as interesting as the case of the farmer who bartered his wife for a pig."

"Aye, truly, me either. I will see you in a bit."

"Good luck to the lass," James said, Niall and Angus offering well-wishes to her also.

When Dashiell arrived at the chamber, he found Ella sitting in bed, eating a slice of buttered bread. Relief washed over him. She looked so much better. "Ella has finally become accustomed to the notion that she will stay here with us."

"Aye."

"She has not spoken yet?"

"Nay."

Dashiell approached the bed and asked, "Would you like to eat supper with us?"

Paige cleared her throat. Dashiell and Ella looked at her. "Do you no' think the healer would object?"

"She slept for several hours. She seems to be eating well. Why could she no' eat with us?" Dashiell asked.

"Do you wish for me to ask Mai?"

"Aye, do it."

Paige curtsied, then left the room.

Dashiell sat on the chair beside the bed, then took a deep breath. "You smell like violets. Do you collect the flowers you place in the stream from the meadow by the loch?" Ella looked back at her bread, then took another bite and nodded. "I am glad to see you are eating so well. Would you like to eat with us?"

She nodded, looked at Dashiell's shirt, and reached out to touch it. He leaned forward to allow her to feel it. "Do you like my shirt?" She stared at his face for a moment, then frowned. Dashiell sighed. "I wish I knew what you were thinking."

She drank mead out of a mug.

He reached over, took her hand in his, and turned it over to examine it. "Your hands are so calloused. It appears you do much hard labor with them. You are a mystery. I wish to know who your people are. You wrote MacAfee in the soil by the stream. Do you belong to his clan?"

Her eyes widened, and she shook her head vigorously.

He frowned. She seemed frightened at the mention of his name, but he was glad he had brought it up. Maybe he could get to the bottom of the mystery now.

"Why did you write his name in the soil then?" He thought for a moment and guessed he would have to ask her in ways in which she could answer yes or no. "Was he in my forest?"

She quickly nodded.

"For what purpose?" He couldn't believe the man would be in his forest and had not asked permission. It just wasn't done.

She drew her hand across her throat.

"To...kill?" He frowned. The land he gave to MacAfee had plenty of game to hunt. Why would he travel this far to hunt on Dashiell's lands illegally?

She nodded.

"So he was hunting on my lands?" He couldn't understand it.

She nodded, drew her hand across her throat again, and mouthed, *"Me."* At the same time, she pointed to herself.

Dashiell just stared at her. He had to be "hearing" her wrong. "You? He was hunting for you?" Dashiell couldn't believe it as he tried to clarify the matter.

She nodded.

Then again, *Dashiell* had hunted for her, though not with the notion of killing her. Mayhap, she was confused about MacAfee's intent. He would have no reason to hurt the lass unless she had witnessed him hunting in the forest without Dashiell's permission, and MacAfee wanted to silence her. "Why? When?"

She held up two fingers.

"Two days ago?"

She nodded.

He didn't know what to think.

Then the lad he'd seen in the inner bailey before rushed into the bedchamber, startling Dashiell and Ella.

"What are you doing..." Before Dashiell could finish his sentence, Finnegan fled. Thinking the boy knew Ella, which was why he had plowed through the men to get closer to her when she'd been wounded, and Dashiell had held her in his arms on his horse in the inner bailey, Dashiell hurried out of the chamber.

The lad had disappeared down the hallway. Dashiell took off running, priding himself on being fleet of foot, but when he reached the stairs, he found the boy had disappeared.

No one else was in sight who could tell him where the boy had run off to.

Then the redheaded maid, Flora, headed up the stairs and frowned at Dashiell. "My laird, what ails you?"

"Did you see a wee lad race down the stairs? Blond-haired, blue eyes? They say his name is Finnegan, and he's working for the blacksmith."

"Nay, but it sounds like the boy who came to see Ella earlier. I chased him away."

"Did you ask him what business he had in the woman's chamber?" Dashiell asked as Flora climbed the stairs.

"Nay, I'm sorry. I thought it best to chase him off as quickly as possible. I believed him just to be curious."

"I believe he may know the lass."

"Och," Flora said, framing her face with her hands in surprise. "Do you want me to search for him?"

"Nay, I know what he looks like. I'll find him." Then Dashiell returned to the room to see Ella for a bit longer. He wished she could tell him who the lad was. "Is the lad kin of yours?"

Ella didn't say anything for a moment. Then she slowly nodded.

"Cousin? Son? Brother?" He rephrased it. "Is Finnegan your cousin?"

She shook her head.

"Son?"

With another shake of her head, she told him no.

"Your brother?"

She nodded.

"Has he been living with you?"

She nodded.

Dashiell sighed in exasperation. He was certain her condition of not being able to speak was just as frustrating for her as it was for him, he reminded himself. Then he remembered the young girl. "What about the young lass you were protecting in the forest? He sighed. "Is she your daughter?"

Ella shook her head.

"Sister?"

Again, she said no in her way.

"A cousin?"

She nodded.

The young girl couldn't be in the woods on her own. "Is she alone?" Dashiell asked.

Ella hesitated, then shook her head.

At least he was glad someone was taking care of her. But who and where were they? "Aye, well, get your rest until the meal."

"Mai believes it best she remains here for supper as she is still so weak. Perhaps tomorrow will be better. She doubts she would be comfortable with all our people in the hall during supper."

"She wants to eat with us. She will have supper with us, and if she begins to feel poorly, we'll return her to her chamber."

The supper bell rang, and Dashiell said, "Can you have her dressed and brought down to the great hall then?"

"As you wish."

Dashiell returned to the great hall and asked his cousin, "Do you remember the lad who approached me when I carried Ella in on my horse in the inner bailey? Finnegan, apprentice to the blacksmith? He's new here."

Fallon frowned, appearing to try and recollect the lad.

This made Dashiell wonder what was going on. She lived in the forest, and now her brother was working for them. She said he had lived with her also. He had to know where the girl was and who she was staying with. Then there was the mystery about MacAfee. Was that why the lad had sought work at the castle? To flee from danger? What had the brother and sister done?

"Nay. I noticed the gathering of our men, but I was on the other side of you and missed seeing the lad. Is he trouble?" Fallon asked.

"He's Ella's younger brother."

"You dinna say."

"Aye. If she canna talk, I must speak with the lad and learn why they lived in the forest and more."

"Do you see him in the great hall now?" Fallon asked.

"No' that I can see. He might miss the meal to avoid me. He ran out of Ella's bedchamber when he saw me there."

Lady Yvaine tsked. "You must have given him one of your fiercer scowls."

"I reserve those for battle."

"So you say," Yvaine said.

James said, "I've seen his scowls. When I've beaten him at chess."

"Nay, that's when you've knocked over the table when I was winning," Dashiell said, everyone laughing.

Dashiell delayed the serving of the meal until Ella was carried down to supper and brought to the head table. Dashiell motioned for her to sit between Niall and himself while Lady Lynette sat to his right on the other side of James and Angus and glowered at the situation.

"I canna believe you have brought this...this forest creature here like this after what she had done to me," Lynette said, scowling at Dashiell.

Now *she* scowled more fiercely than Dashiell ever did, even in battle.

12

Anxious about how Amelda and Mina were faring on their own, Ella couldn't stay here. She was already feeling better but had to return to Mina and Amelda as soon as possible.

She could not believe how terrified she was of the parchment, but when she saw it, it appeared to have been covered in blood. When Dashiell asked her if she wanted to dine with him and his people, she wanted to see what they would be like and if Dashiell might take her cousin and Mina in.

What if he didn't want to get between her and MacAfee? What if he owed more of an allegiance to him than some family living in the woods? She had wanted so badly for Finnegan to race to their hut and make sure Mina and Amelda were all right.

But Dashiell being there had thwarted her plan to tell Finnegan to attempt to return to the forest briefly and then bring her word. She feared Dashiell would be mad that Finnegan had come to the woman's chambers. He didn't seem to have been, thankfully. However, she hadn't been so sure when he took chase after him.

She hadn't expected to be seated at the high table next to Dashiell, though it felt right somehow. She was glad she had told

Dashiell about MacAfee's plans for her. If only Dashiell believed her.

Not only that, but she'd wanted to see Lynette, and she knew the lady was furious. She was sitting at the head table between the man named Angus and Dashiell's aunt and not next to Dashiell. After Lynette's lies about Ella, she was happy to irk Lynette thoroughly.

Lady Yvaine told Ella around Lynette, "We welcome you to Cairn Castle, dear. You have been the topic of conversation here for several weeks now."

Ella glanced around to see everyone watching her. Then, as the pork was served, she took her knife and poked at it.

"Do you like pork?" Lady Yvaine asked.

Ella nodded and proceeded to eat it. Besides fish, it was one of her favorite meals.

"Well," Lady Yvaine said to Dashiell, "I believe she is eating very well, considering."

"Aye, she doesna seem to mind being here so much after all. Though I dinna think I would leave her alone without someone to watch her," Dashiell said.

"Do you think she would try to run away then?"

Nay, not run away, but she would see her family and then return with them if she could.

"If we were to put the temptation in her path, she would." Dashiell smiled at her. He had the most charming smile, and his blue eyes consumed her. She swore he was as intrigued with her as she was with him.

His aunt ate some of her bread. "She still doesna speak, I hear."

"Nay, she seems to want to sometimes, but the words willna come."

"I am pleased you allowed our people to see her."

"I hope not everyone will dream of the lady tonight for doing so."

"My brother, cousin, and I have no' dreamed of her," James said.

Dream of *her*? That was odd, Ella thought as she watched the minstrel begin to sing a song.

"I believe Ella likes you," Yvaine said to Dashiell.

Oh, aye, she thought he was the brawest of men.

"Well," Lynette said as she raised her voice, "I have never heard such nonsense. Some wild woman is served supper at the laird's table and seated next to Dashiell, no less, then we must listen to this drivel..."

"I am sorry, Lady Lynette," Dashiell said as he ran his knife coated with butter over his bread, "if you are uncomfortable sitting at the high table, there is room at one of the lower tables over there, and I am sure my clansmen sitting there would very much enjoy your company. As to the drivel you speak of, you say that Lady Yvaine and I are speaking such?"

Lynette's cheeks grew red as if she had spent too much time in the noonday sun while Ella looked around Angus to see Lynette's response to Dashiell's suggestion. She smiled at Lynette, who slammed her tankard on the table and turned away.

Ella loved it. She touched Dashiell's arm, showing him that she agreed with him and was glad he said what he had, though she wished she could say the words aloud.

Lady Yvaine watched as most of his clansmen and women did, and then she said, "Your people are observing you."

"She isna harming anyone, and I have done her a great injury. I dinna think anyone would criticize her for her actions here today." Except for Lynette.

"What will you do with her after she has healed?"

"The healer said it will take her several weeks to recover fully. We will see." Dashiell observed Ella eating stewed blueberries. "At least she is eating well."

No way would she be here for several weeks. Mina and Amelda would never survive without her. She wanted to tell Dashiell that they had to bring Mina and her young cousin here, but without some way to write the words, she wouldn't be able to. She had to get word to Finnegan somehow.

AFTER THE MEAL CONCLUDED, Dashiell had Ella carried back to her guest chamber, whereupon Lynette approached Dashiell. "She has made a spectacle of supper. Will you play a game of chess with me?"

"I will spend a moment with the lass before she retires for the evening. After overexerting herself at supper, she will need her sleep."

"Poor thing," Lynette said, her voice bitter.

"Aye, well, I will see you in the morn." To tell her she was going home. He wouldn't spend any more time in the woman's presence.

"In the morning? We could stroll in the gardens this evening..."

"Nay, I will be tied up." He wanted to send her home immediately, but it was too late at night to do so safely.

The woman looked furious. He could imagine how awful it would be to be married to her.

When Dashiell arrived at the guest chamber, Flora met him at the door. "I am sorry. We have removed the lady's gown and put her back to bed. I believe she overtaxed herself this evening as she seems to be having some discomfort with her arm."

"Has my healer..."

"Mai has already seen to her, but Ella seems to be in some distress."

"May I see her?"

"She is feverish."

"From the injury I did to her?"

The maid nodded.

Dashiell frowned. "I wish to see her."

"Aye."

The maid pulled the door aside. Dashiell walked in and paused in the doorway as he saw Ella roll over onto her side and moan.

Dashiell strode over to the bed. "I am so sorry I have caused you such pain, lass. What can I do to help?" Ella closed her eyes as she held her arm with her good hand and moaned again. Reaching down to touch her cheek, he felt she was burning up. Dashiell said, "We must reduce her fever. I fear infection has set in."

Flora applied a poultice Mai had prescribed, and Dashiell took a seat.

After two hours, Flora said, "It will be a long night. Do you no' think you should get some rest?"

"You will no' be able to watch her all night long."

"Nay. Three other ladies will take turns watching her. I will return for the two hours before everyone rises to break their fast in the morning."

"All right, but have someone wake me if her condition worsens tonight."

"Aye. We will."

Then he left the room to spend time with James and his kin.

"We were leaving on the morrow with our bulls," James said, "but a situation arose."

As if Dashiell could think of anything but Ella right now. The twinkle in James's eye said he had something humorous to share. He sure hoped he would think it was funny.

"We have no' agreed on a price for using our bulls for stud service."

Dashiell frowned. "What?"

Angus shook his head. "Canna you see Dashiell is worried about the lass? He has more important things on his mind." However, he was smiling when he said it.

A maid served them all some ale.

Niall took a swig of his. "We should just gift him it and no' charge him."

"What?" Dashiell was thoroughly confused. If Ella hadn't been on his mind, he might have gotten the message quicker.

"Our bulls were moved into your cattle pen and got quite rambunctious with the lassie cows." James leaned back on his chair and raised his mug of ale to him.

Dashiell's jaw dropped, then he smiled. "Whose fault was that?"

"Our men's. Think naught of it. As Niall told you 'tis our gift for all your generosity. We had planned to return to our keep first thing in the morning. If you need us to stay here because of the lass, we will," James said.

Dashiell shook his head. "You need no' stay. I know you need to get back home and you still have a couple of days' journey ahead of you."

James drank some more of his ale. "We'll stay. We want to be here for you should you need us."

"Aye," Angus said.

Niall agreed.

Dashiell appreciated it. They had always been there for each other, and he had always enjoyed their company. He also knew, from the way James and his kin had been smiling, that James had been the one to tell his men to put the bulls in the pens with the receptive females without any thought of payment.

His men wouldn't have made the mistake. Dashiell's people would have known about it and must have vowed silence until James revealed what had happened.

"Just dinna let the lass get away from you again," James said. "I predict she is just the one for you."

Dashiell didn't intend for her to leave ever. He wanted to share his life with her. He just had to know what was going on with her and MacAfee, where she and her brother had been living all these years, where her young cousin was, who she was staying with, and where they were from.

Later that night, Dashiell checked on Ella. She was still feverish, moaning, and not doing well. He felt awful about it and stayed up with her for a few hours, trying to cool her down with a wet cloth.

"My laird, let me take care of her," Flora said. "You need to get some rest."

"If her condition changes, send word at once."

13

"Ella, Ella! Wake up!" Finnegan said to Ella, shaking her in the bed at the castle, but she felt like she was on her deathbed and couldn't rouse enough to even look at her brother.

Then her heartbeat kicked up a notch. "What...what do you want? What are you doing here?" she whispered, fearing that the maid, Flora, would alert the guards that a lad was in the bedchamber with her.

But she soon worried that something was wrong, which was the reason he was there in the first place. He wouldn't be otherwise, she realized, so foggy headed, that she was having trouble thinking straight.

She glanced around the room. To Ella's surprise, Flora sat in a chair next to the table, her head on her arms where she slept.

"I skipped supper and left the inner bailey, returned to the woods, and found Mina in a deep sleep, and I'm worried she is dying."

"No...no...no, she canna be." Ella scrambled out of bed, throwing the furs aside, but dizziness overwhelmed her, and she grabbed the mattress to steady herself.

"Before the gates are closed for the night, I came to get you so you can heal her before we canna leave here."

She touched her hot forehead. She was burning up.

"Everyone is asleep. The guards, everyone." Finnegan ran his hands through his hair.

"All right. Let me get dressed. Wait for me beyond the chamber door."

"Aye, but hurry. They could close the gate at any moment."

She wished they could take Mina to see Dashiell's healer, though Ella had her own abilities. But she thought the two of them would be more successful than one person.

Ella found her clothes and hurriedly put them on. She was burning up but then felt like she was freezing. She left the chamber and grabbed her brother's arm to steady herself.

She was so dizzy that her vision blurred as they descended the curved stairs to the first floor. Thankfully, they hadn't encountered anyone on any of the floors or the stairs when they reached the first floor. They hurried to the front doors.

"Where is everyone?" she whispered, holding her brother's arm tight.

He looked at her, his brow wrinkled with worry. "I dinna know. You dinna look too well yourself, Ella."

"Aye, I could have slept for a fortnight."

They opened the castle doors, stepped into the inner bailey, and glanced at the wall walk. No one was on the wall walk watching for danger. The gates were wide open, the portcullis up. It had been too easy to leave, which worried her.

"Where are the guards?"

He shrugged.

They hurried across the inner bailey, then to the outer one, and through the open gates. She knew someone would shout they were escaping, and men would chase after them on horseback, questioning who Finnegan was and where she thought she was going.

They crossed the drawbridge, hurrying as fast as she could. Then they made their way through the woods.

She continued to feel hot and chilled at the same time. Her brother offered support as she stumbled along through the forest. She usually was spry as a deer. She couldn't lift her feet high enough to navigate the fallen limbs, and pushing through the tall bracken seemed a monumental feat. Her vision was blurring, and she felt weak, unlike her usual self.

Then they saw Wolf, who greeted them like they were members of his wolf pack returned from a long absence.

"Do you think Mina put everyone asleep except for us so we could return home?" Finnegan asked.

She nodded. She didn't know for sure, but she thought it might be so.

"Amelda is all right; she's just scared because she felt alone. I told her we were coming home."

They finally found their way to the stream, but it had all dried up. They stared at it for a moment, then looked upstream, expecting the water to flow any minute and sweep them away when they tried to cross it.

They didn't have time to ponder this and hurried to the hut. Wolf followed them all the way there, then saw a weasel and chased after it.

As soon as they reached the hut, they entered it and found Mina still sound asleep, her heart beating steadily, and Amelda sleeping beside her.

Ella breathed a sigh of relief. But then she collapsed on her own bed, feeling as though she had traveled for miles and couldn't stay awake a moment longer.

Had they made a mistake in returning to the hut? Nay, Ella knew they all needed to be together, one place or the other.

∾

DASHIELL FINALLY RETIRED to bed while the maid stayed with her. He didn't believe he could sleep. But that morning, Dashiell stretched, stared at the sunlight filtering through the window, and frowned.

"Christopher," he said as he still slept, tucked under the furs on his bed.

"Aye." The boy clambered out of bed.

"Did the bell no' ring this morning?"

"I dinna know. I believe I must have slept through it if it did," Christopher said.

"Me as well." Dashiell pulled his covers aside but immediately thought of Ella and hoped she was better this morning. "By the position of the sun, I would say 'tis late. I canna believe that no one would have come for us."

Dashiell hurried to dress.

Quinn arrived at his bedchamber a few minutes later. "I must apologize for oversleeping. I didna hear the bell ring this morning."

"Nor did I." Dashiell straightened his belt. "Perhaps the bell was not rung. Why did someone no' wake us to break our fast?"

"I dinna know. When I didna see you downstairs, I grew concerned that you had left the grounds without me."

"Now, why would I have done that when I already have my forest nymph in hand?"

"I wonder how she is faring."

"I wasna informed if the lady was any worse in the middle of the night. I hope that is a good sign." Dashiell headed out of his bedchamber with his advisor at his side. "Did you dream of Ella last night?"

"Nay. I slept soundly throughout the night for the first time since I saw her."

"I had no dreams either. I had hoped I would get that kiss finally."

Dashiell left Quinn at the door and entered the room, causing Flora to jump up from her chair.

"How is she doing this morning?" Dashiell asked. "She didna turn into an owl last night and fly away, did she?"

"I havena checked on her yet. I must have dozed off." Flora walked over to the bed and pulled the curtains aside. She gasped. "Oh, how could she have escaped?"

Leaning over the bed, the color purple caught his eye, and after pulling the covers away, he found violets lying on top of the feather mattress. "She could not have walked out of here in a state of delirium, could she have?"

"I wouldna think so. She was very weak."

Dashiell frowned. "When you relieved the last lady who watched her earlier this morning, was Ella still running a high fever?"

"I dinna remember even leaving here last night."

"I thought you said you would take turns with a couple of other maids to watch her."

"Aye, but I dinna remember anyone ever having come to relieve me."

"You slept the whole time, I imagine, as the rest of us had." Dashiell turned and rushed from the chamber. He entered the hallway, grabbed Quinn's arm, and led him down the hall. "Have the castle and grounds searched at once. The lass has vanished."

"I thought she was feverish."

"She was. Someone must have helped her to leave from here," Dashiell said.

"The lad? Her brother?"

Dashiell frowned. "Aye, mayhap."

As Quinn strode to the stairs, Lynette came looking for Dashiell. "I see you are still entertaining Ella."

"She is gone."

"Gone? She should be locked in one of the towers."

"Did you dream last night?"

"Nay, come to think of it, I had a wonderful sleep. I believe I overslept as I never heard the bell—"

"I dinna believe it was rung this morning. Perhaps you can spend time with the other ladies, as I must handle business." Then he would tell Lynette it was time for her to return home.

"Another hunt?"

Dashiell frowned. "I must know why my servant didna wake the staff before sunrise to begin their daily chores." He had to find the lass right away.

AFTER AN HOUR of searching for Ella at Cairn Castle, Quinn found Dashiell getting his mount ready to ride with James and his kin.

"We have found no sign of the lady. And no sign of the lad either. The blacksmith said Finnegan was supposed to work early this morning, though he had overslept, but the boy wasna on his straw bed when he woke."

"I suspected you wouldna find either. Gather our men. We will search the area around the stream. My healer tells me the lady willna survive with the wound she received as feverish as she has been if she returns to the forest this soon." Not to mention, he was worried for her safety if what she said about MacAfee wanting to kill her was true and he found her first.

When fifteen of Dashiell's men mounted their horses, Quinn said, "My wife pleaded with me no' to go. She says that she fears for our safety as you have wounded a magical creature who will want to punish you and those of us who aid you for injuring her."

"I think Ella knows I wish her no harm." When they entered the forest, Dashiell said, "Listen."

"I hear nothing except for the sound of our horses," Quinn said.

"Is that no' odd? No birds are chirping or rabbits or squirrels scurrying underfoot."

They rode deeper into the forest, and the men stared in disbelief when they came upon the stream.

"Where is the water?" Dashiell rode his horse onto the dry stream bed and stared north, then turned south to observe the dry stream bed in that direction. Glancing down at the rounded stones, Dashiell spied violets, and he dismounted from his horse and picked them up. "She has been here."

"The deer willna come here without water for them to drink," Quinn said.

Dashiell and his men were determined to uncover why the water had stopped flowing towards the sea. They followed the dry streambed until they discovered a dam blocking its path. Some of Dashiell's men were convinced that magic was involved in this unusual occurrence.

However, upon closer inspection, it was clear that men had placed logs, twigs, and rocks in the way to stop the water's flow. Dashiell immediately dismounted from his horse and began clearing the blockage, with his men joining in to help. Once the debris was removed, the water could resume its journey towards the sea.

"You dinna think the lass had something to do with this, do you?" one of his men asked Dashiell.

"Nay." Dashiell drank from his flask. "It had nothing to do with magic." He pointed to the footprints across the stream on the other side. "Do you see the prints left by men's sized boots? We have no' been on that side of the stream. Men have done this."

That's when he thought of MacAfee.

After spending hours clearing the stream and searching for Ella, they were forced to return to the castle without her as night fell. As they sat down to eat, one of Dashiell's foresters approached him with news.

"We saw Ella and her beloved deer returning to the stream," the man reported.

Dashiell jumped up from his seat so quickly that he knocked over his ale. "Is she alright?" he demanded, already heading towards the door.

He signaled for Laird Whittington, Fallon, James, and his kin to follow him as he rushed out of the great hall.

"She was favoring her left arm but otherwise seemed well," the forester replied.

"I must find her."

"She slipped back into the forest as soon as she saw us. She seems more skittish than before."

"I must see her," Dashiell said as he headed for the stables. He wouldn't believe she was all right unless he saw her, and then he would try to convince her to return with him. He truly feared for her safety should she stay in the forest.

When Dashiell mounted his horse with the others, Lynette joined him and said, "I wish to go too."

"Nay, you will stay here. I dinna wish any further incidents between the two of you."

"What is *that* supposed to mean?"

"The lady is mute. She canna speak."

"She speaks when she wishes to." Lynette tilted her chin up haughtily.

"Even when she was in a great deal of pain, she said no' a word. I believe she canna speak."

"Then you are saying you do no' believe me?" Lynette folded her arms in a huff.

"Something akin to that."

"Well, I canna believe you would take her word..."

"She canna speak."

"Och!" Lynette said, then stormed back toward the castle.

"You will be leaving with your escort as soon as you are

packed," Dashiell called after her. He hoped her da wouldn't take up arms against him, saying he'd treated his darling daughter horribly, but she was a holy terror.

"I wish to know Ella's version of the situation between her and Lady Lynette in the woods. I imagine it will be quite different," Dashiell said to Quinn as he watched the lady rush into the castle.

"Then the lady lied as we suspected."

"Precisely. I mean what I say. I want her sent back to her people posthaste."

"Truly, I believe most will feel that way about the woman. I've heard rumors that you never take a woman on the hunt and did so with Lynette because you wished to wed her.

"That is the farthest thing from my mind."

"Aye, but you know how rumors go. One little thing incites them." Quinn let out his breath.

"What?" Dashiell asked, figuring there was more that Quinn had not told him.

He usually didn't put much stake in rumors unless it had something to do with someone planning to hurt another person, and he could prevent it. Quinn had never mentioned them to him, so he knew something else was bothering him.

"Some say that Ella terrorized MacAfee and their men when they stayed here after the celebration."

Dashiell raised his brows, giving Quinn a look of incredulity.

"I know it's preposterous, but they believe she made them dream of terrifying things."

"Is that so? Well, I heard that some believe ghosts were the cause of MacAfee and his men leaving in the middle of the night." But it made Dashiell wonder, since several had dreams of the elusive woman in green, could others have nightmares that had anything to do with her like Lynette had?

Dashiell shook his head. "I dinna believe it." Then he frowned. "Why would a couple of men beat up Geoffrey MacNeill, trying to learn if he knew the lady of the forest? And then why would they block up the stream if they had been the same people involved in the other action? Did MacAfee or his men mention Ella to our people when they were here?"

"No' that I know of."

Dashiell rubbed his bearded chin. "I saw Ella when MacAfee and his men arrived at Cairn Castle for the celebration."

Quinn raised his brows, then smiled. "Did you now? And you didna tell me?"

"None of you had told me about her at the time, so I didna know she was the mysterious woman of the forest."

"Yet even then, you were intrigued."

"Aye. But my point is she was watching when MacAfee arrived. She disappeared as soon as I saw her. If they returned here, hoping to hunt her down—that she was their whole purpose in coming to celebrate with us—"

"Instead, they left the castle in terror and never returned."

"But what if they had? What if they, or some of MacAfee's men, have been visiting the forest trying to locate her?"

"For what reason?"

"To kill her—like she said."

14

Ella's arm hurt, and she was still burning up from a fever, but she had been desperate to see Mina and her young cousin. She worried about them but also felt Mina could make her feel better.

Mina's eyes opened, and she said, "Och, you were at the castle. You are sick. Come here, child. To bed with you now." Mina pulled the covers aside. "I will make a healing tea for you. Once you're settled, I'll check your bandage." Then she frowned at Finnegan. "You are a blacksmith's apprentice. You must return to the castle at once before they miss you."

"They already know I'm Ella's brother," Finnegan explained.

Mina glanced at Ella. She nodded, her whole head hurting from the movement.

"Och, 'tis no' good. When you return, they will question you. Maybe even torture you to learn where Ella is. And MacAfee? He is up to no good. He dammed the stream, believing we couldn't fetch water or fish. He is a bad one." Then Mina tsked. "You need to heal. I told you that you will bring Dashiell here, and you will, but you need to get well."

"There was no one about the castle. I couldna believe it was so easy to leave there," Finnegan said.

Mina frowned. "They all needed to sleep."

"You made them sleep?" Finnegan asked.

Mina only sighed. "You needed to return here because you wouldna have gotten any rest unless you came and made sure Amelda and I were all right, and I needed to care for Ella."

"You knew she was hurt?" Finnegan asked.

"Aye, of course."

So she had made them sleep. Ella knew the villagers called Mina a witch. She seemed to be able to do things others could not do. Ella was glad for that. Though she had to admit she had loved living at the castle and hadn't feared it like she thought she might.

Then she realized it didn't matter how old Mina was. She did have powerful healing skills a clan could use. Besides, she'd taught Ella most of the things she knew how to do.

Ella was curled up on her palette, still burning up from her fever. Mina put wet cloths on her forehead to cool her down while Finnegan and Amelda gathered firewood.

THAT NIGHT, Dashiell retired to his bedchamber early. "I canna believe I slept so late this morning and am so tired this evening."

"Everyone is feeling the same way. I understand you had no luck with finding Ella." Christopher hung Dashiell's shirt and great kilt on a wooden peg on the wall. "They say she is more wary of men now than ever."

"Do you blame her? I still canna believe I shot her. My men said she was still injured. Perhaps she had healed magically...at least I had hoped so."

"I have heard no one dreamed last night, not even those who always dream of the lady. Several were disturbed by it."

"Why? You would think they would have been content to have slept without her disturbing their sleep."

Christopher laughed. "She is perfect in every way."

"Except she doesna speak."

"In a woman, that could be a good quality, can it no'?"

Dashiell smiled. "I would like to hear the lady speak, Christopher, at least to tell me her full name." He climbed into bed and frowned. "I surmise that all of us who dream about the lady will dream about her this eve."

"Why is that?"

"I believe everyone slept so soundly last night so that she could make her escape. The gates were wide open this morning with the gate guard still sleeping beside it."

"She has magical powers then."

"I dinna know. I hope to dream of the lady tonight." Dashiell tossed and turned in his bed for some time, finally falling asleep.

That night, in the world of dreams, Dashiell found himself in the misty forest. He walked for miles, then finally came to the stream. Seeing it dry but piled four feet high with purple blossoms, he stared at the sight. "Where are you, lass?"

He examined the forest beyond but saw no sign of her. "I dinna wish you any harm. I only wish to see you again." He sat down at the edge of the stream bank and said under his breath, "I must see you again."

Dashiell grew weary of his vigil, and then a sudden movement in the trees made him stare at the spot. A deer appeared, and he watched the buck. "I willna harm you. Tell her to come to me. I willna hurt her either."

The deer watched Dashiell, then bolted into the woods, making him frown. "She willna come. There is no water in the stream." He stood. "A dam has blocked the water."

Dashiell walked for what seemed like an eternity. When he came to the dam, he stared at the insurmountable task. He set about moving a branch at a time and, by early morning, had started a trickle in the dam.

He worked on the dam all that day, taking only a break from time to time as he wiped his brow or drank from his flask. Then he pulled another limb from the dam and tossed it to the bank. He did this repeatedly but stopped when he saw a deer drinking water from the stream above the obstruction.

He watched the deer as he continued to pull sticks from the dam, and at one point, the barricade gave way, and Dashiell was caught up in the flowing water and laughed as he swam toward the bank. Then he saw Ella rush beyond the fringe of the forest, concerned for his safety, and he smiled.

Soaking wet, Dashiell climbed out of the stream on her side of the bank. He stood still and watched her. "Though I have injured you, here you are, coming to my aid when you fear for my well-being. You didna hurt Lady Lynette, did you?" Ella said nothing as she observed him. "I think you might care for me as I care for you. Is that not so?"

He watched as she looked down at her pouch and reached in, then pulled out violets after opening it. She looked at the stream, and he stepped back and waved his hand at the stream. "You may place your flowers in the water, lass, if desired. I willna harm you."

Ella glanced back at the stream but would not move closer to the water. Dashiell waited as he watched her, trying to decide what to do. "You may go to the stream, lass. I willna..."

"My laird!" a voice yelled from some distance away. "My laird! We have seen Ella!"

Christopher said, "One of your foresters is here. They have seen the lady at the loch in the meadow."

"In the meadow?" Dashiell said, climbing out of bed. "What time is it?"

"It is dark still, several hours before dawn. I beg your pardon for waking..."

"Is she still there?"

"They say she is bathing."

"Help me get dressed."

"May I come too?" Christopher asked.

Dashiell sighed. "Nay, you are too young."

"Mayhap she willna be afraid of me."

Shaking his head, Dashiell pulled his tunic over his head. "She may fall in love with you. That wouldna do." To the forester, he said, "Have Fallon, Quinn, and the MacNeills aroused at once. Have our horses saddled."

"Aye."

Christopher handed Dashiell's *sgian dubh* to him and said again, "Are you sure you dinna want me to come? Perhaps she will come to me because of my youth."

Dashiell scoffed. "Very well. We will try."

Christopher smiled.

The two hurried down to the stables and found Fallon and Quinn waiting for them on their mounts. "That was quick, lads."

"Aye, well, nobody had to tell us twice to get ready when we heard Ella was bathing in the loch," Quinn said.

Dashiell smiled. "I considered going alone, but I am afraid my cousin wouldna have permitted me to."

"You are right about that, my laird," Fallon said. "It isna safe for you to be alone at this time of the morn..."

"For me...or for her?"

The men all laughed as James and his kin joined them, and they headed for the loch by the woods. The forester led Dashiell and his entourage to the loch while everyone remained quiet. When they reached the meadow, Dashiell smiled at the sight.

With the moonlight glistening off her hair and skin, the lady swam, disappearing beneath the water and rising some distance beyond. "We thought of stealing the lass's gown so that we could catch her for you, but we didna wish to upset you, so we came for you instead."

"You did the right thing," Dashiell said. He and the other men continued to watch the lady, but as one of the horses whinnied, the lady looked at the meadow and, seeing the men, stared at the sight. "She has seen us."

"Should I get closer and try to talk to her?" Christopher said.

"It willna hurt for you to try. Perhaps you should dismount from your horse first. You will appear smaller and less threatening than that way."

Christopher dismounted from his horse and cautiously walked toward her as he made his way to the bank of the loch. Ella watched the lad walking toward her, then glanced back at the others who still observed her but made no motion to move.

"We dinna wish you harm, my lady," the young man said, with a voice still that of a boy's. "Dashiell," he said as he crouched at the water's edge, then pointed back to him, "was very upset that he hurt you and wished for his healer to take care of you until you were well. He wishes to know who you are and where you come from."

Ella looked at her clothes on the bank, then back to the boy.

"I believe," he said, turning to Dashiell, "she wishes to get out and get dressed."

"If we turn away, she will vanish." Dashiell was sure of it.

The men watched as she treaded water in the deeper part of the loch, but then she swam to the opposite shore, sat in the shallower water, with the water lapping at her shoulders, and rested.

The sun began to rise, and she continued to watch the men who had dismounted from their horses and stood observing her. "I dinna believe she will leave the water with us watching her like this."

"She canna stay in there forever." Dashiell glanced over at the meadow.

James scoffed. "If you wish to marry the lass, you will have a time keeping her at Cairn Castle."

The forester suddenly yelled, "A wild boar is charging toward us!"

The foresters' spears gleamed in the sunlight, their tips sharp and glinting with deadly purpose. The archer's bow was taut, a sleek weapon ready to release its arrow at the beast.

Dashiell quickly ordered Christopher to mount his horse and prepare for the attack. "Christopher, get to your horse! A boar is coming this way."

Dashiell and his men hurried to mount their horses. They all readied themselves, spears in hand and arrows at the ready. The ferocious beast came into view, and the men fought fiercely to take it down.

Dashiell glanced back at Ella, worried about her safety.

Ella had hastily put on her gowns. They rustled and swirled as she ran, her long hair streaming behind her as she disappeared into the green of the forest. He nearly forgot the mission of killing the dangerous boar.

Then he helped to kill the beast.

Glancing over at the loch, Christopher noticed Ella was missing. "She is gone."

Dashiell shook his head. "If I didna know better, I would say she summoned the beast to distract us."

"If so," Fallon said, "she was successful."

"Aye, that she was," Dashiell said.

"Well, at least we will have boar for the meal," his advisor said.

"Perhaps she will return to the stream. You three take the boar to the castle and have the cooks prepare it. The rest of you come with me."

The foresters dressed the boar, then headed for the castle while Dashiell and the rest of his party rode for hours, following deer tracks that led them to several different areas they hadn't traveled to.

They finally arrived at the spot where they usually spied her but found no sign of the lass. Dashiell's heart sank, and he could feel his comrades' spirits dimming.

They waited by the stream, hoping that the lass would return soon. But as the sun began to set and the sky turned a deep orange, they knew it was time to turn back.

The journey back to the castle was quiet and somber, though their spirits were higher after a successful hunt. At least they had seen the lass in the loch. Dashiell wished he could catch her and return her to the castle.

When they arrived back at the castle, they were greeted with the welcoming aroma of a cooked boar. Dashiell's stomach grumbled at the thought of a warm meal, and he couldn't help but feel relieved that their hunt had not been in vain. Though catching the lass would have made the excursion so much better.

"I canna believe that boar distracted me so that I didna see the lass leave the water," Dashiell said. She had already dressed by the time he glanced back at the loch. Once she ran off, he'd had the greatest urge to chase after her if it hadn't been for the boar!

His advisor smiled. "I believe all of us were quite disappointed, even though we have fresh meat on the table."

James said, "I've never seen such an extraordinary creature. You will have difficulty taking her as your wife, I suspect."

Angus and Niall agreed. Dashiell thought the same, as much as he didn't want to admit it.

After the meal, Dashiell and his men returned to the stream, hoping to catch the lass this time if they had no other deadly distractions!

15

E lla couldn't believe the forester had seen her bathing in the loch, her fever finally broken. She'd desperately wanted to wash—and she hadn't even seen the man! Even if she'd wanted to see Dashiell, she wouldn't ever have left the loch naked as the day she was born. She could imagine their disappointment when they didn't see her once they had killed the boar.

She raced to the hut and found her brother, cousin, and Mina still sound asleep. She felt so relieved, but she noted Mina seemed to be doing worse, slowing down, eating very little, and sleeping a lot. Her mind would drift off when her brother and cousin spoke to her.

She always knew who they were, which had worried Ella, but she had seemed more frustrated that Ella and her kin had not gone to the castle, beseeching Dashiell to take them all in.

Ella thought herself stubborn at times, but when it came to Mina, she was even more mule-headed about going with them. She feared Mina would soon join Ella's family in heaven, and they would welcome her for having taken care of their kin for so many years.

FOR A WEEK, Dashiell and a regular group of his clansmen hunted for the lass before and after dinner but never found her. He feared MacAfee had gotten ahold of her, but they hadn't seen any sign of him or his men. James and his kin finally had to leave for home with their men and their bulls to take care of matters at home, wishing Dashiell well in finding the lass.

"Let us know what you learn and if we can further assist," James said, hugging him.

Niall and Angus embraced him, offered their help, and wanted to know when Dashiell had a resolution.

"Aye, I will send word."

After they left, Dashiell summoned his advisor. "Quinn, I know I need to marry someone soon. I am ready to begin considering a lady should one interest me sufficiently."

"MacIntyre will be pleased to hear this. His daughter, Lantana, seems pleasant enough. If you dinna mind, may I continue to look for Ella?"

"You may look. If you find her," Dashiell walked over to his window and looked out of it, "she is naught more than a dream, and every night, the dream seems to fade further from my mind. I can barely see her now for the mist and shadows of the trees. The light rarely shines."

"I see the same. Everyone says the same. Their dreams of her are dying."

"Aye, well, I must get on with business. The temptress has taken too much of my time. Lady Yvaine was right. Ella held my dreams at night and my thoughts during the day. I am finally breaking her bond over me, and I willna let her take hold of me again." Yet he truly didn't feel that way. He yearned to find her with every fiber of his being.

"Aye. Macintyre has said that he is sending Lantana to see you.

The timing could not have been more perfect since you have had such a change of heart."

Dashiell nodded but didn't care to see anyone other than Ella.

His advisor said, "I will make arrangements for the lady's arrival then, and if you dinna mind, will make a trip to the stream afterward."

"If your wife doesna mind."

"She has given up on me."

"As long as you dinna neglect your business with me…"

"Of course no'."

Christopher joined Dashiell and bowed. "May I go with Quinn?"

"No' you, too?"

"Aye."

"Very well, but dinna stay too long."

"Aye, thank you."

Christopher ran after Quinn, and Dashiell entered his solar and sat down. "You will always be a forest nymph to me, naught more, lass."

But he could not stay away either. Losing her and the lass's dreams was too much to bear. He'd also kept waiting for her brother to return to work. If anyone saw Finnegan, they were to take hold of him, and he would force him to show him where his sister was hiding. Dashiell was certain Finnegan and Ella knew that, so the lad hadn't returned.

That night—unable to forgo searching for the lass—Dashiell took five men, including Quinn and Fallon, into the forest. To their shock, they soon became engaged in a battle. Thieves? Dashiell became separated from his men, and two blackguards fought him until one managed to stab him in the chest.

He collapsed and didn't remember anything after that. Not until he opened his eyes to see Ella crouched over him. He knew he was dreaming. She bandaged his chest, and then she rolled him onto a toboggan and carried him further into the woods, but all the jostling over the rough ground made him lose consciousness again.

When he woke, he saw an old woman peering down at him and Ella wringing her hands nearby, looking anxious, her brow furrowed.

"Who are you and the lass?" He still wasn't sure if he was dreaming or not.

"I am Mina and this is Ella. You two have met."

"You have always lived here?" he asked Mina, looking around at the small hut.

Mina glanced at Ella. She shook her head. "I was the healer for the Gunns. MacAfee slaughtered Ella's people. She, her brother, baby cousin, and the blacksmith were the only ones who survived."

Dashiell immediately thought of Lynette's nightmare. She had seen everyone killed in battle at the castle, all but Ella. "And you?"

That was what Ella had been trying to tell him. That MacAfee would kill her, not because she had done anything wrong to him. She had been a witness to the massacre.

Mina frowned. "Aye. The blacksmith had been badly wounded. I had been caring for a woman in labor in the village and later gathering herbs in the forest. The gates were closed, so I returned to the hut and escaped the attack. Tannon, the blacksmith, barely made it out alive. Ella came to Tannon's aid, fighting the brigand battling him, and at some point, she lost her ability to speak."

Dashiel couldn't believe it.

"If it hadna been for Ella, Tannon wouldna have made it. She'd brought her baby cousin Amelda and her five-year-old brother Finnegan through the secret tunnels. Before the onslaught, Ella had spoken, laughed, and played and had grown into a lovely young lady."

Dashiel would make it his duty to make MacAfee pay for his deeds.

"She was fifteen summers when it happened. We helped

Tannon recover in the makeshift lean-to I stayed in when I had finished my business in the village if the castle was closed for the night."

"I'm surprised the gate guard wouldna have let you in, given the importance of your job." For any healer who was as important as she was, most chiefs would leave word to allow them in at any hour.

"I didna want to disturb them. When Tannon was well again, he, Ella, and I created this hut, building the fireplace with stones gathered nearby to keep us safe should MacAfee look for any of us who had survived and fled the ordeal."

"And the blacksmith?"

"Tannon knew it was too crowded for us to stay at the hut and too many of us to visit the woods without being caught. He moved into the village and met a maid, and for a time, he helped us out."

Which would be dangerous, Dashiell could imagine.

"Eventually, he worried MacAfee's men might be looking for us, and he was afraid they would recognize him and attempt to force him to reveal where Ella was. He married the maid and moved away. He did everything he could to make the hut comfortable and well-hidden for us before they left," Mina said.

"How old is Ella now?"

"Twenty summers."

"Where did the battle occur?"

"The castle you call yours is hers." Mina applied a poultice on his wound, and it burned something fierce.

He didn't even remember passing out, but then Ella was gently wiping his brow and then his bare chest except where the bandage was covering his wound.

Ella motioned to Mina, who was sleeping now on her pallet. Then Ella wrote in the dirt—*Mina is frail. Will you...* She paused.

"Will I what?" he asked, unable to sit up.

Let us stay with you?

Dashiell couldn't believe Ella wanted to stay with him after she vanished from the castle. He realized then that Mina was why Ella had returned here. And because of her young cousin, who must be five now. He hadn't seen her yet.

He couldn't believe MacAfee had killed her kin. Mina would be just as much at risk if MacAfee had also learned she was alive and had seen what had happened. Mina was a witness too, but MacAfee must have realized Ella had escaped his ruthlessness and was hiding in the forest.

"Aye, you will stay with my clan." Dashiell would send a missive to the king to see if anything could be done to MacAfee. It would help if Ella could explain everything to the king. "I must get word to my men to come for me and you, Mina, your brother, and Amelda."

He didn't want to delay this because he was sure now that the men who had attacked him and his party were some of MacAfee's men, not common thieves as heavily armed and skilled with the sword as they'd been.

He wanted to ensure the lasses' and lad's safe passage if MacAfee and his men were still roaming through the forest, and he hoped the rest of his men had survived the ambush.

Ella wrote in the dirt: *When it is safe for us to send word, I will tell your men to come for you.*

He didn't want her to go out on her own. She was the real target. "Nay. I must return home and bring a force to bring you there."

16

D ashiell might be a chief, but Ella was doing this her way. She was the reason he had been attacked and had to get him help the best way she could. Her brother had been out gathering firewood and food with Amelda when Dashiell came to his senses.

She wasn't going to send her brother through the woods to the castle, fearing harm might come to him. Though they both had practiced sword fighting, she was still taller than him and had a hefty swing when she put her mind to it. Still, Finnegan could also protect Dashiell while he remained here.

As Dashiell slept, she slipped out of the hut, having already told her brother to guard him, Amelda, and Mina at all costs. He'd wanted to go because he could speak, but she was afraid Dashiell's men might return him to the castle, maybe even punish him for leaving his post like he did.

She moved like a wolf through the woods, staying low and quiet until she came to the stream. The full moon was shown across the ripples of water, making it seem so bright. She was afraid if she crossed the stream, MacAfee's men would see her if they were still about.

Then she saw some of Dashiell's men across the stream. The one named Fallon shouted, "There's Ella!"

Instead of fleeing, she waved at them and motioned to them to come with her into the forest. She tried to say Dashiell's name. Her lips parted, and she tried to push a word out. She was nearly in tears for failing him.

The horses were already riding her way. Before she could run to where the hut was, one of the men grabbed her onto his saddle. "Dashiell? You know where he is?"

She nodded and said, "Aye."

Fallon said, "You...you spoke. Say the word again."

She motioned for him to go in the direction of the hut.

"What if it is a trap?" one of the men asked.

She shook her head and pointed to the east.

"Say the word again," Fallon implored as he rode toward the hut.

She couldn't. She didn't know how she'd managed to whisper out the word or how he'd even heard it. She'd barely heard the word herself, and it had sounded strange to her ears.

"I see naught here," one of the men said.

"Go," she said, much more forcibly than she'd spoken before. She couldn't believe she had said another word. She pointed at the brambles. They couldn't see it in the darkness, even with their torches, until they dismounted.

Fallon handed her down to Quinn and held her wrist as if he feared letting her run again. Not when they finally had her in custody. But she wasn't running this time. MacAfee had now made an enemy of Dashiell, so she and Dashiell were on the same side.

She pulled Quinn toward the entryway, and he bent over low to get into the hut. Once inside, he could only bend over—unable to stand his full height. She thought that was another reason the blacksmith had said he couldn't stay with them.

"He's in here!" Quinn shouted.

"No need to shout," Dashiell said, then he smiled to see Quinn, his hand firmly grasping Ella's wrist. "She and her kin are coming with us. MacAfee is the one who killed her family, the late chief of Cairn Castle, and ambushed us. Are our men all right?"

"Aye, we killed the brigands, but we couldna find you," Quinn said.

Fallon poked his head into the shelter, their torches lighting the small hut.

"Ella brought me here and cared for me. She and Mina are healers," Dashiell said.

Mina was sitting up on her bed, her arm wrapped protectively around Amelda's shoulders.

"As you all know, Finnegan is our blacksmith's apprentice. The wee lassie, Amelda, can help with the gardens. Do we have enough of a force here to protect everyone on the way to the castle?"

"Aye. More than enough," Quinn said, "as soon as we discovered you missing." He glanced at Ella. "Can we move him?"

Mina said, "Aye, gently. He will be abed for days, mayhap longer."

Then they moved Mina, Ella, and her kin out of the hut. Fallon and Quinn searched it for clues about the family's history.

THEY LOOKED through the drying herbs hanging from the thatched roof, then examined the empty cauldron still situated over the fireplace, the ashes grown cold. Fallon touched the edge of a rusty well-worn ax resting on its side against one of the walls. Quinn lifted the straw mattresses on each of two beds placed beside two of the walls. A fireplace built of locally quarried honey-colored limestone was situated against one wall.

"You would have thought someone would have seen the smoke

from the hearth at some time or another," Dashiell said as he considered the stones of the fireplace.

Fallon touched it and pulled a loose stone free.

"Whew," Quinn said, "I was afraid the whole thing would come tumbling down."

Fallon reached the opening and found a black bag embroidered with fine stitching and beads.

"What is in it?" Dashiell asked.

Fallon dumped the contents onto one of the beds and ran his hand through the items. "Violets, dried and withered, thirty gold sovereigns, around the same in shillings, a gold brooch encrusted with diamonds, a hair comb set with pearls, and a note." He examined the note but then handed it to Quinn. "I canna read it as it is so faded."

"I can only see the name at the beginning of the letter. It appears to be addressed to a Lady Marg...I canna make out the rest," Quinn said.

"Margery? Or perhaps, Margaret?" Dashiell said as he looked at the letter.

Fallon pushed at the rest of the items and said, "There is a key as well."

"A key?" Dashiell examined the small, ornate brass key. "To a chest, I suspect. See if the chest is here."

The men searched for a chest but found only a girl's blue woolen shawl folded beneath one of the beds, a few other articles of clothing, and a couple of new gowns being sewn. Dashiell examined the fine material.

"Take everything with us that you can. They willna be returning here," Dashiell said.

"Aye," Quinn said and had a couple of men gather everything together.

Fallon pulled Dashiell on the toboggan out of the hut, and Dashiell groaned. "Gently, the healer said."

"He has always been the worst when he is abed, and a healer has to see to his wounds," Fallon said to Quinn.

Fallon climbed onto his horse, and one of the men helped lift Dashiell onto his lap. Amelda was handed up to one of the men. Finnegan took the helping hand of another man and sat behind him on his horse. Mina was gently lifted into another mounted man's waiting arms.

"Dinna drop me," she said, serious as could be.

Quinn mounted his horse, and another man lifted Ella up to him. She planned to ride behind him like her brother did with the other man! "I hate to say this because the timing is so bad, but Lady Lantana has arrived from the king's court in Edinburgh, sweet and attentive, nothing like the spiteful and malicious Lady Lynette," Quinn said.

"'Tis up to her, but I willna be entertaining any lass." However, Dashiell glanced at Ella as she and Quinn began crossing the stream on horseback. He would make an exception in her case.

Everyone was watchful, on alert in case they were attacked further, but everything seemed quiet now. They finally reached the castle walls, the gates were opened, and the whole party of men and Ella and her kin entered the outer bailey.

The gates closed, and they headed for the stables while the grooms took hold of the horses and would feed and water them. Dashiell was so relieved they had finally all arrived here safely.

Dashiell was taken inside and up to his chamber, where Mai soon joined him. But he wanted to see Ella.

"What about Ella and her family and Mina?" Fallon asked.

"Find a bedchamber for Ella and Amelda. Mina can stay with them. The lad will stay with Theo."

"So will he still be an apprentice for the blacksmith?" Fallon asked.

"If Theo is agreeable. We'll talk about it on the morrow. For now, see that he gets settled in. If Mina tells the truth, they are a chief's family, and we'll treat them as such."

"Aye."

"If Ella isna too tired, I wish to speak with her," Dashiell said before his cousin could leave.

"Aye. You do remember Lady Lantana is here?" Fallon mentioned again.

"What has that got to do with anything?" Dashiell wasn't about to tell him he wanted desperately to speak with Ella, to thank her for coming to his aid at great risk to her and her family, and for going for help while facing the same danger.

"Aye." Fallon smiled and then left. Before Dashiell could give his advisor orders, Fallon poked his head into the bedchamber again. "She spoke."

"What?"

"Ella. Two words. Very softly. Barely audible. Hesitant. The words she spoke were: go and aye."

Dashiell's jaw dropped. Then he looked at Mai, and she smiled. "'Tis a good sign. I've heard tell that when someone goes mute over a tragedy, if they begin talking again, before long, you willna even know they couldna before."

"Send her here." Dashiell was desperate to hear her speak to him.

"Aye." Fallon hurried off, and Dashiell swore Ella had gifted Fallon something special before anyone else heard her speak.

Quinn said, "She said them in desperation as she wanted us to find you and get you to safety."

That declaration made Dashiell feel all the more love for the lass.

～

ELLA STILL COULDN'T BELIEVE she had been able to utter two words. It had been such a struggle to get them out, and she was afraid that was all she could ever do. For now, though, she, her cousin, and Mina were taking turns bathing in warm water in a tub in the bedchamber, which was unbelievably wonderful.

They'd been given clothes and one large bed to sleep in, and Mina had a trundle bed next to one of the walls covered in furs. This was just heavenly. Ella was still worried about Dashiell's wound and recovery and wanted to see him again soon.

A knock sounded on the door, and Flora opened it, came in, and shut it. "Beg pardon, my lady, but Dashiell is asking to see you," she said to Ella.

Ella hurried out of the tub and dried herself off, but before she could put on the borrowed gown, Flora came over and helped her. She vaguely remembered how a maid would help her dress when she was younger, but those times were gone.

It seemed strange to have someone assist her. Ella was worried Dashiell was ill from all the jostling while they moved him from the hut to the castle. She was eager to see him and glad he had called for her.

"He wishes to see you. I believe he is grateful that you saved his life."

Relieved, Ella nodded. Once she was dressed, Flora led her to Dashiell's quarters. The bed was even bigger, with a chest against one wall, leather armor, great kilts hanging on pegs on the wall, and a tapestry of a hunt on another. She stared at the tapestry, remembering it was hanging in her parents' chamber.

This was their room. Dogs were chasing a boar on the tapestry, and men were racing after them on horseback, pikes readied.

"Ella," Dashiell said, "come here, lass."

Flora moved a chair next to the bed and motioned to it.

Ella sat down on the chair. Rarely had her siblings been allowed in this room, except when her mother gave birth to her brother when she was ten winters and when her da had been accidentally shot in the arm during a hunt.

Her da had been of good humor about it. The man who had accidentally shot him had worried he would be dead for the mistake. Her da had shown what a good leader he had been and excused him for the accident. Everyone loved him except for his brother, Lennox.

"Ella?"

She glanced at Dashiell again, lost in her thoughts.

He reached out for her hand and groaned.

She quickly took hold of his hand and gently squeezed, reassuring him she was there for him.

"I want to thank you for saving my life in the woods. If you hadna, I would have died. And again, when you went to fetch my men to bring me home, despite my telling you not to, I thank you."

She inclined her head and glanced around the room again.

"Fallon said you spoke a couple of words. Can you speak to me? Unless you are too tired." He moaned a little, and she quickly pressed her hand to his forehead and uttered silent words, as she had done when Lady Olivia gave birth to her son. It was instinctive to stop his pain, something Mina had taught her.

"Can I get you something?" Mai asked.

Ella shook her head at her and said in a whisper, "Nay."

The healer's eyes widened, and so did Dashiell's.

Ella couldn't believe she had spoken again. She was shocked at herself but hopeful she could continue to talk, even more than just a word. It would be so wonderful to speak with people and not have to write everything in the dirt.

Dashiell smiled. "You have come home, lass, and here you will stay."

17

The next morning, Dashiell was burning up, sweating, chilling, and hot again. Now he knew how Ella had felt after he had wounded her—miserable. To his surprise, he saw she was asleep in the chair beside his bed, a fur blanket covering her.

Then he noticed Mina preparing something for him to drink. It appeared Mina had relieved his healer to care for him, which he appreciated.

Mina whispered, "Ella wouldna leave your bedside, but alas, she could no longer stay awake. I would have had one of your men move her to the guest chamber's bed, but I feared she would wake."

"Tell me more about the family and what was going on. Why would MacAfee kill her family?"

"I dinna know. I wasna at the castle when the massacre took place. Ella was clueless."

Dashiell couldn't believe it. "But Ella and her brother and cousin escaped."

"Aye. I was in the forest gathering herbs and making poultices for anyone who needed them: the farmers, the villagers, and those living in the castle. I also delivered babies."

He hadn't thought of sending his healer to the village to take care of people there also. Ella's da was a good leader.

"MacAfee and his people were there at the castle at a feast. When I returned from the village, the castle gates were closed. I went to my hut to dry herbs. And then I heard the screams and fighting."

"You were lucky to have been away from the castle, and Ella and her family were fortunate to escape," he said.

"Aye. I heard the fighting and wanted to help my clansmen however I could. That's when I found Ella, her brother, her cousin, and the blacksmith making their way across the stream. I'm a healer, no' a fighter, though I know how to fight. The blacksmith wasna privy to what had happened either. He had been working at his forge."

"Ella carries a sword."

"I had learned how to defend myself, no' to go into battle, unless I had to. My da taught me. I watched the young lads learn how to fight and wanted to learn. I taught Ella, who taught her brother."

"MacAfee must have planned the siege, so he brought a large enough force to overwhelm her da's people at the feast. What was her da's name?" Dashiell said.

"Coinneach Gunn."

"Ella believes MacAfee wants to murder her because she was a witness to the whole massacre," Dashiell said, trying to remember who Coinneach was, but he didn't believe he had ever met him.

But Coinneach had a brother up north, and Dashiell had met him. Lennox had a son named Michael, who would be Ella's cousin, and Lennox, her uncle.

"I'm sure once MacAfee learned she might live in the forest, he was afraid you would find her first and fight him next to protect her."

"Would he believe I might marry her? He would be right in thinking so," Dashiell said.

Mina smiled.

"Does Ella remember everything that happened that fateful night?" He realized Ella had been staring at the tapestry on the wall.

The bed had been here when he had bartered for the castle. Had they been her parents' things then? Had it brought back any memories?

"As far as I know, Ella doesna remember everything that had happened unless she is no' speaking of it. She cries out in her sleep or is crying in the middle of the eve. When I've comforted her in the past, she says 'tis naught, but I ken differently."

"Have you been here in this bedchamber before? When her da and mother were still here?"

"Aye." Mina looked sad, tears filling her eyes. "'Tis the same furnishings as when her mother and da were alive, if that is what you seek to ken."

"Aye." He rubbed his chin in thought. "Since her da was Coinneach Gunn, Ella has other kinfolk. Her da has a brother named Lennox, who has a castle up north," Dashiell said.

"They were no' on good terms. Her uncle led an uprising against Coinneach when Lennox still lived at Cairn Castle. Coinneach was the eldest of the two brothers and took over as chief of the clan when their da died. Their mother had died giving birth to Lennox, and their da had never remarried."

"The brigand."

"Aye. Lennox was furious that Coinneach was put in charge. His son, Michael, was close in age to Ella, and they adored each other like a brother and sister would. Once Lennox led the revolt against Coinneach, he and those who had sided with Lennox were banished. Michael left with his da and the others."

"Then Lennox eventually married a woman, whose da was chief, and once the woman's da died, Lennox took over the clan," Dashiell said.

"I dinna ken that. I had spoken to Ella about living with them, thinking he would provide her protection against MacAfee. When the uprising was carried out, she said Lennox was spiteful. She didna trust him and had even cut him when he tried to cut her da. She'd even wondered if he had been behind MacAfee killing her family."

Dashiell wondered about that. "And the reason MacAfee was living here for so long?"

"For four and a half years, he had been searching for Ella. They hadn't found her body, nor her brother's, or their cousin's. I believe he felt they had lost her for good, and mayhap he didna feel comfortable where he wasna wanted." Mina wiped Dashiell's brow with a damp, cool cloth.

"Can you elaborate?"

Mina just gave him an elusive smile. "The ones who were so grievously set upon."

"Spirits?" Dashiell shook his head. He didn't believe in such a thing. "But MacAfee or some of his men returned and battled with us in the woods."

"I'm sure he still had spies searching for Ella since you took over the castle. I'm certain there have been rumors about the young woman who hasna spoken since the time her kin were murdered."

Ella suddenly opened her eyes and appeared shocked that she had fallen asleep. She quickly sat up and saw Dashiell smiling at her. She was beautiful, and he realized just how much he wanted her for his own.

Someone knocked at the door, and Dashiell said, "Come." However, his voice sounded much weaker than he wanted to admit.

Quinn stepped into the room. "Laird, we have another visitor.

What do you want me to do about Lady Lantana? She is concerned for your health and wishes to see you."

Dashiell thought about the situation, knowing there was no way he would wed the lady when the Nymph of the Forest had stolen his heart. "Give the lady my sincerest apologies and tell her there will be no match between us."

Quinn glanced at Ella as if she was the reason for the upset in the plans.

"Who is the visitor?" Dashiell asked.

"Michael Gunn. He's—"

"My...my cousin!" Ella exclaimed.

Quinn just stared at her.

"Is his da with him?" Dashiell asked, for the moment forgetting that Ella was barely speaking and had spoken more words than ever. Though her voice was still soft, as if she was unsure how to speak or her voice was so unused to being used that she was having difficulty relearning how to talk, every word she spoke was precious to him.

"Nay. He came with three armed men. We disarmed them."

Dashiell began to rise from his bed.

"Nay!" Mina said, Ella rushing back to the bed to ease him back against the mattress.

"We...we sewed you up. You're...feverish. Stay in...bed until... you're better," Ella said with authority.

Dashiell was so surprised that she had spoken so many words, and they had been so much clearer now that he was slack-jawed. In fact, so was Mina. Quinn only smiled. Maybe he had forgotten she wasn't speaking but a word occasionally. Or mayhap he was just amused that Ella had taken charge of Dashiell as if *she* was the chief of the clan!

Dashiell was so taken aback that he rested his head against the pillow and stared at her. For the first time ever, he was completely speechless.

Ella must have realized she should have addressed him with more respect when he said nothing, but then she turned to Quinn. "I...I must...see him."

Again, her voice was soft and sweet, yet it didn't matter how she spoke; she had the voice of an angel, as far as Dashiell was concerned.

"Bring him here." Dashiell normally would never have had a guest come to his bedchamber when he was wounded or ill, but he hated admitting that he didn't want Ella out of sight. As far as her cousin was concerned, Dashiell wished to meet him and see what he had to say.

How had Michael, most likely his da, known Ella was here? Was he in collusion with MacAfee, as Ella had wondered?

"Aye." Then Quinn left the bedchamber and hurried off.

"Stay, Ella," Dashiell said because she looked desperate to see Michael immediately, and he wanted her safely by his side. He hoped Quinn would bring a couple of guards with him and Fallon to ensure her safety and his if Michael or his men were up to mischief.

Ella took over Dashiell's care. "Mina, why...dinna you...get some...rest?"

Mina sighed. "Aye. I'll lie down for a wee bit." She hugged her. "I knew you would speak again." Then she walked slowly out of the room.

"Ella," Dashiell said, reaching for her hand. "You're talking."

She nodded and took hold of his hand.

"Speak the words," he said, encouraging her to use her voice more.

"'Tis...'tis hard...to remember...to speak...sometimes. I forget I can."

"I'm sure, but I love hearing your words."

Fallon ushered Michael into the bedchamber, accompanied by two guards. Quinn was also there.

Michael had the same blond hair as Finnegan and the same blue eyes. Dashiell could see the resemblance at once.

Michael inclined his head.

Ella held back, appearing to want to run to him, yet she stayed next to Dashiell's bed as if willing herself to remain calm.

Michael smiled at Ella. "Margaret."

That may have been the name her mother and da had given her, but to Dashiell, she would always be Ella.

No one had called Ella by her real name in the five years she'd lived in the forest. It sounded strange to her ears, yet it seemed oddly familiar. Michael had grown so big, from a fifteen-year-old boy to a man she didn't know.

Yet she could see the resemblance in his smile, the color of his windswept hair, and clear blue eyes, and she thought her brother would look so much like him when he was that age. Then she remembered—the shirt that she was so fond of that Dashiell had worn was like the one she had made for Michael for his fifteenth birthday.

"Margaret, I dinna ken what to say. I learned from the villagers that you were here," he said.

She supposed that word might have gotten to someone in the village, but she wondered if her uncle had a spy at the castle. What if one of the men Dashiell had hired worked for her uncle?

"Why...are...are you...here?" she asked, her voice so hesitant and soft. She realized she was afraid to speak the words incorrectly. She needed to practice speaking every chance she got, but she felt it was a struggle every time she spoke.

"Margaret, you're speaking! 'Tis a miracle," Michael said.

"Why are...you...here?" she asked again, annoyed. She realized she didn't trust him. Not after the uprising Michael's da had created, and because Michael had remained loyal to him.

She understood why he would have because he had only been seventeen, but still, he worked for his da even now and never once had come to seek out the rest of their kin. At least, she didn't think so.

"I wanted to make amends to Coinneach. 'Twas a long time in coming. I had no idea that all the rest of our kin were *gone*."

"Dead. Murdered...by...by MacAfee," she said, her words angry despite being hushed. They were not just gone.

"MacAfee?" Michael sounded surprised.

She still didn't trust her cousin. What if Michael was pretending to be surprised? She wanted to ask if he knew MacAfee was now searching for her and that his men had injured Dashiell.

"May I have a word with Ella alone?" Michael stood tall and imperious as if he didn't have to ask but was doing so for Ella's benefit. He looked just like his uncle would when he wanted his way.

"Nay," Dashiell said.

"Why...did you...steal Dashiell's...bride away?" Ella pointedly asked.

"It wasna like that." Michael sounded annoyed with her.

"Then you fell...hopelessly in...love with her...and...stole her... from her intended."

Ella watched to see what Michael would say. Dashiell had probably never had the chance to question Michael himself.

"It's no' a matter that I need to discuss with you."

She recalled now how Michael could be so haughty with her. He was somebody important while she was just the daughter of a chief at the time.

"But you are here seeking me to grant some concession, and you owe me an explanation," Dashiell said.

"Then Lady Margery will need to leave the chamber."

"She stays," Dashiell countermanded.

Michael appeared frustrated. "Aye, we fell in love."

"You...couldna live...without her? Or...her dowery?" Ella asked.

Michael's stern gaze turned worried as he glanced at Ella.

"It seems to me that Ella knows you better than you think."

"*You* didna love her!" Michael countered.

"Nay. The marriage was arranged. But I lost an important alliance as well, you know. In any event, it was the best thing that ever happened to me. I am weary," Dashiell said. "You can speak with the lady later."

Ella was surprised that he didn't tell her to go with Michael to talk further.

Michael inclined his head and left with the guards.

"What do you want us to do with them?" Fallon asked.

"They can eat and stay with us, but I want them watched while they're here," Dashiell said. "I want a guard on Ella and her kin, Mina too, at all times."

"Aye." Fallon left to carry out his orders.

"What about Lady Lantana?" Quinn asked.

"Has she no' left here with her entourage already?" Dashiell sounded annoyed.

"Nay, she says she wishes to remain here until you are well enough to speak to her and tell her yourself that you wish her to go home."

"That is what I have you for." Dashiell sounded exasperated.

Ella didn't blame him. She knew he had to be in pain and feeling out of sorts from his injury. She sat on the chair beside him, put her hand over his forehead again, and concentrated, trying to ease his suffering. At once, he relaxed against the bed, and she was glad she could help him in some small way.

Dashiell closed his eyes, and he seemed to drift off to sleep.

Quinn studied her with Dashiell for a moment, then bowed his head and left the chamber, shutting the door.

A few minutes later, the door opened, and Dashiell's healer entered the chamber. "I am relieving you, my lady."

Ella glanced at Dashiell, confirmed he was sleeping, and then she stood. "Tell...me...if he needs me."

Mai smiled. "Oh, aye, he needs you."

Ella smiled at her, left the bedchamber, and checked on Mina and Amelda. She was surprised that a man was following her everywhere.

"Guard duty, my lady," the red-haired man said. "My name is Ruadh. I'm on the first detail."

She inclined her head. In the chamber where she would stay, she found Mina sound asleep, and a guard was posted there. Amelda wasn't there. "Where is Amelda? And my...brother?"

"I dinna ken, but I'll take you to see Fallon and mayhap he kens where they are." Ruadh took her downstairs, and he asked another man where Fallon was.

"In the inner bailey," the man said, smiling at Ella.

They headed outside and she saw Amelda helping a couple of maids gather dried laundry. As soon as Amelda saw Ella, she raced to hug her, the task at hand all but forgotten. Ella saw a guard watching her cousin, and she was glad that Amelda was being protected, just in case there was any trouble.

"Ella, I've been helping the washerwomen. They said I didna have to but 'tis fun."

Ella smiled. "I am...glad."

"I canna believe you can talk. Your voice, 'tis strange."

"You...you have...never heard...it...before."

"Aye."

Then Ella saw Michael heading their way. Immediately, Ruadh and Amelda's guard were there to protect them.

Michael said, "I want to speak with you further."

Ruadh looked at Ella to see if she was agreeable.

"Aye," she said.

"Is there somewhere that we can talk?" Michael asked. "The garden?"

"Aye."

The two guards went with them while Michael smiled down at Amelda. "And who is this?"

"I'm Ella's cousin."

"A cousin. Then you're my cousin also." Michael patted her head.

She looked up at Ella as if waiting for her to say he was. "Aye," Ella said to Amelda. But she didn't say it in a giddy, cheerful way.

Amelda took her cue and held onto Ella's hand. Ella couldn't believe that Michael was here after all that had happened, which made her suspicious.

When they walked into the herb garden, she saw a bench to sit on, and a feeling of joy and loss hit her all at once. She had sat with her mother on that bench, held Amelda as a baby there, and even sat with Finnegan there when he was younger.

One of the maids was snipping herbs for the meal, and Amelda asked Ella, "Can I go help her?"

"Aye." Ella was proud of her cousin for wanting to assist everyone with their chores, just like she did when they lived in the forest.

Ella sat while the guards stood nearby, and Michael sat beside her on the bench. "Speak."

Michael cleared his throat, glancing at the guards, and then took a deep breath. "Da wants you to leave here with me. Your brother and cousin also. You are our kin, and you belong with us. You, Finnegan, and Amelda will be his wards."

"Nay," she said.

"You dinna have any choice. Da is already speaking with the king on the matter."

"Nay." She rose to her feet.

Michael quickly stood. "'Tis good that you are speaking. When you are wed—"

"What?"

"My da will decide this for you. And for Amelda."

Her uncle would not decide this for either of them.

"He'll decide what training your brother will have," Michael continued.

Ella's heart was beating so hard that she felt like she had been running from danger. "Nay."

"You havena any choice." Michael reached for her hand, but she wouldn't let him take it.

She didn't want him to believe she would agree to her uncle's plans. She felt sick to her stomach. She wanted to speak with Dashiell about ensuring he wouldn't let her uncle take them away.

"Why...did you...come here?" she asked.

"I told you. I'm taking you home."

"This...is...my home." Not really, but if Dashiell would allow them to stay here, they would make it their new home. Then she walked over to speak with Amelda. "This man...will watch...out for you. You are no' to...leave the...castle...grounds without...my permission. You must hear...it from...me."

"Aye," Amelda said.

"Tell me...what...I said."

"No' to leave the castle without you saying so."

"Aye." Then to Amelda's guard, Ella said, "Dinna...let her...leave the castle...grounds."

"Aye, my lady."

"Can...can...I see the laird's advisor?" Ella asked Ruadh.

"Aye, my lady. Come this way." Ruadh started walking back toward the castle, Michael following them.

Ella turned to Michael and said, "You have...told...me what... you wished. And I have...told...you we...willna leave...with you."

"You havena choice," Michael said. "We were best of friends when we were young."

"That...was before...your...da tried...to...have my...da and... others murdered," Ella reminded him.

They ended up inside the castle, but Michael was still following her. Once they were in the great hall, Ruadh motioned to a lad, and he ran to join them. "Find Quinn or Fallon and tell them the lady wishes to speak with them about something of the utmost importance."

"Aye." The boy raced off.

———

18

Banging on Dashiell's bedchamber door was accompanied by, "My laird! I need to speak with you. My laird!"

"Paden?" Dashiell had been in a deep sleep.

"Aye, aye, my laird!"

Paden, a lad of ten, often brought him news when urgent matters needed to be resolved.

Mina tried to stop him at the door, but Dashiell said, "Come. What news have you?"

Dashiell was already awake; he might as well learn what was so urgent that the lad wanted to see him.

"Ruadh told me to get Quinn or Fallon right away."

Dashiell raised a brow. He was neither man.

"But, laird, the request was from the Nymph of the Forest. Her cousin Michael follows her everywhere. Ruadh said it was of the utmost importance."

That concerned Dashiell. What was Michael here for? Dashiell instantly wondered if Michael's da believed he would take Ella and the others under his wing. Dashiell wouldn't allow it unless she wanted to go there, but he didn't want her to leave. Not any of them.

Especially after her uncle was banished from the clan, Dashiell didn't trust him or his son.

"Find Quinn or Fallon and have him bring Ella here at once," Dashiell said.

"Aye." Paden rushed out of the bedchamber.

"Och. Lennox will surely take them and make them stay with him until he can marry Ella off to someone who would benefit him in battle," Mina said, wiping Dashiell's brow again.

"No' if I have any say in it," Dashiell said.

"She willna want to leave here. This is her home," Mina said. "'Tis her castle."

Dashiell smiled at Mina.

"'Tis true," Mina said, unsmiling, serious.

PADEN WAS QUICK; before long, he was bringing Quinn and Fallon to Ella, concern etched in their furrowed brows and unsmiling lips.

"Come with us at once," Quinn said to Ella. To Michael, he said, "You stay here."

"I wish to speak on Laird Lennox Gunn's behalf," Michael said.

"Stay. Here," Quinn said.

Ella loved hearing Quinn's commanding Michael to obey when her words had fallen on deaf ears. Most likely, Michael felt he was the chief in his da's place, and no one would ignore *him*. Then she saw another guard arrive to watch over Michael.

She, Quinn, and Fallon headed back up the stairs. "Nay," she said. "The laird...needs...his...rest."

"He insists. If he falls asleep, you may sit beside him until he wakes. He'll heal even more quickly if you are by his side," Quinn said.

"Michael says his da...his da will make...my brother...and Amelda...wards of his."

"He is gravely mistaken," Fallon said. "I ken my cousin well enough, and he will no' allow it."

Ella still didn't want to disturb Dashiell. When she arrived at his bedchamber, and Quinn opened the door, she saw he was awake, waiting on her. She hurried into the chamber. "You should be sleeping."

"You are more important. What has Michael said to you?"

Ella explained what he had said.

"Nay, you are no' going anywhere." Dashiell sounded tired.

Then she sat beside him, wishing they had not disturbed his sleep. He reached for her hand. She held his hand and felt his strength, warmth, and protectiveness. "Aye. But I know he will go to the king about it. He is my kin." She loved Dashiell for taking them in, but she was afraid there was no way out of this nightmare for her or her brother and cousin.

"But you will be my wife."

Her jaw dropped. She couldn't help it. She cared about Dashiell and wanted to be with him more than anything else, but she had never expected him to marry her. Not when she would bring nothing to the marriage.

"If 'tis what you wish, but maybe we should discuss this at another time," Dashiell said because she didn't jump at the chance to say she wanted to marry him.

"Nay," she quickly said. He would be her husband and protect her and her family. She would be the lady of the castle, just like Mina said she should be. She would care for him and his people whenever they needed healing because she loved him with all her heart and soul.

Her mother had already taught her some of the duties of being the lady of the manor when she was young. Even Mina had taught her some of the things she had seen Ella's mother do when Mina had been at the castle taking care of the sick, wounded, and mothers giving birth.

She thought Dashiell was a good man, never having seen him act harshly toward anyone. And she knew he was the only one for her.

"You dinna want to discuss it later?" Dashiell asked.

"I will marry...you...and...gladly. I dinna...need...to think... on it."

He smiled and squeezed her hand.

Fallon folded his arms and shook his head. "Several of our kinsmen were interested in the lass. They will be sorely disappointed. Even I had high hopes."

"Nay, you dinna," Quinn said. "You ken as soon as our chief was searching for the lass day and night, she would be his."

Ella laughed. "As long...as...I had...been...out here, no...one... had ever...intrigued me...like...you...do." Not to mention, she had only ever dreamed of him as if he was the man who was the one for her, making love to her, loving her as she loved him in return.

Paden came to the bedchamber and knocked on the door frame. "Michael has left with his men."

"Good," Dashiell said.

Ella worried they hadn't heard the last from her uncle.

WHEN DASHIELL WAS ASLEEP, Ella left his chamber with her guard to see Amelda and ensure she was fine. She also wanted to check on her brother. She found Amelda weeding the garden with a maid, her guard watching out for her.

"I am Agnes," the maid said. "Your cousin has been teaching me about the plants in the forest."

"Good. But she must no' go there."

"Nay. Quinn brought all the things from the abode where you were living, and she was showing me the dried herbs and other plants."

Ella smiled, glad her cousin proved helpful even at her young age. Then a beautiful fair-haired woman headed their way, dressed in a blue gown and looking like she was someone of importance.

"That is Lady Lantana," Agnes said. "She's concerned about the laird's injury and no' happy that he willna speak to her about sending her on her way."

It appeared to Ella that the woman intended to speak to her instead. "Aye. Amelda, keep up the good work. I'm off to see Finnegan and learn how he is doing."

"He is all dirty," Amelda said.

Ella chuckled. "From working as the blacksmith's apprentice." She knew he loved the work and was glad for it. "I will see you later. If you need to see me before that, tell your guard."

"Aye, Momma."

Then Ella headed for the blacksmith's workplace, which took her in a different direction than Lady Lantana was coming. She didn't mean to avoid her but wished to see her brother. If the lady wanted to join her, that would be fine.

The lady took a detour and quickened her pace to catch up to her. "Excuse me, Lady Margery, is it?"

Ella glanced at her. "Aye, but you may call me Ella."

"The fey from the forest," Lantana said. "I've been told you are why Dashiell wants me to return home." She eyed Ruadh for a moment. "Must you attend us?"

"Aye," Ruadh said. "It is my laird's wish."

Lantana shook her head. "Rumors are that you are the daughter of a former clan chief who had been in charge of Cairn Castle."

"Aye. Coinneach Gunn was my da."

"Do you believe it is your place to retake the castle?"

Ella smiled at Lantana. The woman was pleasing to look at and not unpleasant to talk to. If the circumstances had been different, she might have even been a friend.

"This is my home, aye. I have no illusions that the castle is mine to 'take over.'" She wasn't about to tell Lantana that she and Dashiell loved each other. That was not for her to say.

She continued to walk to the blacksmith's shop, and Lantana kept up with her.

"I have heard you have...influenced the chief using some magic," Lantana said, but she sounded a little worried her words might annoy one of the fey kind.

"I am just like you, I suspect, Lantana. Raised as a clan chief's daughter, taught how to manage a castle staff, learning the skills of sewing and song."

"No' living off the land, learning to fend for yourself, fighting with a sword, keeping your young cousin and your brother safe from those who would want you dead," Lantana said.

Was that admiration in the lady's words?

"When my family was murdered, I was fortunate to have Mina show me how to live off the land, or we would never have survived." Ella would always credit Mina for the kindness and knowledge she had shared freely with them.

Lantana let out her breath. "I dinna know if I could have survived, living like that."

"Aye, you would have. If you'd had the kind and helpful assistance that Mina provided."

Lantana smiled at her. "You are no' as I had envisioned. A waif of a woman, poorly spoken, with no sense of decorum. You are educated in ways I have never been, and I wish you the best. I dinna know how you could have managed in the forest as long as you did, even with the healer's help. You and Dashiell truly care for each other?"

"Aye."

Lantana shook her head. "I have heard it said that he is a kind and fair man. It appears I have been too late in coming. My da waited to send me until he had learned Lady Lynette had been rejected."

"Oh, the woman is a viper," Ella said before she could stop her words. "I mean—"

"I ken what you mean. I have met her before. She is spoiled beyond repair, and she would be any man's nightmare who wished to wed her."

Ella smiled. "I like you. I hope that we can be friends."

"Aye, I wish it too. Though it seems danger follows you wherever you go." Lantana glanced at the guard with them to make her point.

"Until MacAfee is held accountable for his reprehensible actions, aye."

"Where...are we going?"

Ella was amused that Lantana was following her all this time, as if they were friends and having a nice chat. "To see my brother. He is the blacksmith's apprentice, and I have not seen him in a while."

"You dinna mind if I meet him also?"

"I appreciate the company." Then they reached the blacksmith's workshop, and the blacksmith smiled at Ella and Lantana.

"I am truly humbled to welcome two ladies to my workshop. I am Theo."

"Thanks be to thee for taking time out of your day to welcome us. How is Finnegan doing?" Ella asked.

"He is a superb apprentice, except for the time he slipped away with you into the forest, and I was sorely lacking for an assistant. But I understood his reasoning. I'm glad to have him back."

She was glad to hear it.

Finnegan came running out of the back of the workshop when he heard Ella speaking and hugged her.

She should have objected, as dirty as he was, but she loved his hugs no matter what and hoped he would never be too old or think himself too manly to share them. She hugged him back. "I hear you are doing good work, and I'm proud of you."

"I have made my first sword. Master Theo said it was mine to keep." Finnegan darted off to the back of the shop and, quick as a deer, bounded back to her with the sword in hand.

She took the sword from him and turned it over, studying its quality. "Well done, Finnegan."

He beamed. "I have to get back to work."

"Aye. You have much to learn."

"He is scheduled for sword practice this afternoon," Theo said. "And then back here to work."

"Thank you for taking him in when he needed to learn such a skill."

"He had learned much from his previous master in the village. I am just honing his skills. He is a good lad and like the son I never had. You must be proud of him after having instilled such a great work ethic in him. Most young men his age are no' so inclined."

Ella smiled. "He has always been eager to help, even when he was too young to do the tasks. I will let you get back to work before I am in trouble for keeping you from it."

Theo smiled. "I believe you could get away with anything as far as his laird is concerned."

Ella laughed. Then she and Lantana walked back to the keep.

"I can see your home is here. No' just that the castle is your home, but you have truly won the people over. That is something that oft canna be done easily."

Ella appreciated Lantana for saying so.

"I see it in everyone's expressions as they look at you. Some women, like Lynette, inspire fear, and people will revile her. I've seen her kind treat others with disrespect and lie to get their way. Staff members would avoid someone like her altogether."

"Aye." Ella knew Lynette would have been a horrible person to live with.

"But with you, everyone smiles and greets you, eager to have a word. I heard Lynette lied about you, saying you had injured her."

"I wanted a friend, someone my age, a woman I thought I could trust. Since losing my kin and friends, I hadna had a friend like that again." She didn't want to think of what had become of her friends who had played with her and spoken mischievously about which lad they wanted to kiss or even wed someday.

At the time, though, she knew her da would decide her fate.

"Lynette was envious and hated that you intrigued Dashiell. You have my friendship. I will admit I might be a wee bit envious of your relationship with the laird, but—"

"You wouldna treat me ill. If you wish it, I will see if Dashiell will speak with you." Ella was thrilled that Lantana wanted to be her friend and would do anything she could to encourage their friendship.

Lantana sighed. "I would like to hear Dashiell tell me that he wishes me gone, but I know he is gravely wounded. Men in such a position of power dinna like to show weakness to outsiders. Even among their own people. If it is all right with you, I will stay for a few more days, only because the journey home will take so long."

"Aye, he would wish it, and I can visit with you longer." Ella knew Dashiell wanted Lantana to leave, not wanting her to believe he had any interest in marrying her.

But she understood Lantana's reasons for wishing to stay a bit longer. Maybe by then, Dashiell would feel more himself and speak with Lantana.

Lantana hugged Ella, surprising her, but she quickly hugged her back. "Thank you."

"Aye. I'm glad. I havena traveled on horseback for many years, but I remember the last time I went such a long distance, I didna want to return right away. Would you like to join me in the solar where I was working on embroidering a gown?"

"Aye. I would like that." Lantana cleared her throat. "Because of your issue with MacAfee, do you think he will continue to come after you?"

19

"My laird." Quinn cleared his throat, waking Dashiell in his bedchamber.

Dashiell opened his eyes, no longer feeling feverish, thank the gods, and saw Quinn standing over him, *not* who he wanted to see. Where was Ella?

Quinn glanced at Mina, telling her silently he had private business to discuss with Dashiell.

"I'll return in a bit." Mina walked out of the chamber, closing the door behind her.

"What is wrong now? Ella isna gone, is she?" Dashiell was ready to throw aside his furs and hunt her down.

"Nay, it's Lantana."

Dashiell let out his breath and rubbed his eyes. "Is she still refusing to leave until I personally tell her to?"

"Nay, it's Ella."

Dashiell frowned. "What about Ella?"

"She told Lantana she could stay longer to rest before her long journey home. They have become friends."

Dashiell stared at Quinn. "What?"

Quinn smiled. "The lass makes friends easily, except for

MacAfee and her uncle or Lady Lynette." Quinn lost the smile and frowned. "I must bring up another issue though."

"Aye?" Dashiell knew from how Quinn was so serious that the issue was troubling.

"Ruadh overhead Lantana speaking to Ella, asking if she thought MacAfee would continue to come for her."

ELLA HAD PLANNED to break her fast in Dashiell's bedchamber with him, but he was ready to join her in the great hall to show he was getting better. She understood his need to prove he was still in charge of the clan and could lead them.

She still thought he should be in bed for the meal, but she could not change his mind.

Lantana was sitting beside Lady Yvette and talking to her about her work while on the king's staff. Though she smiled at Ella, she only inclined her head to Dashiell.

"What say you?" Dashiell asked Ella as they broke brown bread. "Did your cousin marry for love?"

"Nay. Michael married her because of who her da was and for the dowry. My uncle probably convinced him of it. My uncle doesna care about who he hurts in the process."

"I meant what I said. I'm glad I hadna wed the lass. That meant I could meet you."

"You still know so little about me."

"I know you are fiercely protective of your kin and mine. That you have suffered greatly though continue to be kindhearted. That you are the legitimate heir to this castle."

She laughed. "As if anyone would believe that."

"The only one who needs to believe it is me. Mina says we were fated to meet in the very way we met."

"She did? She hasna told me that."

"Aye. Though most dinna know it, my grandmother had visions like Mina does. She told me I would fall in love with a bonnie lass who would mean the world to me and that she would speak to me in her special way at first. Of course, she didna tell me you couldna speak."

"That was a shock, I'm sure." She drank some of her mead.

"Aye, for certes. She said we would have many children and fill the castle with their laughter. I thought she meant the keep up north. I never expected she would be talking about this one and you."

"I've dreamed of you." She felt her cheeks heat just from even mentioning it.

"As I have dreamed of you. Of trying to catch you and gain a kiss from your sweet lips that I had the hardest time capturing. But do tell, what did you dream of me?"

"That I danced with you and captured you with a kiss."

He smiled. "Do you think Mina made us dream of one another?"

"Some. But I believe some of our dreams were of our own making."

"Some say you turned into an owl at night."

"No' me."

"And you run with the deer."

"That is true."

"And you live among wolves."

She sighed deeply. "It depends on the type of wolves you are talking about. Then aye."

THREE WEEKS LATER, Dashiell was finally up and about, feeling his usual self. Now that he was doing better, he hoped to wed Ella in a fortnight. He wanted to make love to his bonny bride once he was fully healed. Everyone was still preparing, sending invitations, even to James and his kin, cleaning, and gathering enough food for the celebration.

For the time being, while Ella was with the ladies in the herb garden, Dashiell was in the forest with his men hunting boar, the first time since he was so badly injured when a flushed and horrified Paden rode to meet up with him. "What's wrong, Paden?"

"Uh, well, er..." Paden's gaze focused on the ground.

"Speak up, lad," Dashiell said.

Paden's gaze shot up to fix on Dashiell. "That...woman, er, Lynette and her, uh, da is at the castle, demanding to see you, my laird."

"God's wounds." Dashiell didn't need this right now. He turned to Quinn. "Why does my word mean naught?"

Quinn shook his head and smiled a little. "With that woman, if you had married her, she would have been the death of all of us."

"There was no way I would have married her. Even if I hadna fallen in love with Ella." Dashiell looked back in the direction of the castle. "I would just hunt like we planned without thought to their arrival, but mayhap I can speak with her da while we're in the forest. Any man cheers up during the hunt. Then I will tell him why I'm no' marrying his daughter."

Fallon smiled.

"No' the reason that she's a shrew but because Ella is the only one for me, and she belongs at Cairn Castle with what's left of her family. It's her castle every bit as much as it is ours. And I love her and wouldna give her up for anything."

"Aye, I'll tell him you want to hunt with him if you wish," Quinn said.

"Aye. And leave the woman behind." Dashiell didn't want to hear any more of her biting words.

Quinn laughed. "That is easier said than done." Then Quinn rode back to the castle with two of their men and Paden.

Fallon shook his head. "I thought that woman was gone for good."

"So did I."

"Do you think she will come with her da on the hunt?"

"I hope no'." Dashiell could imagine her raging on about him marrying her instead of the woman of the forest, how she was evil, and anything else she could throw out there.

ELLA, Paige, and Flora were in the herb garden gathering lavender and sage when they heard a commotion in the inner bailey.

"Oh, nay," Paige said, glancing that way.

"What?" Ella looked in the direction Paige was watching, and her heart sank to see Lynette with a man and an entourage. She suspected the man was Lynette's da.

"Och, nay, no' that woman." But then Flora smiled. "You can speak now and tell her off for lying when she said you had hurt her, Ella. She wouldna even let Mai look at her supposed injury. When we learned you couldna speak, we knew she hadna been telling the truth."

"What is she doing here?" Ella assumed they would try to convince Dashiell to marry her instead of Ella.

Flora studied Lynette's haughty look. "Well, she has her da with her, so I suspect he's going to create problems with Dashiell now over not marrying her."

"Who is the most insufferable? Her or her da?" Paige asked.

"I wouldna be surprised if Lynette is the one who is, and she rules her da," Ella said.

Quinn rode into the inner bailey with Paden and two other men and spoke to Lynette's da. "Dashiell is hunting for a wild boar with some of our men. He asks that you join him."

Lynette's da glanced at her. "Aye, let's go."

"He just wants to speak with your da," Quinn said.

Ella almost laughed at seeing Lynette's mutinous expression. She was probably really miffed that Dashiell didn't want to see her and only invited her da on the hunt.

"I. Am. Going." Lynette scowled at Quinn.

Lynette was definitely in charge. Then she glanced in the ladies' direction, saw Ella and her jaw dropped. Her eyes narrowed. "You! She's the one who injured me! Da, do something about her!"

Her da asked Quinn, "Is this true?"

"Nay. Lady Lynette suffered no injuries. Lady Ella did naught to her," Quinn said.

"You are saying my daughter lied?" Her da sounded like he couldn't believe Quinn would say that and was ready to defend her honor.

"That woman has twisted my words, and she's the devil," Lynette said, her tone of voice haughty. "She's naught but a wild woman living in the forest."

"Lady Margery to you," Ella said.

"Lady Margery. Your da was Coinneach Gunn?" Laird Cameron asked.

"Aye, before MacAfee and his men murdered my people," Ella said.

Lynette's da looked at his daughter. "I'm joining Dashiell on the hunt. You will stay *here*."

"What? Nay. I want a word with Dashiell also."

"You will stay here. Take me to see the chief," Lynette's da said to Quinn.

"Aye, my pleasure." Appearing relieved that Cameron told her to stay behind, Quinn led her da through the gates while Lynette looked slightly panicked.

Ella noticed she wasn't so sharp-tongued when she had no man to boss around. And she couldn't boss Dashiell's staff around. Ella wouldn't let her.

"Join us if you want," Ella said, trying not to show she held grudges. The woman had to feel uncomfortable because Ella was sure no one liked her. Not when she had lied about Ella. Who else would she lie about to further her interests?

Lynette finally dismounted from her horse with the help of one of the stable hands. The lad took her horse with him to feed and water him. "My da will wage war on Dashiell if he doesna wed me. It will be an insult to our clan. Dashiell canna afford for that to occur."

Ella frowned. "I wouldna wish that to happen. Too many good people die over lost causes."

"What do you mean?"

"You willna win. Dashiell would be prepared, unlike my people, who let the snake into our castle and were taken by surprise." Of course, she was referring to MacAfee.

Lynette turned her chin up. "You are calling me a snake now?"

"MacAfee."

"Oh." Lynette put her hands on her hips. "You lied about not being able to speak. You put on an act to gain sympathy from Dashiell so that he would feel kindly toward you. And then so you could get your hooks into him, you suddenly can speak like you've never had trouble with it in the past."

"You had nightmares about the castle? About me? About my people? You saw what MacAfee did to them?" Ella didn't wait for her to answer because Lynette's mouth hung agape, and she hesitated to speak.

"Of course, and you know it."

"If you had experienced the actual trauma that day that I had— lost all your kin but a couple, fled from the only home you had ever known while protecting your younger brother and cousin, fearing you would all die, how do you think you would have reacted?"

Fainted dead away, Ella assumed. She couldn't envision Lynette surviving the way Ella and her kin had with Mina's help.

"You...you are a witch!"

"I didna make you dream anything if that is what you believe," Ella said.

"Oh, certes you did," Lynette said.

Ella was so glad that Dashiell wasn't marrying Lynette. Woe to the man who ended up marrying her.

Mina hurried to join them and said, "Ella, we need your help with another woman who is giving birth."

"Aye, of course." Ella was glad to end the conversation with Lynette.

"I'll help," Paige said.

Flora quickly agreed and hurried off with them, none of them wanting to deal with Lynette any further.

Mina told Lynette, "If you dinna want any more nightmares, you'll stay far away from here." She smiled and turned to join the others and saw Ella watching her.

She shrugged at Ella, and Ella smiled. She loved Mina, and she was certain she meant what she said.

Leaving Lynette alone in the inner bailey while everyone was working and paying no attention to her had to have been about the worst thing that had ever happened to her, but the way she treated everyone so poorly, she deserved it.

20

Attempting to smooth things over with Laird Cameron—Dashiell sure didn't need to start hostilities with their clan over not marrying Lynette—he explained about Ella, Lady Margery, and what had befallen her family and hoped he would sympathize with her cause.

Appearing saddened to hear the news, Laird Cameron rubbed his gray beard. "I didna know about any of that until she told me in the inner bailey. Her da was a good man. Her mother was always so gracious. My condolences to her and her family. Does this mean that you feel sorry for her? Do you feel you owe it to her to marry her because you live in the castle that was her family's?"

"Nay, she is the one I love, no other. I'm sure you can understand that." Though not all marriages resulted in a love match, Dashiell knew Laird Cameron's marriage had been.

"Aye, I do. I love my daughter, but I understand how you feel. I would be the same way if I were in your place."

Dashiell wondered if he shouldn't have had Lynette and her da come to speak with him in the forest, though her da was much more reasonable to talk to. But Dashiell realized she might cause trouble for Ella if she ran into her at the castle. He couldn't imagine the woman would hold her tongue around Ella. She hadn't around anyone before.

The hounds barked that they'd located their prey, and Cameron and Dashiell joined the hunt until they took down the wild boar. Then they returned to the castle while others prepared the boar for transport.

Dashiell planned to have Cameron, Lynette, and Cameron's men stay for the feast and hoped that would help smooth things between them. He didn't need to have Cameron on his bad side, but he wasn't about to marry his daughter. He just hoped she would mind her tongue this time at the meal.

When they arrived back at the castle, Dashiell saw Amelda speaking with a perturbed-looking Lynette. Her arms were folded across her waist, and her face was an angry frown as she peered down at Amelda.

"You should see the secret garden."

"Why do you have a guard standing with you?" Lynette asked.

"Because Laird MacAfee wants us dead and so we have to have guards at all times," Amelda said.

Dashiell dismounted from his horse and said, "Lady Lynette." Then he smiled at Amelda. "Where is Ella?"

"A lady is having a bairn, and she's helping."

"We are having a feast. Go tell Ella and the other women so they know we'll be eating if they can join us."

"Aye." Amelda ran off to the stairs.

He hoped Lynette hadn't said mean things to Amelda. He motioned to Cameron to come with him, and they would enjoy some ale with Fallon and Quinn.

"Did you straighten him out?" Lynette asked her da.

Her da looked at her like he was a little embarrassed. Cameron should have straightened *her* out a long time ago.

They went to the great hall to have their ale while the cooks roasted the boar. Lynette stayed with the men, unfortunately. Her da didn't answer her as far as her question to him about changing Dashiell's mind about marrying her.

"What are you going to do about MacAfee?" Cameron asked Dashiell instead.

"I've sent a missive to the king about his despicable actions and their reasons. I'm hoping he will put him on trial." Dashiell took another swig of his ale.

"He would require witnesses. Would Lady Margery speak to the king about it? Would he even believe her?"

Because she was a woman?

"Aye, we're trying to locate the blacksmith who worked for Gunn. Mayhap if the king didna believe a young woman's word, he might realize the blacksmith knew what had happened. However, he wasna inside the castle at the time. But one of MacAfee's men nearly killed him, and Ella came to his aid and helped save Tannon's life."

"Ella did?" Cameron glanced at Lynette with a warning look. Ella wasn't one to be trifled with.

"I'm sure she made it all up." Lynette looked grumpy, probably irritated that Dashiell wanted Ella for his wife when no one was interested in marrying her.

Cameron said, "Hold your tongue, Lynette."

Then Amelda came running into the great hall with her guard and smiled at Dashiell. He loved Amelda as if she were his daughter, just as she treated Ella as her mother. "What news have you?" he asked Amelda.

"Ella said the maid had a baby boy and that Ella would be right down. The midwife and Mai will stay with her. But Mina and the other ladies will be down shortly." Then she waved goodbye, turned, and dashed off for the stairs. Her guard glanced at Dashiell, and he wanted to laugh.

Amelda had enough energy for three of her. Her guard, Bac, raced after her.

"I wish to have an alliance with you," Cameron said.

"Nay, da, unless he agrees to wed me," Lynette said.

"'Tis no' your place to suggest such a thing," Cameron said, looking sternly at her.

Lynette sat back in her chair and stared at her da. He had probably never said no to her in all her life, but it was about time he did.

Ella joined Dashiell at the table, and he leaned over and kissed her. He wanted everyone to know what she meant to him.

After the meal and agreeing to the terms of an alliance, Cameron bid Dashiell farewell and wished Ella and him the best.

Lynette wouldn't even look at them as she and Cameron exited the gates with their entourage.

"What are you going to do now?" Dashiell asked Ella, glad to have an alliance with Cameron and gladder still that he wasn't marrying Lynette.

"I need to speak with Mina and Mai. They need some more healing herbs."

"All right. I need to speak with Quinn about issues in the clan. I'll see you in a little while."

She hugged and kissed him, then headed for the stairs to the upper floors where the ladies were.

An hour later, Paden hurried to speak with Dashiell in the inner bailey while he was speaking to his cousin.

"My laird! My laird! Lady Ella went into the forest with two maids to gather healing herbs that Mina and Mai needed, and I was with them, but we became separated. I heard men approaching, and I dinna ken where the lasses went."

Where was their guard force?

"Tell Quinn to gather more of my men and send them out to the forest, Paden."

"Aye." Paden raced off.

Dashiell and Fallon hurried to get their horses from the stable, his men quickly joining them. "Ella was always supposed to have a guard force, and I didna approve of her going out to the forest anyway."

They mounted their horses and headed out. He feared that Lennox or Michael had come for Ella.

"Do you think Lennox is coming for her?" Quinn asked, his voice filled with concern as he caught up to them.

"Mayhap 'tis naught at all. But what if Michael returned and told him that I wouldna release Ella to his da, and Lennox came with a force to try and convince me that it was in my best interest to turn her and her kin over to him?" Dashiell asked.

"Aye, that is what I fear as well."

"You stay with me. Fallon, take five men east. I want another five to head west. The rest of us will head north." Dashiell couldn't help how his heart was beating so fast.

He feared if Lennox was there, he would grab her, turn around, and head back to his castle fortification.

They hadn't found any signs of her or anyone else, just robins flitting into the undergrowth, the call of birds twittering or cawing a warning that strangers were approaching. And then he saw a deer. The deer didn't seem afraid of him, as if it knew he wasn't there to hunt it.

He stopped and motioned for the rest of his men who rode with him to halt. They watched the deer, and then she walked on a trail to the east. Was she going toward Ella? He prayed it was so.

"Quinn, you're with me. The rest of you keep heading north," Dashiell said.

Dashiell and Quinn followed the deer. She soon disappeared into the forest, and they couldn't find any sign of her. But then a woman screamed. Dashiell and Quinn galloped in her direction. He heard others coming in that direction, but were they his men or others?

"That was Flora's scream," Quinn warned.

God's knees. Then they heard another scream but in another direction.

"Let me go!"

That wasn't Ella's voice either.

"Paige," Quinn said.

"We separate," Dashiell said, wanting to reach all three women simultaneously, but they had separated. Where was Ella?

He saw four men, not his own, and one of them was attempting to drag Paige onto his saddle. Then to Dashiell's shock, he saw Ella emerge out of the underbrush, swinging her sword at the mounted man holding Paige's arm. She cut his leg before another man jumped off his horse to engage her in battle.

"No!" Dashiell rode up to engage the man threatening Ella.

Paige had her dirk out but had scurried back into the bracken.

Ella dropped back so Dashiell could fully engage the man she had struck at. But then, more of Dashiell's men arrived and fought the other men.

He heard more shouting off to the east, where Quinn had gone after Flora. But those he had sent in that direction were also fighting the men, so Quinn wasn't alone.

"Ruadh was with us. He heard a noise and went to check it out," Ella warned.

Once the men they were fighting were dead, they searched for Ruadh.

"Over here!" Fallon called out. "Hell, man. You were supposed to be taking care of Ella."

Dashiell pulled Ella onto his saddle and rode to where Fallon was.

Ruadh had a huge lump on his head and a cut to his arm. He was sitting on the ground, and when he tried to stand, he rocked unsteadily on his feet. His sword was red with blood. Two of the brigands who had tried to grab the women were lying dead by a rock.

Before Dashiell could dismount, Ella alighted on the ground, tore fabric from her chemise, and wrapped the sword cut on his arm.

"Sorry, my lady." Ruadh looked dispirited that he had failed at his mission.

"We should have taken a greater force," she said. "You did all you could."

Dashiell said, "Quinn, take Paige back to the castle. Fallon, you will take Flora. A couple of you can come with us. Bring Ruadh with you. The rest of you search for anyone else in the forest. Did anyone encounter Michael, or mayhap his da, Lennox?"

"Nay," everyone said or shook their heads.

"If you see them, bring them to the castle alive." Usually, Dashiell would have continued searching with his men, but he could still feel the effect of his sword injury. He realized fighting in combat further for him wasn't a viable option.

Then he, Quinn, and Ruadh rode back to the castle, flanked by two of his men.

"Are you all right?" Dashiell asked Ella.

"Aye, we left our baskets of herbs behind."

"They are no' half as important as you ladies," Dashiell said, unable to curb the annoyance in his voice. "You canna be in the woods alone without a proper guard force. And for now—until we are wed—we still have the issue of your uncle."

"With the passage of time, I thought my uncle had assumed he had lost the chance to take me to his castle. And we really need those herbs."

"Unless the men are no' his, I would say he has been planning this for some time. Mayhap they are MacAfee's men though."

"Are you all right?" Ella asked, looking worried.

Dashiell didn't want to tell her the truth about how he was feeling. But he felt he owed it to her. "I must admit my wound is bothering me."

She glanced back at him, reached over her shoulder, and pressed her hand against his head. At once, the ache in his chest and head faded away. She was a Godsend.

"I canna lose you, lass."

She kissed his cheek. "I am here for you."

"As am I here for you, always."

"Can we marry?" she asked.

"Aye, we will."

"Now?"

He looked into her pretty green eyes and smiled. He was surprised but elated. "Aye. We can have a wedding at the castle with just our clan, and then we will have the wedding in front of the guests we've invited."

She smiled at him. "Aye, that will be great."

He agreed. Once he married her, he felt her uncle would have no recourse to claim her as his ward. MacAfee wouldn't either. Dashiell hoped he could also ensure that Finnegan and Amelda stayed with them. They should remain with Ella and continue to be part of her life.

As soon as they arrived at the bailey, Dashiell told Quinn, "Announce that Ella and I are marrying within the hour in the great hall. Have Mai attend to Ruadh."

Quinn smiled. "Aye."

Dashiell handed Ella down to one of his men, and he set her on the ground. Then Dashiell dismounted, and a groom hurried to take his horse.

Ella said, "The ladies and I are off to the ladies' chamber to get ready."

Before she could rush off with Flora and Paige, Dashiell took Ella in his arms and kissed her soundly. "You are the light of my life."

"You are that for me and more," Ella said, hugging and kissing him back.

He couldn't wait to start a family with her.

ELLA WAS glad that Dashiell was going to marry her now. Hopefully, that would end any chance of her uncle getting hold of her. But she still worried about her brother and Amelda. Surprisingly, Mina seemed to be doing much better since she'd had a better place to sleep in the dry, comfortable keep at night.

Ella burst into her bedchamber where Mina was napping, and Ella was sorry she had woken her. "I'm sorry, Mina."

"You are marrying him now." Mina climbed off her trundle bed. She smiled. "I saw a dream of it. This is why I told you no' to tarry while working on your gown."

"You dreamed that I would marry him now and no' later?" The gown was the same one that Ella had worked on in the hut for so long, not believing she would be wearing it to her own wedding. She was glad she would wear it for two wedding ceremonies when she thought no one would wed her here because of her age and because she hadn't been able to speak.

"Aye, now and later."

Ella was glad she had finished her gown. It wasn't that she had been putting it off, but she'd been so busy working as a healer. "I need to tell Amelda and Finnegan also."

"I'll get Paden to do it," Paige said.

"Amelda was in the garden. She loves to work there the most," Ella said. "She loves the outdoors."

"Aye," Mina said.

"Finnegan is working with the blacksmith," Paige said. "I'll send word to him."

Then Paige quickly left the bedchamber.

Flora called on another maid to help her dress Ella in her gown. Then Flora helped Mina dress in the gown Ella and Amelda had helped her finish. Paige returned with Amelda in hand and started to remove her léine and change it out for her new gown.

"You fought one of Lennox Gunn's men?" Mina asked Ella.

"Oh, she was verra braw," Paige said. "She pulled out her sword and began fighting one of the brigands."

"We heard Flora scream. Paige and I dropped our baskets and ran in her direction," Ella said.

"But that's when the men came after us," Paige said. "'Twas frightening."

"Aye," Flora said. "Quinn came and rescued me, and soon more of our kinsmen were there, fighting the men. There were only three, but we had seven warriors on our side."

"Why are you marrying now instead of later?" Amelda asked.

"So that Uncle Lennox canna take me with him," Ella said but then realized saying so might worry Amelda since her uncle might want to take her next. Amelda wished she had never mentioned to Michael that Amelda was her cousin, which meant his cousin also.

"Do I need to marry too?" Amelda asked, very seriously.

Ella hugged her young cousin. She was only five!

"Nay, much later. Dinna worry." But Ella was anxious about it if Lennox made an issue of it. She was also nervous about the wedding. She wanted to marry Dashiell more than anything but was still excited, and butterflies had taken flight in her stomach.

Mina took hold of Ella's hands. "You can do this. You were meant to. I told you. You were meant to be the lady of the manor."

Ella couldn't believe that what Mina had said would really come to pass. "Aye, that's what you said."

"You didna believe me."

Ella smiled. "I should have known better."

"I wonder what Lady Yvaine will say about the abrupt wedding," Flora mentioned. "Though she is not his advisor, he often seeks her advice."

"Aye."

Someone knocked at Ella's chamber door. "'Tis me, Paden."

Paige opened it.

Paden said, "The MacTavish of Glen Affric is ready for Lady Ella in the great hall."

"Let us go and finish this," Mina said, "before I get any older."

Ella smiled. She would probably outlive them all. Then she took Mina's hand and Amelda's and they left the chamber as Paden hurried off, most likely to tell Dashiell they were on their way. The maids quickly hurried after them.

The great hall was filled with clansmen waiting for her appearance. Finnegan quickly greeted her, looking older than his ten years. He was dressed in a shirt, plaid, and boots, his hair combed back. Proudly, he took Ella's arm. His bright blue eyes and mouth smiled. He looked delighted that he would walk his older sister down the aisle to marry the laird.

Ella saw Ruadh wearing a bandage over his arm, and he smiled at her. She smiled back, glad he could stand now, though two men were standing beside him, looking ready to take care of him if he faltered.

Dashiell was smiling broadly, and so was everyone else in the clan. With everyone feeling such great cheer, Ella's nervousness faded.

21

Bac rushed into the great hall where Dashiell and Ella were conducting the simple marriage ceremony, looking concerned, his brow furrowed. Dashiell knew there had to be trouble, or his guard wouldn't interrupt the ceremony.

"Beg pardon for interrupting this most sacred of ceremonies, but Lennox Gunn has arrived at the castle gates with thirty-one men, including his son, Michael. He insists on seeing you."

Irritated that Lennox would interrupt this most special occasion but trying not to show annoyance, Dashiell looked down at Ella. "What say you?"

"We marry, and then he can come to wish us well, but the rest of his men must stay beyond the gates."

"And Michael?"

"He and his father can both wish us well."

"Do as the lady says, Bac," Dashiell said.

"Aye." Bac hurried off.

Then Dashiell and Ella vowed to marry each other, and he kissed Ella soundly as she wrapped her arms around his shoulders and kissed him like she was ready to take this to the bedchamber. But first, the feast.

Everyone clapped and cheered. Then, a much-relieved Dashiell and his wife were ready to celebrate their wedding. He was holding her hand, not wanting to let go ever.

She smiled at him. "I'm so happy."

"Aye, as am I. I will have Lennox sit on the other side of me and Michael on the other side of him. My aunt will sit on your other side," Dashiell said.

"That will be good."

Everyone was getting ready to take their seats, eagerly waiting for Dashiell and Ella to sit down first when Ruadh and three other guards arrived at the great hall. Quinn welcomed them and showed Lennox and Michael where they would be seated.

Michael glanced at Ella, clearly wanting to sit beside her and hoping she would allow him to, but Dashiell remained firm in his decision. Fallon then made a toast to the newly married couple, and everyone cheered except for Lennox and Michael.

They looked shocked, their mouths agape and their eyes wide as they stared at Dashiell and Ella. Dashiell was confident that this would end Lennox's attempts to claim Ella as his ward.

Wild boar and brown bread were served, and finally, Lennox said, "You canna have married her. She's my ward, and I have every right to marry her to someone of *my* choosing. My son already came to see you about that."

"We are married."

"But the marriage has not been consummated."

Dashiell smiled. "Aye, but it will be."

"Amelda will be my ward. So will Finnegan."

"Nay. The family stays together. I ken what you did with the revolt you'd incited against Ella's da, your brother. Did you ken that MacAfee murdered the rest of her kin?" Dashiell took a bite of his boar. He really wondered if they had plotted together since the massacre had occurred only a couple of days after Lennox had been banished from the castle.

Lennox drank some more of his ale and shrugged. "I ken MacAfee. I believed my brother left with the rest of our kin, and Ella had been left behind somehow."

Dashiell shook his head. Coinneach's brother was a liar. "Did you think to give Ella to MacAfee to wed if you had made her your ward?"

"What I plan to do with her is not your concern."

"After MacAfee murdered her kin because her da said no to him marrying Ella—"

"Lady Margaret," Lennox corrected.

"Ella," Dashiell said. "You planned to marry her off to the brigand?"

Lennox ate some of his boar and didn't deny it. So, he was the one Lennox wanted to marry her off to had he taken her back to his castle in the north. Dashiell was now convinced they had conspired together in the massacre of her family.

This would have been Lennox's way of getting back at Coinneach for being the clan chief instead of him. It was a strategy for MacAfee to ultimately gain what he desired—Ella. Dashiell refused to allow Lennox or his son to stay at the castle—not tonight or any other night. He was determined to make MacAfee pay for what he had done to Ella's family.

"I HAD the strangest dream last night, Ella," Yvaine told her. "I dreamt of you marrying my nephew when it wasna even planned."

"Mayhap you had a premonition," Ella told her, though she continued listening to what Dashiell told Lennox. She wanted to say something about her uncle taking her brother and cousin with him, but Dashiell had said they wouldn't.

Yvaine cast her a small smile. "I told my nephew that you are a temptress."

"Really?"

"Aye. He could think of naught else after learning about a mysterious being in the forest. Did you know that some say you turn into an owl at night?"

Ella smiled. "I willna this eve as I will be with the MacTavish."

"Aye. We have heard you run with the wolves."

"But I protect the deer in the forest. The wolves would eat them."

"Certes. Were you no' afraid that my nephew would find you and imprison you for stealing from his lands and living in his forest when 'tis forbidden?"

"Nay, these are my lands too. My forest also. I have never left them, despite MacAfee murdering my people."

Yvaine buttered some more bread and inclined her head. "Do you dance?"

"I...I learned when I was younger. Mina taught me the steps of some of our dances so that I would recall what I had forgotten. 'Twas no' often that we had time for such frivolity."

Yvaine smiled at that comment. "I was saying the same to my nephew. He was always so serious about life until he met you, and then everything changed for him."

Ella hoped that was a good thing.

"You might be a temptress, but you have been good for him. Even suffering from a life-threatening wound that he had received, he healed in no time. I've never seen him so lighthearted or so interested in anything. I'm happy to welcome you to the family, to our clan."

"That means a lot to me," Ella said, genuinely meaning it.

"I ken it does. Family means everything. I'm sorry about what MacAfee did to your family. And I'm sorry that Lady Lynette told an untruth about what had happened between you in the woods."

"She lied."

"Aye. She wouldna have been a good match for my nephew.

Lady Lantana would have been, but you had already stolen my nephew's heart. It worked out in the end."

Ella would have preferred if Yvaine had said that Lantana wouldn't have made a good match.

"Did you like Lady Lantana?" Ella assumed Yvaine had, or she wouldn't have said what she did.

Yvaine waved her hand dismissively. "She would have been a satisfactory wife, but you? You have won no' only my nephew's heart but that of our people. Lady Lantana was still mostly unknown to everyone. You have survived in the woods for years."

Ella nodded.

"You've proven how much you can help others here with their sickness, injuries, childbirth, and other chores. You're not afraid to work hard to live. Lady Lantana has always lived at the king's castle. She has been given everything in life. Aye, she has the proper mannerisms, the right words to say, the beauty, like you have, only a different kind of beauty, but in the end, you are the one my nephew needed in his life."

Ella hadn't thought of it that way, but she agreed.

"I like Lady Lantana, and she would have made him a proper wife, but now you would make him the perfect wife. Though I suspect he willna ever be able to bring venison to the table."

Ella smiled.

"Do you prefer being called Ella to Margaret?"

"Aye. I had been Margaret longer, but Mina's calling me Ella to protect me from MacAfee had become the name I wish to be known by."

"I dinna blame you. About the key that was found in your hut..."

"To a chest?"

"Dashiell told me about it. Do you ken where the chest is?"

Ella thought for a while. "There's a secret garden behind the herb garden. Did anyone find it?"

"Nay, or I would have heard of it. Can you show me where it is?"

"Aye, on the morrow?"

"Late tomorrow, as I am sure my nephew willna let you leave the marital bed until late."

Ella smiled and blushed. She was excited about being with him tonight but also apprehensive.

"You will do well together," Yvaine said.

Mina had already told Ella what to expect in the marriage bed since Mina had been married and lost her husband when she was young but had never remarried.

"Do you remember what was in the box?"

"My mother's journal, mayhap. She used to sit in the garden and write in it. I'm no' sure what else would be in the chest."

The hearty meal had ended, and the clan members settled into their chairs, content with full bellies and warm spirits. As the last few mouthfuls were savored, a group of clansmen emerged, carrying musical instruments. A shawm, lute, and psaltry were brought in and the music began.

The psaltry was gently plucked as the shawm and lute blew out merry tunes, filling the hall with lively energy. The tables were quickly cleared and pushed towards the outer walls, creating a wide-open space in the center of the room. The fire crackled and danced in the background, adding to the ambiance.

The clansmen eagerly made their way to the center, and the joy it brought was evident on their faces. As the first notes of the music began to fill the room, the clansmen joined hands and started to dance, their feet tapping and bodies moving in perfect harmony.

It was a beautiful sight, this celebration of music and dance, and the room was soon filled with laughter and merriment. The worries of the outside world seemed to fade away in that moment as the clansmen lost themselves and embraced the joy of being alive.

Ella barely thought of her uncle and cousin, but she was glad

Dashiell was truly pleased to enjoy the festivities. They danced, forgetting everything but the music, the fire, and the company of their fellow clansmen. For a brief time, they were free from the burdens of life, and nothing else mattered but the here and now.

Ella couldn't help but feel a rush of joy as she and Dashiell finally took a break and drank some ale while watching the clansmen and women dancing to the lively music. It was a rare sight to see, as the harsh realities of life often left little room for celebration. Yet here they were, her husband Dashiell and his and her family, all gathered to commemorate their union.

As she swayed to the beat, her eyes met Dashiell's, and she couldn't help but smile. He was a good, strong, kind man, and she was grateful to have him by her side.

Even Mina began dancing with an older gentleman. Dashiell squeezed Ella's hand, "Joffrey oversees the breeding of our livestock. He is much taken with Mina."

"I wondered about the bloom in her cheeks whenever she was near him and caught her smiling shyly at him."

"Aye. He lost his wife years ago and never showed any interest in another lass. It appears he feels something for her."

Ella smiled. "I'm so glad for her. She looks much better now that she has a comfortable bed and isna working herself to the bone." Ella looked around at the faces of her loved ones, surrounded by music and laughter. She knew that they were in this together. That thought warmed her heart more than any fire could.

At that moment, Ella felt like she was home—not just in the physical sense but also in the emotional sense. This was where she always belonged—just like Mina had repeatedly told her—with her family and her clan, dancing and celebrating the love that bound them together.

Michael stood by, stony-faced, and Lennox wore a disgruntled expression, his arms folded across his chest.

Ruadh and two other guards were watching them. They'd been

disarmed, but they still were making sure they didn't cause any trouble for Ella and her family.

She was torn between feeling like she wanted them just to leave so she didn't have to see or think of them—she couldn't forgive her uncle for his men killing three of their guards as he tried to go after her da to kill him and wanting them to see how happy she was and that he didn't get his way.

She was certain he hated her for cutting him twice.

Ale flowed freely, and everyone was in good spirits until late that night when Mina and Amelda retired to their chamber, two guards posted as usual.

Finnegan was also being guarded. No one wanted Lennox to grab the boy and take off with him.

"Were you no' afraid that MacAfee and the men who laid siege to your castle would come looking for you in the woods?" Dashiell asked Ella as they settled at the head table to take a break from dancing.

He couldn't imagine her, her kin, and Mina living all those years in the forest, trying to stay hidden from the brigands.

He loved Ella and was so glad he had taken her home to her castle where he could keep her safe. But he wanted to know how they had lived that long there without getting caught. He wanted to know if someone living among his people had been tipping off MacAfee that Ella had been living in the forest all that time.

"Aye. Mina wouldna let us out of the hut for several weeks, worried about MacAfee and his men searching for me. She had been hunting for mushrooms and berries when she heard MacAfee speaking to some of his men. She kept hidden and listened, saying that MacAfee swore I had escaped the castle with my brother."

Dashiel wished he had been there to deal with the men then.

"He didna mention my baby cousin. He said naught about the blacksmith, either. I doubt he would have been trying to determine who all had died. He wouldna have known all our people. They never said anything about Mina either, probably for the same reason. But he would have known my brother and was looking for me."

"He willna harm you again." Dashiel would ensure it.

"It took forever before the number of people combing the woods for me finally dropped off. When I finally went to the village to barter for us, I saw some of MacAfee's men looking at wares and hurried back to the forest. I stayed close to the hut, except for gathering wood and water. Eventually, we only saw anyone from the castle when the men hunted for food."

"But you didna try to protect the deer in the forest then," Dashiell suspected.

"Nay. They made themselves scarce, and so did I."

"About the dreaming..."

Ella smiled a little.

"Did you make us dream of you?"

"Nay. I canna do such a thing."

"Mina then?"

"She isna a witch."

"Nay, a very good healer. Did she then make us dream? And then make us sleep the one night so thoroughly that you and your brother could slip out of the castle to return to the forest?"

"Aye. She wasna doing well. We had to take care of Amelda also. She couldna have fended for herself."

"When MacAfee wanted to barter his castle for my land up north, he appeared haggard. So did his men. Also Lynette said she had a most terrifying nightmare when she was here."

"Aye."

"Did Mina make them dream?"

"Of their own making. I didna know about it for a very long time, but she finally explained that's why MacAfee bartered his castle for your land. But it took years of her giving them their just rewards for slaughtering my people. She made them dream of what they had done and they finally couldna live with it."

"And Lynette?" Her nightmare fit in with what had happened to MacAfee and his men.

"She had lied to you that I had hurt her. I thought you had brought her to see me so I would have a female friend my age. I wanted to take her to the meadow and show her the loch and the wildflowers. She climbed off her horse, and I thought she would smell the flowers. But instead, she hit me in the shoulder with her fist."

Lynette was evil. He hadn't realized she was until he knew Ella couldn't speak.

"She tried to slap my face, but I grabbed her arm and threw her on her bum. I was much stronger than her because of all the work I do. Anyway, then she started to scream that I was trying to kill her, and I ran off. So I told Mina. I guess she helped her see what I'd experienced through a nightmare. It served her and MacAfee and his men right."

"I agree, lass. I love you."

She lifted her head and offered her mouth to him for a kiss. He quickly obliged. "I love you too."

"Are you going to tell everyone we're retiring for the night?" she asked.

"Nay. They'll celebrate our wedding until they're ready to retire. They'll see us leave and know just what we have in mind to do."

She blushed beautifully.

Dashiell finally pulled Ella into his arms and asked, "Are you ready to retire to bed?"

Her cheeks heated. She was ready, yet she wasn't.

22

Dashiell whispered to Ella as their people celebrated, "We dinna have to do anything but sleep together on our first night."

She wanted to do everything with him. She was his wife. She was curious. She wanted to consummate the marriage so Lennox had no chance to snatch her away.

"I'm ready."

He smiled. "Good." Then he raised a tankard of ale to his clan and said, "Enjoy the eve."

Everyone cheered them.

Yvaine smiled at Ella in a way that said she was happy she had married her nephew. Ella was glad because she had been a little worried that Yvaine had thought Lady Lantana might have been more suitable despite saying she wouldn't have been.

Ella and Dashiell left and went up to his chamber, a couple of guards following them. She was glad they remained diligent but hoped they wouldn't hear them when they made love.

Then they walked into the bedchamber, and Dashiell shut the door. He pulled her into his arms and began to kiss her. She loved the way his warm and inviting mouth felt on hers, and she loved kissing him just as thoroughly. Her hands were at his waist, but then he unfastened her belt. Then he was running his fingers through her hair.

She ran her hands over his hair, taking his cue. She'd never made love to anyone before, and she wanted to do this right. Before she knew it, he was out of his clothes. She looked at his beautiful body for a moment, so muscled, toned, amazing. He was smiling at her figure, and she felt he was just as much in awe of how she looked as she was of him.

"You are beautiful," he said, kissing her cheek.

"So are you." She hugged him, and then he lifted her in his arms and carried her to the bed. When he pulled aside the covers, they found purple, sweet violet petals all over the bed.

She chuckled. "Mina did that. Or had someone do it."

"I had some of my men collect the flowers," Dashiell admitted. "And they fetched the healing herbs you ladies had gathered."

"Oh good." She was amused and loved him for it. Though thinking of how the men had brought the flowers to their wedding bed—

"Because of Lennox's men camped beyond the castle walls."

"Ahh, now I see."

"The lasses scattered the petals on the bed."

She smiled. He was beside her, not thrusting inside her like she thought he would be. No, he was gently kissing her, licking her lips, unassuming yet arousing. Her breasts felt fuller, heavy, tingling with anticipation.

Her heart beating wilder, she felt the place between her legs was wet with expectation. His fingers combed through her hair before sliding down to her breast, and he fondled her most exquisitely. Her nipples quickly protruded with the contact, reaching out for more of his touch. This was heavenly. She ran her fingers through his hair, and he kissed her again.

Only this time, he pressed his tongue for entrance. Even though she'd never kissed anyone in such a manner, it felt right, natural, and she quickly opened to him but slid her tongue around his, and he smiled a little.

She loved when she could make him smile. Then she captured his tongue and sucked. He groaned. She quickly released his tongue, but he did the same thing to her, and she realized just how erotic that was. She moaned with pleasure.

Then he pressed his warm mouth against her throat with gentle kisses all the way down to her breast. Mina never told her that her husband had done all these moves with her. In truth, Mina had said 'twas mostly kissing and then thrusting. But this was so much more, which delighted Ella.

He kissed her breast and then licked her nipple, had her gasping and then smiling. But then she wanted to do that to him and pushed him onto his back, startling him, his eyes wide. He might have thought she had decided she didn't want to make love with him after all this eve. She wanted to lick his pebbled nipples and give him the same pleasure.

When she did, he moaned, and she sucked on a nipple, and he clenched her hair and groaned. She loved that she could do that to him. He kissed the top of her head while she licked and sucked on his other nipple.

His hand swept down to her breast, and he squeezed gently. He settled her on her back, and he moved his knees between her legs. She spread them further, readying herself for what came next.

Again, she didn't expect him to do what he did—spearing her between her legs with a finger, startling her, making her jump, but then he began to stroke her. At the same time, he was kissing her mouth, and she wrapped her arms around his neck and kissed him back. Her pulse quickened as she gave in to the feelings of joy, building ever higher until she felt a release she'd never experienced before.

Her body shuddered with ecstasy when Dashiell moved

between her legs and pushed into her, and she sucked in her breath, gripping his muscular arms tightly. He held off for a moment before he pushed all the way in. "Are you all right?"

"Aye." She'd felt a pinch of pain, but her body was becoming accustomed to his fullness.

He began to thrust and continued to kiss her. She kissed him back, inserting her tongue between his lips, and he stroked her tongue with his when he suddenly held himself still, then thrust again. She found herself moving her hips toward him until he groaned with deep satisfaction.

He moved off her, kissing her bare shoulder and then her mouth again. But then he left the bed, and she was surprised to see him wash himself with a cloth dipped in a basin of water. Then he took a fresh cloth and cleaned her.

"Do...do we need to save that to prove we did it?" she asked.

He smiled and dried her, leaving the rags on the table. "We have proof." He pulled their covers and furs over them and snuggled with her. "Are you all right?"

She felt languid and happy. "Aye. 'Tis good you married me."

He chuckled. "I feel the same way about you. You're the perfect lass for me."

He sighed, and the way he did it made her think he wanted to change the subject to something that wasn't as pleasant to talk about. "The day that the stream was dammed up, do you know who did that?"

"Aye. Mina saw MacAfee overseeing his men, blocking the stream. She was certain they thought I would try to remove the blockage so the deer could drink there."

"Bastard. I dreamed about the stream being blocked and another time of you crying beside the stream when you put flowers in it."

She sighed. "As a homage to all those we lost. I did it every spring." Then she looked at him. "You dreamed of these things?"

"Aye." He kissed her forehead. "The next time you wish to go, you will have a fully armed escort, and I will be with you. The first time I saw you—"

"I thought you were a friend of MacAfee." She kissed his cheek.

"Nay. MacAfee said he wanted to celebrate the transfer of properties. I suspected something was going on that he was keeping a secret about. He wanted to hunt in my forest."

"For me."

"WE HAVE DELAYED everyone from breaking their fast," Ella said, kissing Dashiell's bare chest that morning.

Her kiss made him tingle all the way to his toes and started his staff to rise. She was enjoying this as much as he was; if he hadn't had a duty to perform, he would have stayed in bed with her forever. If she continued to run her hand over his chest and kiss him like that, he was going to have to take this further.

"They will set something aside for us while they eat and then be off to work." But he knew they needed to join his clan, to show she oversaw the staff now. He reluctantly left the bed and started to dress while she watched him, smiling. "How are you feeling?"

She raised her arms above her head and stretched. "Like I am in love and the luckiest woman alive."

He came over to the bed and kissed her. "'Tis I who is the luckiest man in the world."

She wrapped her arms around him and kissed him deeply. Then he pulled away, and she climbed out of bed while he considered her beautiful body, her perky breasts half hidden in her long red hair. Then she began to get dressed in a léine and brat, ready to start their day.

He placed her shoes on her feet and then finished with his boots.

"What are you going to do about my uncle and cousin?"

"Send them on their way. After what they did to your own da and your kin, he's no' welcome here. Particularly because he might wish to take Amelda and Finnegan with him."

"Good."

"Did my aunt ask you about what the key belonged to that was at your hut?" Dashiell asked.

"Aye. I told her it belonged to a chest that was in a secret garden. Did you find it?"

"Nay. Where is it located?" He ran his hand through her hair.

"At the south part of the herb garden. 'Tis walled in, just a small area where my mother used to sit and write in her journal. It has a little locked garden gate. A hedge conceals the entrance. It makes it appear that it is all just plantings. I have no' thought about it since we fled the keep."

"Do you ken what is in the chest?"

"'Tis my mother's chest. She had it moved there if anything went wrong after my da's brother tried to take the clan over."

"We'll eat first, then look for the secret garden."

"Aye, your aunt wants to come with us."

"She is one of the most curious women I know."

"I asked her if she felt you should have married Lady Lantana instead."

Dashiell was surprised. "Nay, I would never have wed the lady. No' once I had seen you."

"That is just what I wished to hear."

Then she and he were served bread, cheese, and honeyed mead in the great hall. Dashiell saw Quinn and Fallon coming to join them. "Where is Lennox?"

"He and his men left this morn," Quinn said.

"I took a force of men with me and made sure they were truly gone," Fallon said.

"I dinna want Finnegan or Amelda to be outside the castle walls at any time unless they are accompanied by a force that would protect them. Amelda shouldna need to leave. Finnegan will hunt with us when he is a wee bit older." Dashiell had every intention of treating him as one of his kin. The same with Amelda.

"Aye," Fallon said. "What are your plans for the day?"

"This morn..."

Quinn and Fallon both smiled a little.

"Late morning," Dashiell said, "Ella and I are going to find her mother's secret garden, and Lady Yvaine wishes to go with us."

Quinn motioned to Paden, who was waiting near the entrance to the great hall.

The boy came running over to see what Quinn wanted. "Find Lady Yvaine and tell her that our chief, his lady, and I are going to the secret garden."

Dashiell raised a brow.

Paden raced off.

"I wish to see this secret garden that has eluded us since we have been here," Quinn said.

"Like the Nymph of the Forest," Fallon said.

Dashiell smiled and looked down at Ella. "Aye."

"I wasna afraid of you," she said defiantly.

"Nay, you feared for your family. 'Twas understandable."

She sighed. "I was concerned that you might have believed I wished control of the castle and its lands as the rightful heir, which you could not allow."

Dashiell, Quinn, and Fallon laughed.

"And if he had thought so, he would have been right," Fallon said.

Then they heard someone coming and saw Paden and Dashiell's aunt in a rush to get there. Even Christopher soon joined them.

The group headed for the herb garden, and at the back of it, Ella frowned, peering around the vegetation against the wall but not finding any entrance. "The plants have overtaken the entrance in my five years away."

"Send for the master gardener," Dashiell said and was glad Paden was with them as he ran off to fetch him.

After a while, the master gardener hurried to join them and asked where he needed to cut back the vegetation.

"There," Ella said. "The path should be right there."

The master gardener clipped away until they saw an iron gate behind the vines and ferns. Once he had cleared the plants out enough, Ella approached the gate but then frowned and turned to Dashiell. "Do you have the key to the gate? The one I have is to the chest. It willna open the gate."

"Fetch the locksmith, Paden." Dashiell felt he would have half their clansmen here before they reached the chest inside the secret garden.

"Do you need me to stay?" the master gardener asked.

"Aye. The garden probably needs a good cutting back also," Dashiell said, having every intention of making it as beautiful as it had been when Ella's mother had come here to write in her journal.

It took even longer for the locksmith to arrive. Dashiell looked up from examining the lock and smiled to see the locksmith. "Prithee, open this lock for me, my good man."

The locksmith examined the lock and then used a key to unlock all locks of unknown origin. As the lock clicked open, Dashiell smiled.

Dashiell opened the gate, but Fallon said, "Let me go first, in case of snakes."

"Very well, but if you see something like a chest let us ken at once."

Fallon unsheathed his sword and then walked into an over-grown mess of weeds. He turned to the master gardener. "You have your work cut out for you. Come in and chop some of this back so the ladies have a path to walk on."

"Aye." The master gardener strode forth, and while he cut the plants back, Paden hurried to pull them to one side of a growing pile.

Once there was a narrow path, Dashiell took Ella's hand and walked into the garden. Quinn and Yvaine followed them.

Vines covered the stone walls and wrought iron trellises in the garden, letting in enough light for the plants beneath them to grow. Violets bloomed in profusion around a large oak tree, while pansies and violets smiled amongst several flat rocks that seemed to be there for seating.

As everyone explored the garden, Dashiell spied a moss-covered object square in shape that looked out of place. As he approached it, he could see that it was a chest. "Look here, a trunk." Dashiell pulled at the lid, but it was locked. He pulled out the key and unlocked the chest with a click.

Ella bumped heads with Dashiell as they peered inside the chest. She reached in and pulled out a journal.

"This is my mother's." She opened it up and said, "She talks about her garden, the weather, how her husband has been preoccupied with the Crusades and fighting for the King of Scotland and Wales. She worries about her daughter, Margaret, me."

Ella paused, tears welling up in her eyes. "She says MacAfee wishes to wed Margaret, but she doesna like the man." She glanced up from the journal. "'Tis true."

Dashiell couldn't believe they hadn't known about the secret garden before this, but in a way, he was glad that Ella had been with them to show them the location. Particularly because, as she had said, it was her heritage. He wanted her always to feel that way.

He felt her sadness when she was reading her mother's journal, knowing that her mother hadn't been able to see her daughter grow into a woman, marry, and have a family of her own.

The master gardener cleared off a buried stone bench, and

Dashiell guided Ella to sit while she read her mother's journal to them.

He wondered if she preferred reading it in privacy, but she looked up from it and said, "Come, sit with me," to Yvaine.

She was happy to sit beside Ella and patted her lap as if comforting her for being so upset.

In the meantime, the master gardener continued to snip and clip, and Paden soon got some other men to help haul off the plants that the gardener had cut to clean up the secret garden.

Ella continued to read the journal and said, "My mother said she has been ill of late and that MacAfee has come seeking Margaret's hand in marriage again, but Coinneach said no again."

"MacAfee was persistent," Dashiell said.

"Aye. There is much about gardening. Besides managing the staff, her love of gardens takes up much of her time. More ladies talk about who is marrying whom and whose baby is due when and what so and so said that was inappropriate at dinnertime."

Everyone listened quietly.

"Then all about me and how I was dancing so well and helping manage the staff and how much I loved gardening with her and Finnegan and all the mischief he was getting into."

Ella skimmed through the book further, then stopped again. "Earlier, she discussed the account concerning my uncle's revolt. Fifteen men, in addition to Lennox, took part in the fight. She said we were eating dinner when Lennox told my da he was taking over."

Dashiell knew then that it had to be near the end of her mother's journal.

"My mother thought that Lennox believed that when he led the uprising, most of the clan would follow him, but other than the men he'd convinced to do it, everyone else stuck with my da."

"That was a good thing," Dashiell said.

"Aye. She mentioned how proud she was for me cutting Lennox

to protect my da. I didna know that. She said that in two days, MacAfee was visiting. That was the last note she made. She must have secured the journal, and then MacAfee struck." Ella closed the journal, and Yvonne patted her hand resting on top of the journal.

"Is there anything else in the chest?" Fallon asked as he peered over Quinn's shoulder.

"The lady did some sketches of people," Dashiell said as he unrolled a piece of parchment and examined it.

Ella wiped away the tears that had gathered and spilled down her cheeks, and he stopped what he was doing and hugged her.

"This appears to be of Finnegan when he was about five years old." After pulling another from the chest, he smiled. "Ella, you have always been beautiful. This must have been done shortly before your mother died. You look to be around fifteen or so here."

"Aye, thank you."

Dashiell stared at the pictures and planned to have them framed on the wall in their bedchamber.

He pulled out the next drawing, then said, "Perhaps this is your da."

"Aye, that is my da," Ella said, looking it over.

He pulled out more drawings and showed them to her. "Who are these of?"

"My other aunt and uncle. She's the one who had Amelda before MacAfee massacred everyone. My mother didna have a chance to draw the baby."

Dashiell leaned into the chest and found flower seeds, a dagger, and an assortment of gold coins.

He pulled out a letter bound with a ribbon and opened it, then smiled as he read it. "This is a love letter from Coinneach to his beloved Catherine. I should have written letters to you. Wait, what frightened you when I handed you the parchment and the pen to write your name to me?"

"I saw blood on the parchment. My mother's blood. The letter from MacAfee stated he would wed me over my da's dead body. That's what I saw. 'Tis the first time I've seen parchment since then. I couldna remember at the time when you showed it to me. Only that it was covered in blood."

"Have you recalled everything that had happened that fateful day?" he asked.

"Most of what I saw. Though you must remember, I was trying to follow my mother's guidance to get my baby cousin and young brother to safety at once."

"Do you still feel your uncle might have sent MacAfee here to kill your family in an act of revenge for being banished from the castle? Of course, MacAfee had the notion he would force a marriage on you if your people were dead. Then he would take over the castle and properties as well?"

"Aye. And I believe my uncle came here to take me up north to see that I married MacAfee, his last act of revenge on the last of his kin. Who knows what he would do to Finnegan," Ella said.

Finnegan walked into the secret garden and said, "He would have to kill me because when I'm old enough, I will avenge our family." Then he stared at the garden as the master gardener was taming the overgrown tangle of vines and plants. "This is the secret garden."

"Aye."

"I guess we couldna have hidden out here," he said.

"Nay. We would no' have been able to escape if we'd come here once MacAfee and his people took over the castle. And MacAfee might have killed you and Amelda once they found us."

"Aye, Amelda would have cried." Finnegan looked at the drawings his mother had done.

"We wouldna have lasted long without water. We would have managed on the food grown here for a while."

Finnegan eyed the drawing his mother had done of him.

"We'll hang them in a special place," Dashiell promised.

"I was so little," Finnegan said. "Too bad we dinna have one of Amelda."

"We have an artist who can make one of hers and one of us." If she agreed, Dashiell wanted to do that for Ella, him, and Mina.

"That would be lovely." Ella took a deep breath, and he knew she was sad over her family's death again.

He ran his hand over her back. "Tell me if you want to move anything out of our bedchamber and replace it with anything else."

"I'm fine with the tapestry, bed, and everything. All the items still in the keep make me feel I am home," Ella said.

"Aye, me too," Finnegan said. "So many things are just like they were. It's like MacAfee came in, murdered everyone, stayed here, then left, and all that was gone was our kin."

Dashiell thought Ella's uncle would no longer be a problem—at least he hoped not—but he wanted to make sure MacAfee wouldn't be either.

23

As they strolled through the tranquil secret garden, Ella couldn't help but ask Dashiell a pressing question after dinner that night. Ruadh and Christopher were stationed at the gate to protect her, so she felt safe enough to bring it up. The moonlight streaming down and torches lighting their way added to the romantic atmosphere despite the seriousness of their conversation.

"Do you have reason to believe there's a spy among your staff?" she inquired.

"It's possible."

"I...I think it's too much of a coincidence that MacAfee and my uncle suddenly knew I was here," Ella said. "I truly believe someone on your staff is being paid to spy on everyone. And that he...or she learned the men were hunting for a woman in the woods."

"I've had Quinn and Fallon investigating this undercover."

Ella rubbed her forehead. "Why would anyone in your clan be a traitor?"

"For money?"

"Have you hired anyone after you moved into the castle?" she asked. Bhictoria had said Dashiell would but she didn't know who was new and who had always been with Dashiell. "Besides, my brother."

"Aye, we have. That's one of the things we need to discuss with Fallon and Quinn." Dashiell leaned down and kissed her forehead.

She smiled at him.

"You are the center of the mystery. We need to determine when MacAfee was in the woods looking for you and about Michael's arrival here. Maybe we could put our heads together and learn who might be a culprit."

"Your aunt should be in on this. She is very observant."

Dashiell nodded. "Aye, that's a good idea."

Once they finished their stroll, Dashiell asked, "Are you ready to do it now?"

"Aye, if you are." She knew how important it was to find a spy and stop him or her if there was one.

"I willna be able to sleep until we begin this process."

Then they left the garden, and Dashiell told Paden, who was speaking to Ruadh, "Tell Quinn, Fallon, and Lady Yvaine that Ella and I want to meet with them in my solar."

"Aye, my laird." Paden ran off while Dashiell took Ella's hand and headed for the keep.

When they reached the sitting area next to his bed chamber, it wasn't long before Lady Yvaine, Quinn, and Fallon joined them. Paden stood by, waiting to see if he was needed any longer.

"Can you get us some ale, Paden?"

"Aye, my laird." He rushed out of the solar and through the chamber, shutting the door on his way out.

"We may have someone on our staff working for Lennox, Ella's uncle, who had stayed behind when he and his son and the other traitors who were loyal to him were banished from the clan," Dashiell said. "Or mayhap who works for MacAfee."

"Fallon and I have looked into this possibility since we learned that these men were after Ella," Quinn said. "But we haven't discovered anything yet."

"Mayhap, a former clan member who had been with Lennox when he was banished, remained behind and worked in the village so he could be hired on your staff when you took over," Fallon said.

"Nay. I would have recognized him or her if I'd seen them. If one of MacAfee's men had lived in the village once he sold the castle to you, his man would have notified him earlier about the rumors that we lived in the forest, I would think," Ella said.

"I agree," Dashiell said.

"Since MacAfee and his men killed most everyone at the castle when they were here, I believe it's more likely that the person was hired here later to see if I turned up—once you moved into the castle, dinna you think? Mayhap that I had even sought refuge with your people or planned to tell you what he and his men had done to my people."

"Aye," Dashiell said. "We need to learn if anyone who joined us after we moved here has frequently visited the forest or even the village and heard the rumors there."

"We have to be careful about questioning anyone, or the news will spread through the clan," Lady Yvaine said. "You know how rumors fly when any interesting news is shared."

"Aye. We need to know who joined us after we moved in. It's very possible that if he...or she...gets word we're looking into this, the person will vanish from the castle," Dashiell said. "If someone lives among us is working for MacAfee or Lennox, we need to know immediately."

"And eliminate the threat," Fallon said.

"Aye," Dashiell said.

Yvaine leaned over and squeezed Ella's hand. "I have an idea. I will have you meet all the women. Though you have seen quite a few, you havena had time to meet them truly."

"Oh, I like that idea," Ella said.

"It will appear innocent enough. You will oversee the staff and need to know everyone. At the same time, I can see who is new to me on the staff and then we'll have to determine when they joined us. You willna know who is new and who has been with us forever."

"That is an excellent idea." Ella smiled at her, grateful that his aunt seemed delighted to take part in the venture

"I agree. We can do the same with Ella meeting the clansmen," Dashiell said. "I will take her around to meet everyone because 'tis just as important for her to know the males on the staff, whom she will also be in charge of."

"What about the ones who hunt with you?" Ella asked. "If one of the men is new—"

"None," Quinn said. "Everyone who hunts has been with us since they were bairns and grew up in the clan."

"All right, I'm sure it's someone who has joined the clan after you moved here, but here's another possibility," Ella said.

Dashiell let out his breath. "That someone who has been with us all these years has become a traitor and paid or threatened to spy on us."

"Aye," Ella said. "A disagreeable notion, but it should be considered also."

"Aye," Yvaine said.

Everyone else agreed.

"Do we tell your brother and Mina? No' Amelda. She is too young," Lady Yvaine said.

"I believe my brother should know about it," Ella said.

"Aye," Lady Yvaine said.

Ella put her finger to her lips and then raised it. "I dinna want him to question anyone, but just listen to see if he overhears anything. If he doesna know what we suspect, he might be unaware about a traitor in our midst."

"Aye. He's ten, and after having lived in hiding for all these years, I'm sure he will do well as a spy on his own while learning what he needs to as the blacksmith's apprentice," Dashiell said.

"As to Mina, aye, she needs to know at once that someone might be a spy on the staff," Ella said. "I will tell her before we all retire to bed."

"Aye," Dashiell said, hoping it wouldn't take too long. He was ready to join his bonny wife in bed already. "I believe a man would more likely be responsible, but we canna discount the women. My aunt taking Ella to see the women first is the best way to handle this right after we break our fast in the morn."

"Do you think we should have all the women gathered together, as well as the men, when we do this?" his aunt asked. "If we dinna, someone might no' be accounted for, and we would miss them."

"Aye. And we can ask the others if everyone who is supposed to be there is, in case we dinna see that anyone is missing," Dashiell said.

"Some leave early for the village to do their tasks," Quinn said.

"We will make sure no one leaves the grounds; keep the gates locked until Ella has a chance to meet all the women," Dashiell said. "Everyone will be at the great hall for the nooning meal, and we can do the same then with the men. The men willna return to their tasks until Ella has met all of them. Does anyone else have anything to offer?"

Everyone shook their heads.

"Then on the morrow, we'll carry out the plan."

"I'll return as soon as I tell Mina what is going on," Ella said.

DASHIELL KISSED ELLA AS YVAINE, Quinn, and Fallon said their good nights. "Dinna take too long, or I will come for you, Ella." He sounded anxious that she wouldn't return to him.

Ella laughed. "I willna take too long." Then she kissed him and left the chamber, but Ruadh was still there, and she realized he was her guard along with another. She frowned. "Are you all right? You should be abed."

Ruadh shook his head. "I dinna want to be relieved of my job. Where are we off to now?"

"You wouldna be. I would make sure of it. We're off to my, uh, Mina and Amelda's chamber." She had to remember she no longer resided in her chamber but with Dashiell, and she loved it.

Ruadh escorted her to her former chamber where Bac was standing guard.

When she entered the chamber, Ruadh closed the door for her. "Mina, I hoped you would be awake still."

"Aye. I need my sleep." She motioned to Amelda, who was asleep in the big bed. "As do the bairns. I thought you would be in your chamber with your husband, lass."

"Aye. Quinn, Fallon, Lady Yvaine, Dashiell, and I have discussed that someone may be a spy on the staff who reported our whereabouts to Lennox and MacAfee."

"I have thought the same. 'Tis unlikely that they both move far away, thinking you are gone forever and suddenly are hunting for you in the woods, at least in MacAfee's case. With Lennox, he knew you were at Cairn Castle. Again, how did he know so fortuitously? I believe someone is sending one or both of them missives."

"I believe so. You dinna, um, see anything about it, do you?" Ella asked.

"Nay, I would have told you right away. I will listen and see what I can learn also. Your brother is a good listener. 'Tis good that you are keeping him informed on what is going on. He needs to be aware of it."

"That's what I believe. I'm off to be with my husband before he comes and gets me." She hugged Mina.

"He is good for you. I'm proud of you for going through all you have, finding your voice, and proving to him you can help solve the mystery."

"I just hope we can do it quickly."

"Aye, I do as well." Then she hugged Ella back and wished her a good night.

Ruadh escorted Ella back to her chamber and found Dashiell writing a missive at the table in the room. He hurried to shove it under a book, and she frowned at him. "Are you keeping secrets from me?"

He looked anxious but shook his head, took hold of her, and embraced her warmly. "I feared you would see the parchment and become terrified again."

She sighed with relief, then smiled. "Nay. Who are you writing to?"

"The king. I already sent him a missive, but I wanted to send another to ensure he received the first one. I want him to know what happened to your family. Now that you can speak, and your brother is a witness also, we need to speak with him. If we can find the blacksmith also, that would help."

ELLA DIDN'T BELIEVE she would be so nervous when she went to see all the women in the clan the next morning. It wasn't that she was afraid of meeting them. Maybe she wouldn't remember everyone when she saw them again, but she prayed that no one had anything to do with being a spy for her enemies.

She watched them as Lady Yvaine introduced her to all the staff, even those she knew, like Flora and Mai, their healer, Paige, and Olivia, holding her baby boy in her arms. Olivia was so sweet to offer her son to her, and Ella loved holding onto him and looking into his pretty gray eyes. She kissed his forehead, and he gave her a wee smile. She smiled and gave him back to Olivia.

"He is beautiful." Ella hoped she would have bairns one day.

"We are grateful to you," Olivia said.

"I'm glad that I was able to help you."

Ella was watching to see if anyone acted guiltily, lowering their eyes when they met her or even boldly like they were glad to cause trouble for her. She hadn't expected one of the women to ask, "Do you run with the wolves?"

And another asked, "And fly as an owl in the night?"

Ella laughed. She couldn't help it, though she considered if someone might be looking away from her. It was not because they felt guilty but because they feared her. She hoped no one would.

"I've heard the wolves howling and fed an orphaned wolf pup until he could hunt alone. Flying as an owl would be fascinating, and I often heard them hooting in the night or seeing their golden eyes, but nay. I'm just like all of you."

But the women didn't appear to believe that. One of them said to the others in a hushed voice, "Except she can heal like no other healer can."

Which wasn't true. Mina was more skilled than Ella, she felt. But she ignored the comment, afraid some would believe she could hear like the wolves.

She continued to meet and greet everyone, but when they were done, she finally said, "How many of you are new to the clan...like me?" She wanted to include herself so she did not sound like she had another reason to single them out.

Seven women raised their hands. She assumed that if anyone didn't know who was new, the others would ensure that Ella knew. Lying to the new chief's wife wouldn't be a good idea.

"That must mean the rest of you have always been with the clan?"

The other women smiled and agreed.

"That is always a good sign that you are happy with your

kinsmen and women," she said. "Where are you from for those of you who are new?"

Four spoke up and said they were from the village. "It was hard making enough to live off in the village. MacAfee wouldna hire us because he said he had enough staff. But the other lasses and I sought employment with Dashiell, and Lady Yvaine hired us on."

"Aye," Yvaine said. "You all had skills we could use—a baker, a tailor, and two of you were eager to work at anything we had you do. So one of you has made an excellent gardener, and the other is in charge of our washerwomen. We're happy you're with us and hope you are too."

Since Yvaine had praised them, Ella felt she was trying to tell her that the women were beyond reproach. But that didn't mean that they still might have found other incentives to come to work for Dashiell. Or any of his people, either.

"I came from down south," one of the women said. "My mother died when I was young. Bandits murdered my father. I traveled north with my brother until we reached Cairn Castle and asked for employment."

"I'm sorry to hear about your losses," Ella said. "I know how you feel."

"Thanks be to thee."

Ella glanced at one of the other women who had not said where she was from. "I had been with MacAfee."

Ella felt chilled at hearing her words.

"No' here," she said, "but I joined him and his kin up north after he left here. I overheard him talking to his men about departing his castle and leaving someone behind. He mentioned killing her family, and that's when I left. I had to know if he was speaking the truth or bragging to his men like some would."

Ella couldn't believe the woman would overhear the conversation and not tell Dashiell about it when she was hired here.

"I was also afraid MacAfee would learn that I had overheard

what he had said, and since I was new, he might no' believe I was loyal to him. I didna know if he and MacTavish were friends once they celebrated here together."

Ella recalled Mina always telling her, her brother, and her cousin to speak the truth as close to it as they could, and then they would be less likely to be caught up in a lie. What if that was the case with this woman? She was sent here to spy, maybe not a member of his clan, but hired by him to go to work for Dashiell and to listen, to learn if Ella had survived.

"So why come here then?" Ella asked.

"I wanted to know if it was true. I believed that MacAfee wouldna return here, but after the fights in the forest, I realized I had assumed wrong," the woman said.

"That is Jennie," Lady Yvaine said as if giving Ella her name to say she believed she might be the spy.

"Did you learn if it was true? That MacAfee killed the woman's family?" Ella asked.

"I believe you are the lady MacAfee lost. And that he did kill your family, or you wouldna be living in the forest with only your brother, cousin, and the healer. I was afraid, once I learned of all of you and didna tell anyone, the laird would have me fired."

Ella nodded, then turned to the last woman. "And you?"

"I'm Rita, and I lived on a croft near here. My family forced me out because I wouldna marry a lad they wanted me to, and so I came here to seek work. I work with the sheep."

That would be simple to verify. Ella looked at Lady Yvaine. She nodded.

"I thank you for helping me to meet the ladies in the clan, Lady Yvaine. Ladies, I look forward to getting to know you better. If anyone has any concerns or issues, please feel free to come speak with me."

Most of the ladies smiled, and then she dismissed them to do their duties. All the women but Paige started to leave. "Amelda and I will work on the secret garden today if it pleases you," Paige said.

"Aye. Thank you for taking her under your wing."

"She is a hard worker but cheerful and fun to work with. And inquisitive? Oh, aye, and yet she has taught me many things about the plants in the forest—which are safe to harvest and which are no' that she is a wealth of information."

"She loves to be out-of-doors. I'm glad she has you to watch over her." And a guard. They still had guards always posted for each of them.

Once everyone had dispersed, Lady Yvaine said, "I will investigate Rita's family situation immediately. What about Jenny?"

"She seems the most suspect, but she may be telling the truth. It's hard to say. I need to meet with the men as well."

"And the other women who are new to the clan?" Yvaine asked.

"I wouldna write them off either. And truly, anyone, yourself no' included, could be the culprit. Does anyone seem to have nicer things or extra money to spare that would be beyond their capability in the position they hold?" Ella wasn't sure they could discover that either.

"The only way to know that would be to enlist the help of a couple of maids who could look into it without appearing suspicious."

"The more people who know what we're doing, the more likely someone will catch us at it and learn the reason for it." Ella didn't think that would work at all.

"Aye. If the person is afraid that we are onto him or her, the spy may vanish, and we'll no longer have any issues."

"However, I want to know what they are getting out of the situation. I'm off to see Dashiell, but we'll talk later."

"You know you have brightened his outlook on everything since he found you and brought you home. I'm glad he did. He is happier than I have ever seen him. We will get rid of this spy one way or another," Yvaine said.

"I'm sure we will. Oh, I wonder if the person will decide to try to remain here and not be a spy for MacAfee anymore."

"'Tis possible, but I suspect that willna be the case. Besides, he or she has already involved Dashiell and his men in the skirmishes."

"True," Ella admitted. "If no one had said I was in the forest, MacAfee wouldna have returned there looking for me, I'm certain. And Dashiell and later Ruadh wouldn't have been injured."

"I agree."

Then they hugged, and Ella saw Paden and called him over. "Do you know where your laird is?"

"Aye. He went on a hunt, my lady."

"When I am now here?"

Paden smiled. "For wild boar this time. A farmer was herding a couple of cows through the forest, and a wild boar attacked him."

"Has the farmer been brought in to see the healer?"

"Aye, and his cows are in the corral. He's in the barracks. Mai went to attend to him, and then Mina too. We are lucky to be with this clan. We have more healers than in any other clan."

"I will see to him also." Then Ella hurried off to the massive keep doors, and a guard opened one for her.

She and Ruadh headed for the barracks. "I take it you have been with Dashiell always."

"Aye, my lady. He knows all my faults just as I know all his."

She smiled at him. "I will have to question you about them."

"Mine or his?"

She laughed, glad that many of Dashiell's people seemed fond of her. But when she reached the barracks, she grew serious and walked inside. Mina and Mai were caring for a man lying on a bed, bandaging his legs, and giving him ale, while three men were there to help with whatever they needed.

"Is it bad?" she asked the healers.

"Nay. He was lucky that the bore grazed him, though he bled a lot, and we have to watch over him to ensure he doesna end up with an infection," Mina said. "We've already applied the poultice."

The man was lying there looking tranquil, unlike someone a boar had just gored. Maybe it wasn't as serious as it seemed. Mina tended to downplay injuries with small untruths to help them feel better. Was that what was happening now?

Perhaps the man had drunk so much ale that he was simply numb to the pain, or maybe Mina had calmed him like she had taught Ella to do. Would she teach Mai the same technique?

Then Mina took Ella aside from the men's hearing and said, "I meant to be with you when you met the lasses of the clan. Do you suspect anyone?"

"There are seven women who didna belong to the clan until after Dashiell moved into the castle. Any one of them, or anyone in the clan who wanted more money, might have told MacAfee where I was. Even some of the villagers, truth be told."

"Aye. What about the men?" Mina asked.

"I will meet them after the meal. I was going to speak to Dashiell about what I learned, but then I was told he went on a hunt to take down the boar with his men."

"Aye. Another lass is in labor. I was going to see her. Do you want to come with me, or stay here with Mai? Or have you other duties to perform?"

Ella smiled at her. It would take some time for them to understand that she oversaw the staff and wasn't just a healer for the people now. However, if an emergency arose, such as an injury or the birth of a child, she would drop everything to help.

"What would you have me do?" Ella asked.

Mina smiled. "You are in charge now. I would have you do what you think is best. But I will say since staying in the castle, I have had a decent sleep and food, and I willna speak of dying soon any longer."

Ella hugged her. "You have no idea how much that pleases me." Then she frowned. "Is the woman in childbirth alone?"

"Nay, two other women are with her. Mai and I were there until the farmer was injured."

"I will go see her then. You can come with me if Mai doesna need any assistance. I havena met the woman giving birth then, and I need to learn if she has been with the clan all along or has no' been."

"Aye." Mina told Mai, "If you are good with us checking on Zella, we are returning to the castle."

"The farmer is sleeping now. I will stay here and make sure he doesna have a fever, but go. I'll be up to check on things in a while."

Ella wished she could ask Mai if the woman was new to the clan, but she didn't want to speak about it in front of the other men. Then she and Mina returned to the keep and climbed the stairs to the chamber where Zella was having the baby.

She was in labor, and the other three women there quickly bowed their heads to Ella.

"I havena met any of you," Ella said, smiling. "I was able to meet everyone else below the stairs."

Mai checked the woman in labor to see how she was progressing. "It willna be long."

"Have you been with the MacTavish clan all along, or at least before he came to Cairn Castle?" Ella asked, applying a cool, wet cloth to the pregnant mother's forehead.

"I have been," one of the women said. "My sister, who is having the baby, has been also. We were shocked when we learned Laird MacTavish had bartered his land for the castle. But once we saw it, we were thrilled."

"I havena been with the clan all along," another woman said.

"My brother and I had worked as butchers in the village, but there are two other butchers, and they were causing us trouble."

"Oh?"

"Aye. We spoke with MacTavish about the matter since he oversees everything that goes on and he hired us to work for him. He is much more generous than what we earned in the village."

"Oh, I'm so happy for you." Ella was glad that Dashiell was fair, though she expected no less from him.

"I am...the daughter of one of...the men who betrayed your... uh, da," a meek, red-haired woman said, freckles bridging her nose and dotting her cheeks. She had to be about Ella's age. "I take... care...of the babies when the women...work."

Ella frowned at her. She didn't remember her. "If you were with Lennox, why did you come here?"

Tears filled her eyes. "I'm Venetia. You probably dinna remember me. I was sixteen when we left. My mother had died the year before that. The other men with Laird Lennox that had tried to overthrow your da didna have children or wives, except for Laird Lennox's son, Michael."

Ella studied her expression to determine whether she was telling the truth.

"My fifteen-year-old brother and I were the only younger ones with them—besides your cousin, Michael. My brother and I had to leave with our da. I wanted to stay at the castle where my friends were," Venetia said.

Ella felt bad for her unless this was all a made-up story.

"This was where I belonged if it hadna been for my da and your uncle's treachery. When I saw Michael come here and then Lennox, I was afraid they would see me and want to kill me for leaving their clan and coming here."

Ella wondered why she had not told MacTavish that she had been with Ella's clan initially but had gone with her da, Lennox, and the other traitors and had lived there for the last five years.

"Michael saw me and gave me the coldest glower. Our da had died, and my brother and I found our way here with a caravan of farmers who had gone to market. They offered us a ride. I was surprised when I learned your da and the rest of you were gone, with no word about where you had gone. But then MacTavish hired us."

Ella was still frowning at her. If they thought her da still ruled, why would they have thought her da would have allowed them to return to the clan? Could MacAfee have sent her to spy on them? A woman who appeared terrified of her own shadow? Could Lennox have hired her and her brother to spy on the situation there?

"You are welcome here," Ella said. "But I wish to speak with you further."

The woman's lower lip quivered.

"Come. We'll speak in my old bedchamber in private."

Venetia nodded, looking like she was bound for the dungeon. The other women appeared just as anxious for her but said nothing. "Will you be all right without me for a wee bit? This shouldna take long," Ella asked Mina.

"Go. I can handle this, and when you're finished, you can join me."

"Good. Come, Venetia." Then Ella led her out the door, and they walked to her bedchamber. "I'm serious about you staying here. I need to ask some questions because of what I went through, though."

"Aye, of course."

Then they walked into Ella's former bedchamber and took seats in the solar. "Tell me, did you ever witness MacAfee visit my uncle?"

"Aye, often. Or Laird Lennox would visit Laird MacAfee at his castle. MacAfee is still building the keep on his land, but the first two stone towers and the wall between them are complete. The rest is built of wood until they can be replaced with stone."

Maybe someone would attack him when he was more vulner-
able before he could build a better-fortified fortress. Ella could only
hope for all his treachery that he wouldn't live to do anything evil
like that to anyone else.

"Did you ever overhear anything that was said?"

Venetia wrung her hands. "He said he would do whatever he
could to ensure he got the woman he wanted for his mate."

"Me?" Ella asked.

"I didna know who he was talking about. I was never privy to
who MacAfee wanted to wed."

Was Venetia being honest? Or not?

24

A fter Ella dismissed Venetia, she was about to head out of the chamber and immediately speak with Venetia's brother to see if he had a different version of what his sister had told her when Mina walked into the bedchamber and closed the door behind her. Ella knew from Mina's dark expression something was wrong.

"Zella had a healthy baby girl. But I need to speak to you about Venetia. Do you believe everything she said?" Mina asked.

Ella was taken aback that Mina might know what they had talked about in private, but then she had ways of knowing things, so it shouldn't have been such a surprise. "I listened to what she had to say. I might sound like I believe her, but I know I should be wary of anyone other than you, my brother, and my cousin. We have endured so much, and I dinna know the woman."

"Aye. 'Tis good that you keep an open mind."

"What do you feel about her? Do you think she isna speaking the truth?" Even though Ella would keep an open mind, she felt Venetia hadn't told her everything she knew.

"Do you remember her? In the clan?"

"Vaguely. I think I blocked a lot out of past events that had occurred before the massacre."

"Do you know what she was like before the massacre? I mean to say, was she good to you, or did she scorn you for your position in the clan if you can remember anything?" Mina persisted.

"I dinna remember her all that well. I remember seeing her at meals at one of the lower tables once, but I remember...wait." A flash of memory hit Ella all at once.

"What do you remember?"

"She and a lad were laughing and joking, and when I drew closer as I was on my way to the stables behind them, she gave me a scornful look. The lad didna. He was interested in me, as several were because I was the chief's daughter. For no other reason."

Mina narrowed her eyes. "Then I would worry that she hasna changed and that she actually came here as a spy for your uncle. It could be that she hasna, but still, I would be wary of her motives."

"Aye. What about her brother?"

"The same thing. He is family and she would be more loyal to him likely as no'. If he is here with her, I wouldna believe them. She may be speaking the truth, but you shouldna trust them until you know for sure," Mina said.

"Why did you no' think of them when we were discussing who might be a spy?" Ella asked.

"This is the first time I've seen her since I've been here. She has been out of sight, most likely fearing we would know she was with our old clan. Then, she was in the room with the women helping Zella with her baby. I swear she looked like she was about to faint when she saw me arrive. She knew I recognized her."

"You...dinna have a, um, feeling about them, do you?" Like Mina had read their minds, Ella was thinking. Because she swore there were times when Mina had read hers or her brother's about something she shouldn't have known about. "Wait, did you see something about the brother and sister that would make you think thus?"

Mina had been at the castle any number of times. Maybe she had overheard something that made her suspicious of their motives.

"Remember when you were on the boat on the loch racing against other youths your age?" Mina asked.

"Aye. We did that several times since the time I was thirteen."

"But one time was disastrous."

Ella struggled to remember. Then, memories of Lennox's attempt to overthrow her da's rule and her mother's attack reigned over her. But the mention of trouble while in a boat race made her remember an incident.

"Michael and I were in a boat rowing together. One of the boats rammed into ours, sending me into the water. I was an excellent swimmer, but my boat was again struck, and it hit me, knocking me out."

"Aye. You nearly died."

Ella's mouth gaped. She shook her head. "I never knew who struck my boat. Was it Venetia and her brother?"

"Aye. They sounded so contrite about it, sobbing and truly sorry that your da was certain it had been an accident. No one told you they had done it. I'm sure they felt it was unnecessary. I was fetched to see you because you had swallowed so much water and nearly drowned. Your cousin dove into the loch to rescue you."

"I remember that part." At least back then, her cousin had still been her friend.

"He swam you to shore. The boat had a hole in the side and had nearly sunk before they could bring it to shore to patch it up. Not that the boat was as important as you, but your da wanted to ensure that someone else hadna sabotaged the boat."

"Like someone had already put another hole into it?"

"Aye."

"So why, if everyone believed the brother and sister's stories, did you feel there was more to it than an accident?" She suspected Mina did.

"I heard them laughing about it later. They didna say they did it on purpose, but they mentioned how they thought you were a good swimmer. How could you nearly drown yourself? I couldna tell your da that I suspected more had gone on. No' without real proof."

"And you didna want to tell me either if there was naught to it."

"Right. They were your age, petty children, and it could have been naught more than spitefulness or even a way of expressing relief after what had happened to you that they had no' gotten into serious trouble."

"You stayed at the castle more after that. I remember you being there, saying you were checking on me. You said it was because I had nearly drowned, and you were making sure I was all right. But that wasn't all there was to it, was there?"

"I wanted to see if I could catch them talking further about the 'incident,' but I never could. After that, I figured it was mostly an accident."

"Mostly."

"Aye. I could never rule it out as completely a mistake."

"What about the brother?" That knowledge made Ella's skin chill. "Do you think he has been avoiding us seeing him also?"

"Mayhap. I havena seen him. A lot of staff members work here. It would be easy for them to hide from us. They could even eat their meals away from the great hall once we arrived at the castle. If they are the spies, they might have hoped you wouldna remember them."

A knock on her bedchamber door sounded, and Ella crossed the bedchamber floor and opened it. Paden was standing there, frowning, worried that he might be interrupting something.

"I'm sorry, my lady, but his lairdship said you can meet the men on staff now. He'll meet you in the inner bailey."

"Oh, I'll be right down then." Ella said to Mina, "I'll talk to you later."

Then she headed down the stairs to the inner bailey. She felt just a little intimidated to see all the men gathered together, most of whom she didn't know. She had seen some working at the castle but needed to learn everyone's name and occupation.

Dashiell smiled at her as she joined him and rubbed her back soothingly. She smiled at him and then saw Finnegan standing beside Theo, the blacksmith.

"Let Ella know your names and occupations. Some of you she has met, but I want everyone to go through the process," Dashiell said.

Quinn started. "I'm Quinn, advisor to his laird."

"Fallon, cousin of Dashiell and his tanist."

Finnegan said, "I'm your brother, Ella. And I'm the blacksmith's apprentice."

Everyone chuckled.

Once everyone told her their names and occupations and how long they had been with Dashiell, she realized Venetia's twin brother wasn't among them. But that's who she wanted to speak with. The rest of the male staff had been with Dashiell way before he took over Cairn Castle. Everyone looked her in the eye, and none appeared guilty.

"Thanks," she said. "You are all dismissed."

"Do you want to speak with anyone in particular?" Dashiell asked her.

The men didn't move right away, and she shook her head, then led him away to the gardens. "I need to speak with Venetia's brother, Garrett. He wasna here."

"Garrett? He's training to be a watchman." Dashiell called out to Christopher.

He joined him and said, "Aye, my laird?"

"Find the lad named Garrett."

"The new watchman?"

"Aye."

Christopher glanced at the other men as they began to disperse and go about their jobs.

"He's no' here," Ella said.

"I'll find him," Christopher said.

"And bring him to the gardens. I'll speak with him there," she said.

Christopher hurried off across the inner bailey to find the master of the guards.

"What's going on?" Dashiell asked, sounding worried about Ella.

"I spoke with his sister, Venetia. She and her family joined our clan a couple of years before MacAfee killed my kinsmen and women. She isna related to me by blood. Her da backed my uncle, so when he left, so did Venetia and Garrett."

Dashiell frowned.

She didn't intend to speak of her near drowning since she didn't know for sure if the sister and brother had hit her and her cousin's boat on the loch by accident or on purpose.

"I'll be with you when you speak with Garrett." Dashiell sounded protective as always.

She appreciated it as he took her hand and walked her into the gardens. Amelda and her guard were picking herbs.

"Momma!" Amelda said, handing the basket of herbs to the guard, Bac, then racing to hug Ella.

Bac just smiled, looking sheepish that he was doing this on his guarding job.

Ella hugged her back. "You look like you've been busy."

"Aye. Cook told me to gather the herbs for the meal."

"You are doing a great job!"

"I got to get these to the kitchen."

"You do that." Then Ella released her cousin so she could do her duty.

Amelda waved to her guard to bring her basket of herbs with him. Obediently, he joined her as he cast Dashiell a smile. They headed into the backside of the castle.

"You know, I thought she was your daughter at one point and that you had a husband, but maybe he was dead."

"Nay. Though I have raised her like she is my daughter since she was a baby."

"She is as good-natured and helpful as you."

Finnegan entered the garden and joined them. She hadn't expected that.

"Does Master Theo no' need you in the shop working?" she asked.

"He sent me to tell you that Christopher is searching everywhere for Garrett, but he canna find him. Christopher even came into the blacksmith's shop looking for him. One of the guards said he thought he saw Garrett leave the outer bailey before the men gathered together in the inner bailey at Dashiell's command," Finnegan said.

"Aye," Dashiell said.

"Though everyone had word you were coming to speak to the men soon."

She didn't want to think the worst of Garrett without speaking with him first, but his actions made her suspect he was guilty of being a spy. Why else would he leave the castle grounds if he had no reason to, just before she met and questioned him?

"Stay with your sister," Dashiell said. He nodded to Ruadh, who would watch Ella and her brother.

Now, she felt Garrett and maybe his sister were just as dangerous to their well-being.

∿

Then Dashiell strode off to the inner bailey and called out to Christopher, "Find Fallon and Quinn."

"Aye, right away." Christopher ran off to the keep.

Dashiell couldn't believe his people had hired Venetia and Garrett, who could have been spies for Lennox.

As soon as Fallon and Quinn raced out of the keep, Dashiell joined them and said, "We need to hunt down Garrett."

"What has he done?" Fallon asked.

"He vanished before the men were assembled so Ella could meet with them." Dashiell explained where the guard had seen him and how he was in Ella's clan before the massacre. "They lived with Lennox after he was banished from the clan. Garrett's sister, Venetia, also needs to be watched."

"Gods' wounds," Fallon said.

"Aye. We need to locate Garrett and return him to the castle for questioning. I dinna want him killed."

"Aye," Fallon said. "I'll gather a force to help us search for him. He'll likely know these woods well since he was with Ella's clan." Then Fallon stalked off.

"What about Venetia? Do we confine her before she flees?" Quinn asked.

"Aye. I suspect she willna flee. Unless someone waits for her in the forest to take her to safety. She may no' know the forest as well as her brother as lasses usually were no' allowed to wander through the forest, but the lads would be expected to learn to hunt," Dashiell said.

Quinn called out to Christopher. "Christopher, you're needed."

He came running. "I'm going on the hunt for Garrett?"

"I want you to take Veneita into custody. She can stay in the women's chambers, but I need you to have a guard posted to keep her there," Quinn said.

"Aye!" Christopher ran off.

"Let's go," Dashiell said to Quinn.

They both mounted their waiting horses, and Fallon soon joined them.

"I'm going too," Finnegan said.

Dashiell glanced at Ella.

"Aye, but come back without any injuries," she said.

"Get a mount for Finnegan," Dashiell said to the stable hands. He couldn't promise to keep her brother safe if they had trouble in the forest. But he understood that Finnegan had to prove he was part of the clan and bound to help protect his sister after all she had done for him.

Still, Ella looked stricken to let him go as she wrung her hands.

Then Finnegan ran and hugged her. "I willna get myself killed. And I'll look after his lairdship also."

Dashiell would have laughed if the situation wasn't so serious. "Keep Ella safe, Ruadh." Then he rode out of the inner bailey and beyond the last gate with his men to find Garrett before he escaped for good.

25

"Come, Ruadh. I want to check on Amelda and then see Venetia to question her further," Ella said.

"Aye."

They headed for the kitchen.

Cook smiled and said, "Amelda dropped off her basket of herbs. Then, she went up to see Mina in their bedchamber."

"Thank you," Ella said. Then she and Ruadh went up to her bedchamber but found Mina napping when they entered. "Have you seen Amelda, Mina?"

Mina wiped the sleep from her eyes. "In the herb garden, the last I saw of her from the chamber window."

"She could have been here and used the latrine without disturbing you, aye?" Ella asked.

Mina thought hard, then frowned. "She's with Venetia."

"What? Where?"

"I dinna know. It's dark, and a torch lights the way."

"But it's light out." Ella rubbed her forehead. "Unless it's underground. Do you see this happening now?"

"Or soon, or later. I dinna know."

Ella went back to the door and opened it. "Ruadh, find Fallon or Venetia."

"Is Amelda in the chamber?"

"Nay, and Mina believes she sees her with Venetia in a dark place like...the tunnels!" Ella ran out of the chamber and headed for her and Dashiell's chamber.

Ruadh was right behind her.

She turned on him. "Go find Fallon or Venetia. Make sure she's no' in the castle still."

He hesitated. "I'm supposed to protect you always. Bac is watching Amelda."

Ella let out her breath. That was true. "But you must send someone else to learn if Venetia is guarded in a chamber at least."

Mina came out into the hallway. "I'll check the women's chambers where she should be."

"Forget it. I'll do it." Ella stalked off for the women's chamber, but no guard stood at the door when she arrived. She opened the door and found the chamber empty. This would be the case if all the women were off doing chores, but Venetia was supposed to be confined. "Where else would she be?"

Ruadh scratched his head. "She was supposed to be here."

"We search the tunnels." Ella ran for her chamber, and once inside, she grabbed her sword and sheathed it. Then she crawled under the bed, found the trap door closed as it should be, and opened it. She could see a faint light down there. "Someone's down there," she whispered to Ruadh, who was peering under the bed at her. "Get a torch."

"Aye, my lady." His hurried footfalls raced out of the bedchamber.

"You are no' going down there are you?" Mina asked, standing next to the bed. "No' until Ruadh is with you."

"Aye. Tell Ruadh to follow me. I'm going to follow the light before I lose it."

"Ella."

But Ella had already descended into the dark tunnel, hurrying to catch up to the person wielding the light. She heard two people's hurried footsteps. One of a woman, she thought, and one of a child. Amelda and Venetia, just like Mina envisioned.

Ella was furious because she knew Venetia wouldn't take Amelda for a stroll through the tunnels for no good reason. She had to be handing her over to someone in the forest. Hopefully, she wouldn't meet up with her brother, Garrett, in time and take off with Ella's cousin. Instead, she prayed Dashiell and the others would catch them at it if she didn't stop Venetia first.

FALLON GALLOPED into the forest to join Dashiell, and he assumed he would tell him that Venetia was under guard.

Instead, Fallon's expression was anger-filled. "Venetia must have suspected Ella didna believe her story, and she has disappeared from the castle. Besides me, I had several of our staff searching for her, but we couldna find any sign of her."

"Then when we locate her brother, we'll find her also." Dashiell hadn't immediately believed she would be spying for Lennox and, thereby spying for MacAfee, but he suspected now he'd had it all wrong. He liked to think of himself as fair-minded and not one to make assumptions without knowing the truth.

"Aye. Do you want me to hunt them down with you or—"

"Return to the castle. Check on Ella, Amelda, and Mina. I want to ensure Venetia isna still in the keep and just hiding someplace."

"Aye." Fallon kicked his horse and headed back to the castle.

Dashiell glanced at Finnegan, who was nearby, listening to the conversation. Dashiell had already assigned two guards to keep him safe while they were in the forest, though he was rethinking that decision and wishing he'd left him back at the keep.

But then Christopher rode out to meet up with them. "Ruadh sent me, saying that Venetia took Amelda into the escape tunnels."

"What? Where is Ella?" Dashiell asked, his heart pounding in his ears. He knew the answer before Christoper even gave it to him.

"In the tunnels. Ruadh grabbed some men to go with him."

"Does he know how to navigate the tunnels?"

Christopher frowned. "I dinna know."

"I dinna know either."

"I do," Finnegan said. "We dinna know how to go the way Venetia would have gone, but I know where she'll end up if she doesna get lost."

"Let's go."

Finnegan hurried off toward the tall grasses some distance from the forest, stream, and outer castle walls.

Dashiell prayed they were not too late to reach Amelda and his mate in time.

ELLA REALIZED her mistake in leaving Ruadh behind to get reinforcements. He wouldn't know the way through the tunnels to the forest. But she couldn't let Venetia get away with Amelda either. How would Venetia know the way through the tunnels, though?

Unless—she had been here when MacAfee was here. Had he found the tunnels and discovered that's how Ella had escaped? Maybe Lennox had been here visiting MacAfee after he had murdered the rest of her clansmen and women.

Lennox could have brought the sister and brother with him and shown them the tunnels and the way through them.

Panic filling her, she moved through the familiar tunnels. The musty, cool, damp smell brought back memories of her escape five years ago. But this time, her panic was different. She wasn't leading her family to an unknown future with no plan. Instead, she was on a mission to find her cousin, afraid MacAfee might be waiting just outside the exit to capture her.

She heard Ruadh calling for her, but he was somewhere in the tunnels, and she had no clue where exactly. If she called out to him, Venetia would know she was close behind her, but her voice echoing off the walls would just confuse Ruadh. She hoped he had sent for reinforcements.

Amelda cried out, "Let me go! My mother will come for you, and you will be sorry!"

Amelda's small voice echoed off the walls and alarmed Ella. She tried to move quickly but as silently as possible. Venetia stumbled on the uneven, rocky floor, cursed, and then ran again.

"Just come on. Quit fighting me," Venetia growled.

Ella's heart beat frantically as she tried to reach them before they found the exit. She had never returned to close the hidden exit door, but in five years, the vegetation could have covered the entrance again.

"Get up! Get on your feet!" Venetia sounded like she wanted to kill Amelda.

Ella thought Amelda had dropped to the floor like a sack of wheat. A warrior could lift the five-year-old over his shoulder and run with her. But Venetia was about the same size as Ella.

She could lift Amelda, but carrying her and running long distances would be difficult, especially on uneven, rocky ground. And if Amelda fought her, it would be nearly impossible.

Venetia wasn't running any longer. "Get up, Amelda!" Then Venetia screamed ouch. "You little beastie."

"I hate you!" Amelda screamed back at her.

Ella was getting so close. She thought she would be around the bend to the right and reach them. Then she saw the torchlight wavering against the wall.

Other footfalls approached Venetia and Amelda. Ella's cousin screamed.

Ohmigoddess! The footsteps were heavier. It had to be a man who would easily lift Amelda and take her out of the tunnels.

"She was fighting me like a wild cat. She even bit me," Venetia said. "Is my brother safe?"

The man grunted as if he didn't care one way or another.

Ella held her sword in her right hand and her *sgian dubh* in her left. She had intended to threaten Venetia with it, but now she would have to fight whoever the man was.

Ella came around the bend of the glistening wall and saw Venetia trailing behind, carrying a torch. The man who had Amelda over his shoulder was none other than MacAfee himself. He *had* known the way to the tunnels. One arm held Amelda tight to his shoulder while his other hand carried a torch.

Ella rushed to knock Venetia out just as MacAfee turned another corner in the tunnel. It appeared he didn't care if he lost Venetia. He wasn't waiting up for her. He only cared about getting Amelda out of the tunnel. And then what? He would use her as a bargaining tool to get Ella to accompany him. Then he would kill them both?

She struck Venetia hard on the back of the head with the guard on her sword. Venetia dropped the torch and fell to the rocky floor with a thud, not uttering a sound. Ella didn't bother to see if she was just knocked out or dead. She had to reach MacAfee before he was free of the tunnel.

She assumed his men would be waiting with horses there for him. If he made it outside, all was lost. She quickened her pace, not worried about keeping her footfalls as silent as possible, figuring he would think it was Venetia.

She heard his heavy, lumbering run echo off the cave walls, no longer hearing Ruadh calling out for her. The light from MacAfee's torch shone around the bend.

Amelda said, "My mother will kill you for this."

"Mother? Do you mean Ella? She's your cousin."

Ella dove around the wall and closed the gap between her and MacAfee, planning to dive and slice his leg. He was too tall to cut his throat. Hanging over MacAfee's broad shoulder, Amelda saw Ella, and her eyes widened.

Amelda opened her mouth to speak. Ella put her *sgian dubh* to her lips, telling her not to say a word. Ella had only one chance at this. She saw the light from outside the tunnel and heard the clash of swords and neighing of horses. MacAfee suddenly stopped, and she almost ran into him.

She cut his leg, and he nearly dropped Amelda. Before he could swing around and kill her, Finnegan entered the tunnel, the light from the torch MacAfee dropped on the floor and shining on her brother's face. The sun at his back made him appear like an avenging angel, his sword in hand. But MacAfee would kill him.

MacAfee dropped Amelda, and Ella grabbed her before she fell. Then MacAfee reached for Ella. He would use her as a shield.

Suddenly, large hands pulled Finnegan out of the way, and Dashiell rushed in. He ran at MacAfee, and Ella cut at MacAfee's arm as he tried to grab hers.

"Run back to the keep," Ella said to Amelda. She had to get her away from the fighting, though she was afraid Amelda wouldn't know the way. But she couldn't be here while MacAfee was swinging his sword at Dashiell and trying to kill him.

Then she grabbed Amelda's hand and ran with her toward the bend in the wall. "Stay here. The light from Venetia's torch is right there. Just stay here."

"Stay with me," Amelda pleaded, tears in her eyes, both hands gripping Ella's.

"I have to make sure MacAfee doesna kill Dashiell." She had to make sure MacAfee never came for any of them again.

She hated to leave her cousin when she knew how terrified she was, but she had to end this with MacAfee while she had the chance. She ran toward him again while Dashiell struck at him over and over again as if he were a man possessed. She knew how he felt. She felt the same way about taking MacAfee down.

She struck her sword at MacAfee's back, but his padded leather armor kept her from progressing. His leg and arm were bleeding from the cuts she had made, but they didn't seem to be slowing him down.

Then she saw Michael enter the tunnel at Dashiell's back. She raced past both MacAfee and Dashiell to stop him. She didn't think she could kill him because he was a man and stronger than her. But if she could stop him long enough until Dashiell or one of his men could help her, she had to fight him.

"Woah, I'm on your side," Michael said, his sword out, bloodied, like hers was.

Was he lying to her? She couldn't trust that he wasn't.

"Put down your sword," she said, her sword and *sgian dubh* ready.

"I'm here to help Laird MacTavish," Michael said. "You and I were best of friends always."

"Until you took up arms against my da."

"I didna. I had my sword in my hand, aye, but I didna fight anyone, did I? I had to go with him that day when he was banished. He was still my da."

"And if he had taken over? You would have had an elevated position in the clan. So you would have eagerly gone along with it." She heard the grunting and groaning between the men behind her, hoping that Dashiell would eliminate MacAfee quickly. But she didn't trust Michael.

"Aye, but I didna go along with the plan or set things in motion. That was all my da and his cohorts doing."

"Why are you here? Is Lennox also?"

"Just me."

"With MacAfee and his men."

"I came alone, heard the fighting, and came to help to prove that I'm on your side."

"You, your da, and MacAfee are in league with one another. Drop your weapon," she said.

"I canna help you if I'm unarmed."

"You canna hurt us if you're disarmed."

Michael struck her sword and hit it hard. He knocked it out of her hand, and it flew toward the wall, hit it with a clunk, and fell on the ground. Without hesitation, she dove for it, jumped to her feet, and came up swinging. He hadn't expected that. Instead, he had made a move toward Dashiell.

But once she engaged him, he had to protect himself. She attacked him with such ferocity, he fell back several steps. "Mac-Afee wants you, though why, I have no idea," Michael said, his voice angry and hard.

She struck his sword again and managed to cut Michael's cheek. He growled and came at her, hitting her sword so hard again that she lost it. Gods' wounds!

She darted around him but couldn't reach her sword, and with his sword's reach, she couldn't cut him with her knife. If she threw it, he could easily dodge it unless he didn't know it was coming.

Then she heard men's running footfalls come from Amelda's direction. "Ruadh!" Amelda said.

"Stay here." Ruadh came around the bend in the tunnel with four more men behind him.

With reinforcements at hand, MacAfee glanced back to see them, and Dashiell cut MacAfee's throat. He slumped to the ground and collapsed.

Dashiell turned on Michael, who promptly dropped his sword.

"Your da was in on killing his brother and the rest of our kin, wasna he?" Ella grabbed up her sword and poked Michael in the chest with it.

"Nay, it was all MacAfee's doing. You know he did it because your da wouldna allow MacAfee to wed you."

"But your da wanted to take me in as his ward to marry me off to MacAfee. You tried to take me with you the first time. You knew what it was all about. You knew my family had been murdered."

"Please put the sword down. I didna know. You're no' making sense."

"You knew my da and all our people wouldna just leave. So someone had to have massacred them. You had spies in place to learn when MacTavish found us because MacAfee must have assumed he would take us in, and word had to be sent to Lennox right away. Then your da would have told MacAfee."

"No, none of this is true." Michael glanced at Dashiell as he held his sword, dripping with MacAfee's blood.

"Where is your da?" Dashiell asked, his voice a growl. "Or is he too cowardly that he sent you to do a man's job?"

Michael stiffened, turned, and tried to stab Dashiell, but he cut him down with a hefty swing of his sword.

Ella looked down at her cousin, who had once been her best friend. She was saddened to see what he had become because of his da. But then she ran to join Dashiell and hugged and kissed him.

She quickly released him after he kissed and hugged her back and found Amelda hiding around the bend in the wall, her guard with a bandaged head sitting on the floor while she hugged his arm.

"Are you all right?" Ella asked Bac.

"Nay. Venetia got the best of me, and Dashiell will have my head," Bac said.

"He willna," Amelda said, hugging his arm even more tightly.

"What about Venetia?" Ella asked.

"She was coming to in the tunnel some distance back and Mina is seeing to her, but she will be locked in the dungeon after that."

"I must speak with her."

Dashiell and Finnegan joined them, and Dashiell frowned at Bac.

Amelda gave Dashiell a hard look, not letting go of Bac's arm. "He's my guard, and you willna punish him."

Dashiell tried not to smile, but he was unsuccessful. "We will speak later," he told the guard.

"Aye, my laird."

"I'm glad you found your way to us," Ella said to Ruadh.

"Aye, I finally saw the light from the torch that Venetia had been wielding before you knocked her out," Ruadh said. "And then we heard all the fighting."

"What about Uncle Lennox?" Finnegan asked.

"Dead," Quinn said. "He was with MacAfee's men with a force of his own to back him up. All of them are dead."

Ella thought about the woman who married her cousin instead of Dashiell as it was supposed to be. Now, she was a widow, and Ella had the man she was supposed to marry.

"What about Venetia's brother?" Ella asked.

"He has been captured. He didna fight anyone. He said that Venetia is married and has a little girl. Lennox forced her to do his bidding. Her brother has a girl he was about to marry, and Lennox used that against him also."

"Then send them home to Lennox's castle to care for their families. They can tell Michael's wife that Lennox, MacAfee, Michael, and their men are dead," Ella said.

Dashiell smiled at her. "Do as the lady says. In the meantime, lock that tunnel door. I want it sealed."

Ella understood that because everyone seemed to know where it was now. Besides, she knew another escape tunnel out of the castle and would let Dashiell know that as soon as possible.

Then they left the tunnel, and Mina, Mai, and Ella took care of the men injured in battle. Amelda helped this time, bringing them clean bandages and even washing wounds.

Finnegan stood behind Ella, and she finally turned to see what he wanted.

His eyes filled with tears, Finnegan hugged her. "I thought I had lost you and Amelda."

"You brought Dashiell to the tunnel entrance, which meant you saved us." She hugged Finnegan and kissed the top of his head. "You will make a fine warrior one day."

He smiled a little. "I've got to get back to the blacksmith."

"Aye, thank you, Finnegan. I love you."

"Love you too." Then he dashed off.

Amelda laughed. "He never hugs you first. No' since he was little."

As if Amelda could remember that far back.

"Aye," Ella said.

They turned to see Venetia and her brother walking out of the front gates, leaving Cairn Castle behind.

Once the wounded were patched up, everyone cleaned up and entered the great hall to dine.

"One of my men went to the village for supplies and learned some of MacAfee's men had been questioning everyone about some woman who lived in the woods with a boy and baby girl who would be five now," Dashiell said to Ella.

"When was this?"

"The night he wanted to celebrate with us. He had done it before they came to the castle."

"I'm glad I hadn't been in the village then. I had been there earlier in the day."

One of the maids came with more ale for them, and Ella's jaw dropped. "Bhictoria!"

The woman smiled at her. "Imagine seeing you here at the head table. And here I had told you to sneak—" She glanced at Dashiell as if she shouldn't be telling her secrets.

"He doesna care. Tell me," Ella said.

"Well, I didna realize you had such a highly elevated position. You would have been at the celebration all along."

"Did you enjoy the celebration?"

"Aye." Then she frowned. "Come to think of it, I dinna remember seeing you there." Then Bhictoria's eyes widened. "You can speak."

"Now I can. I'm glad to see you working here." Now that Ella didn't have to hide who she was, she could be friends with the likable maid. "When were you hired? I hadna seen you here before."

"Lady Yvaine hired me a short time ago." Bhictoria laughed at herself then. "Here we thought you were living in the forest as an owl, sometimes as one of the deer, a wolf even. But of course we didna tell anyone about it."

"Like MacAfee?"

"Nay, he wouldna have believed us. We kept it among ourselves. This is good because you've been living here all this time." Bhictoria motioned to two of the men who were serving meals. "My brother is in the bakery, and the other is a cook."

"I'm glad you all are working here."

Then Bhictoria curtseyed to her and left to continue serving the meal.

"She will learn soon enough that you *are* the woman of the forest," Dashiell said, then took a bite of his bread.

"Aye."

Then Ruadh entered the great hall carrying a wolf pup under his arm.

"Warrior!" Ella jumped from her seat and hurried to take the pup from him. Warrior wagged his tail and licked her face.

Finnegan and Amelda hurried from their seats to hug the wolf pup.

Dashiell joined them. "It appears we have another addition to our clan."

The houndsman rose from his seat, frowning. "You want me to put a wolf pup in with our hounds?"

"Aye," Dashiell said, "until he's old enough to fend for himself."

Ella let Finnegan have the pup, and he headed back to his seat. The hounds came to inspect the new "dog" while she hugged Dashiell. "I love you," she said.

"He was part of your family. And for Amelda, we have a cat with kittens in the stable. If she wants, she can play with them whenever she isna busy with chores."

Paden rushed into the great hall, and Ella was worried some other trouble was brewing. "My laird, that woman...you know the one. Lady Lynette? She is back saying that her da sent her to marry"—he glanced at Fallon—"your cousin, Fallon."

EPILOGUE

Dashiell watched as James MacNeill, his wife, Eilis, and the rest of his entourage arrived at Cairn Castle. He introduced her to James's brothers, Dougald and Malcolm, the two Ella hadn't met already, their wives, Alana and Anice, Angus's wife, Edana, and cousin Niall's wife, Anna. Even Gunnolf, who had been raised like a brother, and his wife, Brina—were there.

The next morning, they would celebrate their wedding with their friends.

"I am so excited to meet you," Anna said to Ella. "The last time Niall and the others met with Dashiell, he wasna pleased he would have to find a wife among the eligible maids in the area. When James said Dashiell had found the perfect woman for him, we were thrilled and just had to meet you."

"I'm glad. I'm thrilled you're here."

"I am as well," Alana told her. "When our husbands returned home and told us how you lived in the forest—"

"No' just the forest," Eilis said, "but how you hid yourself as an owl..."

"No' to mention that you ran with the wolves—" Edana glanced at Warrior. "Oh, my."

"We raised him as a pup. He runs wild sometimes, and sometimes he wants to come home and stay with the hounds," Ella said. "I'm so glad to meet all of you."

Anice smiled. "You are welcome to visit us anytime."

"Oh, aye, us too," Anna said.

The other ladies agreed.

Dashiell was glad to see his friends and their wives come to visit but also enjoyed seeing their wives become Ella's friends. She had made many friends among their staff members but after living in the forest for so long and not being able to have friends for all that time, he knew she needed this.

James slapped him on the back. "I hope our wives dinna wear Ella out. They were so excited to meet her, we couldna hold off any longer. Have you had any further trouble from Lennox or MacAfee's people?"

"Nay. I believe that MacAfee was the instigator in wanting Ella. So now that MacAfee and Lennox are gone, whoever took charge of their clans are busy managing things and dinna care what we do."

"Good. Did your cows have their calves yet?" James asked.

Dashiell was amused by how they had bred their bulls from the market with his cows unbeknownst to him. "Aye, they did. They're beautiful. We can see them after the meal."

Niall said, "We didna tell our wives that Ella was of the fey, but they believe she is truly special."

"Aye, that she is," Dashiell said, smiling as she joked and laughed with the MacNeill wives and Gunnolf's.

Then Ella had the wives meet Finnegan and Amelda, and everyone hugged them. Finnegan's face blossomed with color.

~

ELLA WAS THRILLED to meet James, his kin, and their wives. She would love to visit them at their castles. For now, she was just glad she and Dashiell had a fortnight of peace after all that had gone on.

Mina was teaching two other women healing skills, and even Amelda was an eager listener and applied poultices to wounds and the like. Finnegan was still working as a blacksmith and taking weapons training.

Ella continued to practice weapons training with Dashiell and with some of the women, who were eager to learn how to protect themselves if they encountered trouble like she had. Amelda had picked a kitten from the litter and often brought her into her bedchamber, which she shared with Mina at night.

That was fine with Ella and Mina, except the kitten had jumped on Mina in the middle of the night, and she shrieked in terror. Guards had to rush in to protect them—from a kitten.

After dinner, they had a dance to celebrate their friendship with the MacNeills. Dashiell said to Ella, "When my friends would visit, once they all had wives, I was a bit—"

"Jealous?" she offered.

"Envious. Until I met you and would have no other woman in my life. I believe you have always been the one meant for me."

"As I have always known you were the one for me. After, of course, I learned that you were not a friend of MacAfee."

Dashiell smiled. "No' in the least, love."

Paden urgently brought a messenger into the great hall. "My laird," Paden said to Dashiell, "the messenger is from the king's court with a message."

The messenger handed the missive to Dashiell, and everyone in the great hall stopped dancing, talking, and playing music.

Dashiell nodded. "MacAfee tried to take my wife hostage. He paid with his life. The king doesna need to have a trial concerning the matter."

The messenger's eyes widened.

"Stay with us for the night. Rest your horse. Feast with us and you can give the king the news on the morrow."

"Aye, my laird."

Then Bhictoria came over with a tankard of ale and handed it to the messenger. "Drink up. There's plenty of food. And then you can dance with me."

Ella smiled at her, and then she took Dashiell in her arms. "You dinna think the king will be mad about what happened to MacAfee, do you?"

"Nay. We did his work for him."

Then he kissed her, and she kissed him back. He took her to dance with his friends, who were dancing with their wives, and they both felt everything was just how it should be.

Mina smiled broadly at them, and Ella swore she was silently saying, "I told you so."

ACKNOWLEDGMENTS

Thanks so much to Donna Fourier and Darla Taylor for beta reading for me! You all are such a help! Thanks for everything.

ABOUT THE AUTHOR

Bestselling and award-winning author Terry Spear has written over a hundred romance novels. Her first werewolf romance, *Heart of the Wolf*, was named a 2008 *Publishers Weekly*'s Best Book of the Year, and her subsequent titles have garnered high praise and hit several *USA Today* bestseller lists. A retired officer of the U.S. Army Reserves, Terry lives in Spring, Texas, where she is working on her next wolf, jaguar, cougar, and bear shifter romances, continuing with her Highland medieval romances, and having fun with her young adult novels. When she's not writing, she's photographing everything that catches her eye, making teddy bears, and playing with her Havanese puppies and grandchildren. For more information, please visit www.terryspear.com, or follow her on Twitter, @TerrySpear. She is also on Facebook at http://www.facebook.com/terry.spear. And on Wordpress at: Terry Spear's Shifters http://terryspear.wordpress.com/

ALSO BY TERRY SPEAR

Adult Titles

Romantic Suspense: Deadly Fortunes, In the Dead of the Night, Relative Danger, Bound by Danger

***

The Highlanders Series: His Wild Highland Lass (novella), Vexing the Highlander (novella), Winning the Highlander's Heart, The Accidental Highland Hero, Highland Rake, Taming the Wild Highlander, The Highlander, Her Highland Hero, The Viking's Highland Lass, My Highlander, Stolen Highland Dreams

Other historical romances: Lady Caroline & the Egotistical Earl, A Ghost of a Chance at Love

***

Heart of the Wolf Series: Heart of the Wolf, Destiny of the Wolf, To Tempt the Wolf, Legend of the White Wolf, Seduced by the Wolf, Wolf Fever, Heart of the Highland Wolf, Dreaming of the Wolf, A SEAL in Wolf's Clothing, A Howl for a Highlander, A Highland Werewolf Wedding, A SEAL Wolf Christmas, Silence of the Wolf, Hero of a Highland Wolf, A Highland Wolf Christmas; SEAL Wolf Hunting; A Silver Wolf Christmas, SEAL Wolf in Too Deep, Alpha Wolf Need Not Apply, Between a Wolf and a Hard Place, SEAL Wolf Undercover, Dreaming of a White Wolf Christmas, Flight of the White Wolf, All's Fair in Love and Wolf, A Billionaire Wolf for Christmas, SEAL Wolf Surrender, Silver Town Wolf: Home for the Holidays, Night of the Billionaire Wolf, You Had Me at Wolf, Joy to the Wolves, The Wolf Wore Plaid, Jingle Bell Wolf, The Best of Both Wolves, While the Wolf's Away, Christmas Wolf Surprise, Wolf Takes the Lead, Wolf on the Wild Side, Her Wolf for the Holidays, A Good Wolf is

Hard to Find (2024), Dreaming of a Highland Wolf (2024), Wolf Bound, Mated for Christmas (2024) , The Wolf of My Eye

SEAL Wolves: To Tempt the Wolf, A SEAL in Wolf's Clothing, A SEAL Wolf Christmas; SEAL Wolf Hunting, A SEAL Wolf in Too Deep, SEAL Wolf Undercover, SEAL Wolf Surrender

Silver Town Wolves: Destiny of the Wolf, Wolf Fever, Dreaming of the Wolf, Silence of the Wolf; A Silver Wolf Christmas, Between a Wolf and a Hard Place, Home for the Holidays, Jingle Bell Wolf

Wolff Family Lodge Wolves: You Had Me at Wolf, Wolf on the Wild Side, A Good Wolf is Hard to Find

Highland Wolves: Heart of the Highland Wolf, A Howl for a Highlander, A Highland Werewolf Wedding, Hero of a Highland Wolf, A Highland Wolf Christmas, The Wolf Wore Plaid, Her Wolf for the Holidays, Dreaming of a Highland Wolf, The Wolf of My Eye

Billionaire Wolf Series: A Billionaire in Wolf's Clothing, A Billionaire Wolf for Christmas, Night of the Billionaire Wolf, Wolf Takes the Lead

White Wolf Series: Legend of the White Wolf, Dreaming of a White Wolf Christmas, Flight of the White Wolf, While the Wolf's Away, Mated for Christmas

Red Wolf Series: Seduced by the Wolf, Joy to the Wolves, The Best of Both Wolves, Christmas Wolf Surprise

Greystoke Wolf Pack: Wolf Bound,

Wolf Novellas: Day of the Wolf, Seal Wolf Pursuit, Wolf to the Rescue, Night of the Wolf, United Shifter Force

***

Heart of the Jaguar Series: Savage Hunger, Jaguar Fever, Jaguar Hunt, Jaguar Pride, A Very Jaguar Christmas, You Had Me at Jaguar, The Witch and the Jaguar, Dawn of the Jaguar

***

Heart of the Cougar Series: Cougar's Mate, Call of the Cougar, Taming the Wild Cougar, Covert Cougar Christmas, a novella, Double Cougar Trouble, Cougar Undercover, Cougar Magic, Cougar Halloween Mischief, Falling for the Cougar, Cougar Christmas Calamity, Catch the Cougar (Halloween Novella), You Had Me at Cougar, Saving the White Cougar, Big Cat Magic

***

White Bear Series: Loving the White Bear, Claiming the White Bear, Bear of a Halloween

Grizzly Bear Series: Bear in Mind

***

Highland Wolves of Old: Wolf Pack, Wolf Alliance, Wolf Heir

Heart of the Huntress Series: Killing the Bloodlust, Deadly Liaisons, Huntress for Hire, Forbidden Love, Deadly Liaisons, Vampire Redemption, Primal Desire, Huntress Unleashed

Vampire Novellas: The Siren's Lure, Vampiric Calling, Seducing the Huntress

***

Comedy Romance: Exchanging Grooms, Marriage, Las Vegas Style

***

Science Fiction: Galaxy Warrior

Young Adult Titles

The World of Fae:

The Dark Fae

The Deadly Fae

The Winged Fae

The Ancient Fae

Dragon Fae

Hawk Fae

Phantom Fae

Golden Fae

Falcon Fae

Woodland Fae

Angel Fae

***

The World of Elf:

The Shadow Elf

The Darkland Elf

Warrior Elf

***

Blood Moon Series:

Kiss of the Vampire

Bite of the Vampire

Night of the Vampire

The Vampire Chronicles Series:

The Vampire in My Dreams

Demon Guardian Series:

The Trouble with Demons

Demon Trouble, Too

Demon Hunter

Non-Series for Now:

Ghostly Liaisons

The Beast Within

Courtly Masquerade

Deidre's Secret

The Magic of Inherian:

The Scepter of Salvation

The Mage of Monrovia

Emerald Isle of Mists

www.ingramcontent.com/pod-product-compliance
Lightning Source LLC
Chambersburg PA
CBHW030425180626
46812CB00005B/2183